Murder ... go hand in hand...

"Senator Lloyd," I said, counting on my appearance to delay any suspicion of me.

"Yes?" He looked at me questioningly, apparently thinking I was another mourner expressing condolences.

"I'm Sutton McPhee from the *Washington News*. I have a question I'd like to ask you."

Irritation sparked in his eyes, but still he saw me as only one of the more morbidly curious of the press.

"I'm sorry," he said, beginning to turn toward the car again. "Not now."

But I held my grasp of his arm and leaned toward him, to whisper in his ear, where only he could hear my question.

"How well did you know Ann Kane, Senator?" I said, then stood back for his reaction.

He straightened again, this time slowly, and fixed me with a hard look, as if memorizing my face.

"I don't know what you're talking about," he said evenly, and climbed into the limo, pulling the door closed as he went.

But he did. He knew exactly what I was talking about.

MORE MYSTERIES FROM THE
BERKLEY PUBLISHING GROUP...

CAT CALIBAN MYSTERIES: She was married for thirty-eight years. Raised three kids. Compared to that, tracking down killers is easy ...

by D. B. Borton

ONE FOR THE MONEY	TWO POINTS FOR MURDER
THREE IS A CROWD	FOUR ELEMENTS OF MURDER
FIVE ALARM FIRE	SIX FEET UNDER

ELENA JARVIS MYSTERIES: There are some pretty bizarre crimes deep in the heart of Texas—and a pretty gutsy police detective who rounds up the unusual suspects ...

by Nancy Herndon

ACID BATH	WIDOWS' WATCH
LETHAL STATUES	HUNTING GAME
TIME BOMBS	C.O.P. OUT

FREDDIE O'NEAL, P.I., MYSTERIES: You can bet that this appealing Reno private investigator will get her man ... "A winner."—Linda Grant

by Catherine Dain

LAY IT ON THE LINE	SING A SONG OF DEATH
WALK A CROOKED MILE	LAMENT FOR A DEAD COWBOY
BET AGAINST THE HOUSE	THE LUCK OF THE DRAW
DEAD MAN'S HAND	

BENNI HARPER MYSTERIES: Meet Benni Harper—a quilter and folk-art expert with an eye for murderous designs ...

by Earlene Fowler

FOOL'S PUZZLE	IRISH CHAIN
KANSAS TROUBLES	GOOSE IN THE POND
DOVE IN THE WINDOW	

HANNAH BARLOW MYSTERIES: For ex-cop and law student Hannah Barlow, justice isn't just a word in a textbook. Sometimes, it's a matter of life and death ...

by Carroll Lachnit

MURDER IN BRIEF	A BLESSED DEATH

PEACHES DANN MYSTERIES: Peaches has never had a very good memory. But she's learned to cope with it over the years ... Fortunately, though, when it comes to murder, this absentminded amateur sleuth doesn't forgive and forget!

by Elizabeth Daniels Squire

WHO KILLED WHAT'S-HER-NAME?	REMEMBER THE ALIBI
MEMORY CAN BE MURDER	WHOSE DEATH IS IT ANYWAY?
IS THERE A DEAD MAN IN THE HOUSE?	

Corruption of Power

Brenda English

BERKLEY PRIME CRIME, NEW YORK

CORRUPTION OF POWER

A Berkley Prime Crime Book / published by arrangement with the author

PRINTING HISTORY
Berkley Prime Crime edition / July 1998

All rights reserved.
Copyright © 1998 by Brenda English.
This book may not be reproduced in whole or in part, by mimeograph or any other means, without permission.
For information address: The Berkley Publishing Group, a member of Penguin Putnam Inc., 200 Madison Avenue, New York, NY 10016.

The Penguin Putnam Inc. World Wide Web site address is http://www.penguinputnam.com

ISBN: 0-425-16398-9

Berkley Prime Crime Books are published by The Berkley Publishing Group, a member of Penguin Putnam Inc., 200 Madison Avenue, New York, NY 10016.
The name BERKLEY PRIME CRIME and the BERKLEY PRIME CRIME design are trademarks belonging to Berkley Publishing Corporation.

PRINTED IN THE UNITED STATES OF AMERICA

10 9 8 7 6 5 4 3 2 1

For Carey and Meagan,
whose love makes my world
go round.

Acknowledgments

My thanks to Officer Kevin Brown, Fairfax County Police Department, Holly Jones, former Fairfax Hospital Pharmacist, and Sue Brown, Fairfax Hospital Emergency Department, for their efforts in helping me make this manuscript as accurate as possible. Any mistakes that occurred anyway are all mine. There is neither a Great Falls district in Fairfax County, nor a Great Falls governmental center/police substation. They are my own creations for purposes of the plot, not an error.

My heartfelt thanks, also, to:

Mary Stuart Rizk, former Director of Communications, Inova Health System, and my former boss, without whose support I couldn't have written this book;

Joshua Bilmes, my agent and trusted sounding board;

Gail Fortune, my editor at Berkley, on whose advice I rely heavily; Laura Anne Gilman, who liked Sutton when they met; and all the friends and family who've never stopped cheering for me.

Wednesday

One

"So the police have no leads, nothing? Just that Ann Kane is dead and two guys had sex with her first?"

"Nothing, Sutton, zip."

"You'd tell me if you had anything more, wouldn't you, Bill?" I asked in a totally phony sweet voice, knowing it would irritate him. Bill Russell usually found the seldom sweet, frequently cynical newspaper woman I thought of as the real me amusing even when I was annoying. I expected he would know that the sugarcoating on my voice now was really a sarcastic gibe, to which he would respond in kind, just another round in our constant but good-natured picking at each other.

Bill was the forty-year-old public information officer for the Fairfax County Police Department, and he had a job few people envied, caught between the devils (aka, reporters) and the deep blue sea—or gray sea, in this case, since that was the color of the county police uniforms. It took someone with a sense of perspective and a sense of humor to keep both groups happy with him, or at least not too unhappy. He generally gave as good as he got, but he took it all in stride, knowing what was meant seriously and what wasn't, what was important in the bigger picture. But his answer wasn't the biting response I expected.

"Trust me, McPhee," he replied tiredly, not at all at his usual level of sarcastic repartee. "We're still looking at everybody and everything we can find. Senate aides don't turn up dead every day of the week, and the pressure's on over this. But we've got nothing new."

"Okay," I said, taking just enough pity on him to let him off the hook temporarily. "But you know how unbearable I'll be if I pick up the *Post* or turn on Channel Four and see something you haven't told me. Just remember, there's nothing you and I can't talk about."

"I'll call. I'll call. 'Bye, Sutton." The note of exasperation made me wonder—just for a second—if I might have pushed my luck. But I knew Bill. Almost as soon as his irritations reached the surface, they dissipated. It was another reason he was good at his job. He didn't hold grudges.

We both hung up. I went back to my computer screen to write my update, such as it was, on Ann Kane's death, and made a mental note that it was time to take Bill out for a drink to repair any frayed edges that might have developed in our relationship under the pressures of the moment.

Two years ago, when I began covering the Fairfax County police for the *News*, a major metropolitan daily newspaper in Washington, D.C., that competed head-to-head with the *Post,* I set out to woo Bill as a source. It was not exactly an original strategy. The best reporters always try to build relationships with at least one or two people who are key information sources for any beat. As often as not it fails, precisely because every other reporter on the beat is doing the same thing. But this time Bill and I clicked. He grew to trust me, as I did him, and it gave me a leg up on the rest of the press pack. I rarely got favors—

well, okay, one or two—but when I had solid leads, Bill never tried to bullshit me or steer me wrong. He knew I worked hard for what I got, and my leads were often as good as, and occasionally better than, what the police had. He also knew that when I could do it without risking a source or blowing my own scoop on a story, I had passed along a few pearls of information that had resulted in real breaks for a couple of police investigations.

The crass bottom line was that we scratched each other's back. The truth was we liked each other. Given the low regard in which I often held public-relations flacks, I was as surprised as Bill was that we had become friends. Although I frequently needled him good-humoredly, I knew he told me what he could, on and off the record, and I tried not to get him into trouble with his bosses. But the Ann Kane case had a lot of people on edge and aggravated, and I had heard in Bill's voice that it was taking a toll.

"Not much new on Ann Kane," I called across the busy newsroom to Rob Perry, the editor for the local news pages. "I'm doing a brief rehash and I'll have it in the queue in fifteen minutes."

"Make it ten," Rob answered flatly, ever the epitome of the what-have-you-done-for-me-today city editor. There was a 7:00 P.M. deadline—now just two hours away— hanging heavily over his head. It's a mortal sin in the newspaper world to miss a deadline. It screws up the very tight schedules of hundreds of other people in both the production and distribution sections of the paper, not to mention pissing off the readers if their morning papers are late. It also costs an arm and a leg. Double amputees are not unknown in the newspaper business.

Quickly, I wrote my lead: *Frustrated Fairfax County police continue to search for answers in last week's death of Ann Kane, a Senate aide whose body was found in a local wildlife area. But answers are eluding investigators, who say Kane, a top assistant to Senator Rita Wills (D-Fla.),*

*died of a fatal combination of prescription drugs, appar-
ently after having sexual intercourse with two men.*

I rehashed what the police were telling. Ann Kane's nude
body had been found, wrapped in a sheet, a week ago last
Sunday, probably about a day after she died, by bird-
watchers on Mason Neck, a wildlife area a few miles south
of the Mount Vernon Plantation and about twenty miles
south of Washington, D.C.

The medical examiner eventually reached several conclusions. Kane had died after ingesting Demerol, a pain-
killer with marked depressant effects on the central nervous
system. While the amount of Demerol in her system ordinarily might not have caused any problems, in Kane's case
it had been deadly, because she also was taking Nardil, an
antidepressant from a class of drugs known as monamine
oxidase inhibitors, or MOAs. MOAs can be dangerous even
when combined with otherwise innocuous foods such as
wine and cheese. When combined with any of a wide variety of other drugs, the results can be fatal. Ann Kane's
physician, who said he prescribed the Nardil for stress-
related depression, told police he had given Kane no other
prescriptions, certainly not one for Demerol, and that she
was fully versed in the risks associated with the drug she
was taking. That's why the police were working under the
theory that Kane might have taken the Demerol without
knowing it—disguised in food or drink given to her by
someone else.

The medical examiner also found semen from two men
inside Ann Kane's vagina, shallow bite marks on her neck
and breasts, but none of the bruising, cuts, or tissue under
her fingernails that would indicate any resistance. While it
was possible that the sex was consensual, the police pointed
out that an unconscious woman wouldn't fight back either,
no matter how many men were having sex with her.

Her death, the ME said, had been an ugly one. Within
no more than thirty to forty minutes of taking the Demerol,

her blood pressure had fallen drastically, followed by convulsions, vomiting, and heart failure. Chances were, it came as quite a surprise to her two assailants.

The ME's opinion was backed up by evidence in Kane's apartment. Not only were the signs of her death all over the linens on her bed (linens that matched the sheet in which she had been wrapped), but there were wineglasses, newly washed and wiped clean of fingerprints, in the sink, and signs of fingerprints having been wiped from doorknobs and other surfaces throughout the apartment. Even if the sex had begun as consensual, it was clear the men involved feared it wouldn't look that way and had done everything they could to cover their tracks. According to the police, the very least they were looking at was manslaughter charges—if they could find the two men.

Today was Wednesday. Ann Kane had been dead for a week and a half, and so far no one knew who she was with when she died or who had thrown her body out in the woods.

I added a quote from Bill—might as well give him some personal publicity—and from Tim Burke, Senator Wills's PR guy, with whom I'd also talked on the phone. Both confessed they were mystified by the whole thing, that it didn't fit at all with anything the police or her friends knew about Ann Kane and how she lived her life. Bill noted that the consensual-sex theory was not one to which the police gave much credence, that police were going under the assumption that Kane had been drugged unknowingly and raped before she died.

I quoted Bill's plea for information from anyone who might know anything about the case. After reading my copy to make sure it was sensible, I coded in the routing to Rob's computer queue and switched directories to retrieve a longer piece I was working on for a future issue of the paper's Sunday magazine. That article was about increasingly violent teenagers in the suburbs. I was deep into the excuses of these young thugs about how they need guns to show they aren't afraid of each other, when my phone rang.

"Sutton McPhee," I answered, my eyes still on my computer screen.

"Sutton, it's Bill."

"Why Officer Russell," I replied, my voice sarcastic but my mind secretly glad for the interruption. "What a surprise! And so soon after our last conversation. Did you change your mind and decide you had news for me after all?"

"This is news all right, but it's not about Ann Kane."

"Oh?"

"I think you might want to get over to Great Falls. We just got a call from Hubbard Taylor."

"The county supervisor? Not my department, Bill. I cover forthright criminals, remember. But now that you've interrupted me, I might as well listen. What's Taylor's problem?"

"I think you'll want to hear this. He says he just got home from a board meeting and found his wife dead—you know, the one in the wheelchair. He says she's been murdered."

That got my attention. I swung away from the computer and focused on what I was hearing.

"Jesus!" I said, in a voice loud enough to carry across the newsroom. "What happened?" Heads looked up from several of the neighboring desks, wondering what had prompted my raised voice. I ignored them.

"I don't know. Nine-one-one got a hysterical call from Taylor, says his wife's been strangled. There's an ambulance and several of our units there, and I'm going over, too. I guess I was just confused for a minute and called you. Do you have the number of the *Post* handy?"

I laughed. "Kiss my ass and give me the address."

"Forty-eight-twenty-three Wintergreen. It's right next to the river. I gotta go, Sutton."

"I'll see you there."

"Oh, and Sutton?"

"Yeah?"

"You're welcome."

"I know," I said smugly, and heard Bill laugh on the other end.

We hung up again. I grabbed a notebook and my purse and went over to stand behind Rob, who was hunched over his keyboard, making intelligible prose out of somebody's less-than-sterling copy, probably mine.

"Rob, I know we're on deadline, but I think you'd better save some space for me—in fact, you probably should tell the page-one folks to save it. I just got a hell of a story."

Rob turned his head to stare back over his shoulder at me, his unruly eyebrows raised in a question over the top of his glasses. It was the look he gave us when we weren't living up to his standards and he was afraid we were about to sink to a new low. "Withering" just about summed it up.

"Little green aliens land on the White House lawn?" he asked. "Or something else as exciting as this piece of non-news you just turned in on the Ann Kane killing?"

"Hub Taylor's wife is dead," I told him, for once not wanting to take up his challenge to a duel of wits. "He told the police he just found her when he got home from a board meeting. Says she was strangled."

"Holy shit!" Rob replied, his Alabama roots stretching it out to about five syllables. The news got his attention, too, and he swiveled in his chair to face me. "They know who killed her?"

"I don't think so. Taylor just found her body and called the police a few minutes ago. I'm going over there to see what I can find out. I'll call you from there with whatever I can get."

"Christ!" Rob said. "Who would want to kill Janet Taylor? I mean, the woman was a helpless cripple, for God's sake!'' He shook his balding head as if to clear it. "Okay, McPhee, call as soon as you can. I'll get the photo lab to send a photographer out there, and I'll call upstairs and tell them to hold page one." He reached to pick up his phone and stopped, shaking his head in mock disgust. "Jesus, did I really say that? Look at this, McPhee! You've got me sounding like fucking Jimmy Olsen! Next thing you know, I'll be yelling, 'Stop the presses!' " The phone rang under his hand.

"What?" he yelped into the receiver. He listened for a couple of seconds and then looked at me and held up one finger in a signal to wait. "Yeah. Uh-huh. Yeah, we know. Sutton just got a call on it, too. She's about to go over there." He paused to listen again.

"Okay," he continued. "Right. I'll tell her to find you there." He hung up the phone without any pretense of a good-bye and turned back to me.

"That was Hale," he explained. "He just heard it at the county government center. He's going out to the house, too, so touch base with him when you get there. This thing probably will take both of you to cover."

Ken Hale was the *News* reporter who covered Fairfax County government and its board of supervisors. It wouldn't be the first time he and I had collaborated on a story. He was low-key, steady, and absolutely impossible to discourage once he thought he had the bones of a good story in his jaws. Ken was one of the best reporters I knew.

"Okay," I agreed, and then I was out the door, my adrenaline rush in full force.

Two

I love being a newspaper reporter. I love covering cops. I love piecing the stories together, doing my best to track down leads, maybe even beat the police to the truth—or at least some of it, anyway. What I have a hard time with, however, are the innocents: the bystanders who just happen to be on the wrong street corner during a drive-by shooting, the children or the wives who die from the beatings of an abusive man, the father of three who's killed when a drunken driver crosses the center line. It's those people, not the criminals, who keep me awake at night sometimes, wondering if the so-called justice of the courts really is. Maybe, occasionally, it comes close to evening things up. But a lot of the time it fails flat out—the guilty go free and the innocents are still dead. Like Janet Taylor.

And like my sister, Cara.

After the death of my parents in a car wreck when I was still in college, Cara was the only close family I had left. At twenty-six, she had moved to Springfield, Virginia, to be closer to me. A year later—now two years ago—Cara had been shot to death in a cold-blooded and calculated execution disguised as an ATM robbery.

I was covering the Northern Virginia school systems for the *News* at the time, the then-pinnacle of my career as an education reporter that had taken me to newspapers in Georgia and in Washington. And I was bored. But Cara's death, and the Fairfax County Police Department's lack of leads about who might have killed her, shook me out of my rut and sent me on an angry search for the people responsible for her death. I had found them: the minister of her beloved church and his assistant. They were career criminals running a lucrative blackmail scam against several wealthy parishioners, and Cara had stumbled onto what they were doing. And they had murdered her.

Both men now sat on death row in a Virginia prison, and Rob Perry, aware of my growing disinterest in the education beat and impressed with my doggedness in finding Cara's murderers, had moved me over to cover the Fairfax County police. It had been an inspired idea on his part and, in many ways, my salvation. For while I still struggled to deal with the pain of the victims of violence and lust and greed, a pain I now knew firsthand, at least as a police reporter, I had found a way to try to help, to make a little of the world right again. It hadn't brought back my sister, of course, but it had helped keep me more or less sane in a world that sometimes seemed to have completely lost its collective mind.

As I threaded my way out of the District of Columbia in the afternoon rush-hour traffic and toward one of Northern Virginia's poshest neighborhoods, I thought about Janet Taylor and what I knew of her. Mostly I knew what was common knowledge. I knew that she was, as Rob had so sensitively put it, a cripple, although far from helpless. I knew that Janet Taylor had been in a wheelchair for the last seven or eight years, ever since a fall from a horse had severed her lower spine. I knew from seeing her at a couple of very tony social functions that she had full use of her upper body, that only her legs were paralyzed. I also knew she was the daughter and only child of a wealthy, old-line Richmond family and that she was one of those truly good souls of whom the world has too few. Just being in a room with Janet Taylor was all it took to know that. An elegant blond woman with delicate features, she had an inner warmth and graciousness that extended to everyone around her. You could tell she usually saw only the good in others and that was what kept her so involved in a whole string of worthy causes.

It also probably explained how she could stand to be married to Hubbard Taylor, a wealthy-in-his-own-right owner of a chain of car dealerships, who always struck me as someone who had spent his life running away from himself. Adversity can forge children into two kinds of adults: those who lose their fear of what might happen and who grow up determined to be a match for life, and those who never lose that fear and who overcompensate in some way to cover it up. Taylor was one of those insecure self-made men whose bombast covered a gut-deep fear that people still could see the poor and powerless little boy who grew up hard and fast in rural southwest Virginia.

But he obviously adored his wife, as he should, and she genuinely seemed to care for him. She had even put her own health at risk six years ago when, still in an intensive physical-rehabilitation program, she had thrown considerable energy into helping Taylor with his first—and, as it turned out, his successful—campaign for a seat on the Fairfax County Board of Supervisors.

As a supervisor, Taylor was part of the governing board of one of the richest counties in the United States, with a multibillion-dollar annual budget as large as that of some small countries. Four years later Taylor ran again against heavy Republican opposition and money, and won hands down, due in no small part to his wife's popularity among

the people in his Great Falls district. Lately there had been
considerable talk about Taylor running for a seat in the U.S.
House of Representatives, an idea apparently being pushed
by his mentor, Ed Lloyd, the senior U.S. senator from the
Commonwealth of Virginia and the man who had per-
suaded Taylor, an early and heavy financial supporter of
Lloyd, to enter politics in the first place.

Now Janet Taylor was dead, murdered, according to her
husband. As I pulled up to the end of the long, curving
driveway where half a dozen reporters from the suburban
and Washington papers milled among the usual space-
hogging convoy of radio and television remote-broadcast
trucks, I thought about how many people's lives Janet Taylor had touched and improved. If her husband were dead,
his family would miss him, but a week later a dozen other
politicians would be ready to take his place, with little dis-
ruption in the political process. His wife, however, was different—one of the irreplaceables whose absence would
leave the world a meaner, colder place.

I drove beyond the last of the TV trucks in my high-
school-graduation present (at thirty-four, I can just barely
remember that far into the distant past.): a 1976 white VW
Beetle convertible that was used even when I got it and
that I intended to drive forever because I actually could
identify the engine parts. It was unbelievably reliable. It
had never left me stranded, which was more than anyone
could ask of a piece of machinery, and I still thought it was
cute, even after 183,623 miles. I found a place to park a
few yards away from where a uniformed cop was talking
to a small group of people I guessed were neighbors. The
cop wasn't letting them get even as close as the press. As
I got out I heard my name called. Turning, I saw Ken Hale
walking rapidly toward me, his usual buttoned-down and
jacketed Brooks Brothers look now whittled down to a
white oxford-cloth shirt and a tie at half-mast in the welcome warmth of a late afternoon in mid-May.

"Hi, Ken," I greeted, walking over to meet him. Instinctively, we both moved away from neighbors and from the other reporters to compare notes. "What's the story?"

"Man, Sutton, this whole thing is just too weird," he answered. He looked up the drive toward the white-columned house, now dripping with the colored strobes of police-cruiser lights. "What a thing to happen. And to Janet Taylor! I mean, I can see why any number of people might go after her husband, but why her?"

Just then I saw Oren Young, one of the *News* photographers, walking up behind Ken.

"Hey, y'all," Oren said, chewing his ever-present Dentyne gum. None of us had ever seen him without a wad of it in his mouth, even at lunch. How he ate a sandwich and still kept his gum intact was one of the great newsroom mysteries. Some of us believed he had a hollow tooth in which he secreted the stuff while he chewed. We joked that the gum was probably a tension reliever and the only thing that kept Oren from becoming a serial killer. "I take it that we can't get up to the house?" he asked.

We all eyed the uniformed policeman who leaned against the side of the police cruiser that blocked the end of the drive, his arms crossed over his chest and a take-no-crap expression on his face.

"Nope," Ken answered, running his hand through sandy-brown hair. "The cop over there says forget it. But he did announce a few minutes ago that someone will be down here in a while to tell us whatever they can."

"Which will be next to nothing," I opined, knowing how the police, always convinced it will put their investigation in jeopardy, hate telling news reporters anything unless it serves some purpose of their own. "I heard Taylor was at a board meeting when it happened?"

"Yeah, him and at least fifty other people, including me. It ended about four, and he left. I was still there interviewing Rhodes Gray, the Mount Vernon district supervisor, when his secretary ran in to tell us. Apparently, after Taylor found his wife, he called Mannie Sims, his assistant, who was still in the office, and Mannie told him to call nine-one-one. I got over here as fast as I could.''

''I was told Taylor said she'd been strangled. You hear anything like that?''

''Beth—that's Gray's secretary—said Taylor told Mannie the same thing. Said he found a scarf wrapped around her neck.''

''Any sign of Taylor since you got here?''

''No, he's still inside with the police. They—''

Ken was interrupted by a piercing whistle from the cop in the driveway.

''Okay, listen up, people,'' the cop said, his hand dropping from the small radio attached to the left shoulder of his shirt and over which he had just been speaking. He put his thumbs in his belt and moved away from the car, then planted his feet in a wide-legged stance that told us he thought he had something of importance to impart to us.

''Bill Russell will be out in a couple of minutes to answer your questions,'' he said, his voice booming out to reach all of us. ''So just hang tight.'' Then he stepped back to the cruiser and resumed his sentry duty.

Ken, Oren, and I moved in the direction of the driveway, along with the rest of the press pack, and as we got there I saw Bill come out the large double front doors, along with two other men. One, I knew, was Chet Stewart, head of the police department's criminal investigations bureau, who could be expected to show up where a supervisor's wife had been murdered. The other was a stranger and one of the most gorgeous men I had ever seen.

''Okay, okay, settle down,'' Bill said, once he, Stewart, and the hunk reached the end of the drive and we all pressed closer and began shouting questions at him. ''If you folks will bear with us, we're going to tell you what we can. When we're done, you can ask questions and we'll tell you the same things again.''

Chuckles and groans issued from the reporters.

''And then,'' Bill continued, deadpan, ''we'll be available for a few minutes for you TV and radio people to tape us saying the same thing for the third time.''

The newspaper reporters in the group laughed out loud at that, always happy to see someone take a dig at our electronic colleagues, whom most print journalists consider lightweights and prima donnas. We were rewarded with a few glares, a couple of obscene gestures, and widespread hissing. They didn't share our opinion.

To an outside observer, our low-key levity probably would seem completely inappropriate, considering the circumstances that had brought us together. But most of us had held this same vigil, outside some house or other location where murderous violence had put in an appearance, too many times. We all—reporters and police alike—learned quickly to defend ourselves by stepping back emotionally, often through humor, in order to keep the horror of the things we saw and reported from burrowing inside where we lived. As soon as the cameras rolled, as soon as the first genuine question was asked, however, we all would be serious professionals again.

''Officer Russell,'' I said, elbowing my way in front of a Barbie doll from the cable news channel, ''I believe I already have notes on this same press conference, where you don't know anything, from when Ann Kane's body was found. May I just go home now? I have laundry to do.''

''We'd all appreciate it if you'd go home, McPhee,'' Bill said, his mouth serious but his eyes telling me he still knew exactly how to take my digs at him. ''Dirty laundry is what you do best.''

From time to time I also deliberately needle Bill in front of other reporters, because it squelches complaints of favoritism. He knows why I do it and always responds in kind, so I was prepared for his comeback, and for the hoots of laughter at my expense from the other reporters. What I wasn't prepared for, however, was the reaction of the good-looking guy in the charcoal-gray suit and who now was standing to Bill's right. As the words left my mouth his attention locked on me, dark blue eyes glaring out from under black brows and a thick shock of equally black hair, pinning me to the spot, searing me with a look I usually got only from people who personally had felt the sharp point of my pen. His mouth, ordinarily probably quite appealing, had tightened into a grim, straight line that spoke volumes of disapproval—of me. I was riveted, by the ferocity of his gaze and the unexpectedness of his reaction.

And then there was my own reaction. He was looking at me with a fierce expression. I was looking at him in shock. His eyes had filled me with an overwhelming sense of recognition, of familiarity. It left me confused. I knew perfectly well I had never met him. I was sure of it. But there was the feeling that I knew him from somewhere.

"Most of you already know Chet Stewart from the criminal investigations bureau," Bill said, looking at Stewart to his left, who nodded to the press. "And this is Detective Noah Lansing, who will be in charge of the investigation. He'll answer your questions." I dragged my attention back to my surroundings, trying to focus on the fact that Bill had been speaking again.

Detective Noah Lansing held my look for another heartbeat, which I realized was very loud inside my ears, before turning away to listen to a question from Paul Carlson, the inept morning-show cohost at Channel 3 and a mental dead ringer for Ted from the old *Mary Tyler Moore Show*.

Christ, I thought as Carlson stuttered his way through the twisted syntax of the reportorial-challenged who is lost without a TelePrompTer, what did I do to him? Him being Noah Lansing, total stranger, whose hostility had just left me speechless and whose presence left me off balance.

"First, maybe I should just tell you what I can, and then I'll try to answer questions," Detective Lansing said, looking away from me to the rest of the group, his expression now perfectly neutral and professional. He appeared unperturbed, in spite of his glare at me, as microphones waved in front of him and red on-the-air lights came to life on TV remote cameras, whose operators were happy to be able to get Lansing's live comments on the tail end of the local six-o'clock-news shows. He opened his small notebook and thumbed backward for several pages.

"The call to nine-one-one came in at four thirty-seven P.M.," Lansing began, once he found the notes he wanted. "The caller identified himself as Hubbard Taylor and said he had just found his wife dead. The dispatcher asked if he was certain, and Mr. Taylor responded that she had no pulse and wasn't breathing. The dispatcher immediately sent police units and an ambulance to the address.

"A police unit arrived first, and the officers found Mr. Taylor sitting on the front steps of the house, very distraught and saying he couldn't go back in the house, that Mrs. Taylor was dead.

"The ambulance also arrived at about that time, and the paramedics and police officers entered together, bringing Mr. Taylor with them. They found Mrs. Taylor inside. The paramedics confirmed that she was dead. Cause of death will be determined by the medical examiner, of course. I can tell you that there were signs of trauma to the upper body, so we are investigating this as a homicide. We haven't located any witnesses at this time. The Taylors' maid was not in the house because it was her day off. Officers are searching the property and those next to it. They're also checking to see if any neighbors were home during the afternoon and might have seen anything suspicious. But at this time we have very little to go on. All we can say for certain is that Mrs. Taylor is dead, and foul play is being considered. Okay, I'll take questions now.''

All hands waved at once, mine included. Detective Lansing pointed to a reporter from Channel 7.

"Did Taylor try CPR?"

"We don't know," Lansing told him. "Although the nine-one-one dispatchers are trained in giving CPR instructions over the phone, the call was cut off before the dispatcher was able to do that."

Lansing looked back at our side of the group and waved a hand at Ken Hale.

"Mr. Taylor was at a board of supervisors' meeting this afternoon. Can you tell how long his wife's been dead, and is he a suspect?" Ken always knew what the most important question in any story was.

"At this time we have not identified anyone as a suspect or ruled anyone out," Noah Lansing answered carefully. "We have confirmed Mr. Taylor's attendance at the meeting, which was televised, and his wife appears to have died sometime during that time period. Mr. Taylor is quite upset, as you can imagine, so we will be talking with him at greater length later. It will take a while before we have official word from the medical examiner on the exact cause and time of death." He pointed to Trudy Gernrich of the *Post* and nodded.

"Was she raped?" Trudy, like me, could be refreshingly direct. Well, I considered it refreshing.

"Again, we won't know until after the autopsy," Lansing answered.

"When do you expect to have those results?" I called out my question without raising my hand, a move calculated to get an answer without drawing attention to the fact that I was the questioner, since Lansing didn't seem inclined to acknowledge my existence. It worked.

"In twenty-four to forty-eight"—he began answering automatically even before he finished turning toward me, then realized who had asked—"hours." He bit the last word off and looked immediately to another reporter. But not before I felt the ice of his blue eyes again. And not before I was hit once more with a feeling of undeniable and powerful familiarity, like a fist in the stomach.

After a couple more questions from the group, each answered by Lansing in equally brief fashion, Bill Russell interrupted to call a halt.

"Ladies and gentlemen, the investigation is continuing," he said, gesturing up toward the house, where a medical examiner's van had moved up to the front door, "and we all need to get back to it. So we'll take a few more minutes to give you radio and TV folks anything else you need for your news shows and then we have to go."

The print reporters, Ken and myself included, hung around to listen, just to make sure someone more quick-witted didn't ask a question that elicited new information. When Bill finally cut off the individual interviews, several of the members of the press began to drift toward their cars and remote trucks for the drive back to their offices and studios. I stood against my car, cell phone in hand, to dictate a story to Rob Perry, who would send it up to the page-one desk. Oren got into his own car, waving—and chewing furiously—as he drove off, but Ken waited with me, to give Rob what he knew for the story whose byline we expected to share. Bill, Stewart, and Noah Lansing were walking briskly up the drive to the house, deep in conversation, none of them giving us a backward glance.

"Here's the deal," Rob Perry was saying. "The two of you are on this story for the duration."

It was 7:30 at night, and my workday was in its fourteenth hour. Ken and I had returned to the paper from the Taylor home and Rob was sitting on his desk, feet up in his chair, coffee cup in one hand, unlit cigarette being used as a pointer in the other, talking to us as we stood facing him. The only place Rob could smoke these days was in his private office on the west side of the newsroom, but he couldn't function without a cigarette, even an unlit one, in his hand. He also had a habit of loosening more and more of his clothes as the deadline got closer, a habit attested to by his current dishabille: tie loosened and halfway down his chest, the top two buttons undone on his shirt, and his sleeves unbuttoned and rolled up.

"Was there some question?" I asked slightly caustically, but not expecting an affirmative reply.

"As a matter of fact, there was," Rob said, using his irritated-parent tone of voice. "Mark Lester tried to take over the story and give it to Sy Berkowitz. He said it was page-one news and deserved page-one reporting."

Mark Lester is the editor for the front page. Sy Berkowitz is the so-called special-projects reporter who followed Lester from their previous paper in Philadelphia. I knew I had just been chastised, even if indirectly, for being too cocky and presumptuous.

"He can't do that!" Ken barked, standing up straighter in outrage. Ken looks mild-mannered, but he can be ferocious when it comes to his stories. "We cover the board of supervisors and the cops. It's our story!"

"You're damned right it's our story," Rob told him, "but I had to drag Lester into Mack Thompson's office and have a little hand-to-hand combat before he would believe it."

Mack Thompson is the managing editor, which means he spends a lot of time settling internecine wars among various sections of the paper, all of which have to vie with each other for a limited amount of space.

"So both of you had better be balls-to-the-wall on this one," Rob went on. "Forget anything else you're working on short of an earthquake or World War Three. I want us right on top of this thing, and I don't want to see any surprises when I pick up the *Post*. I used up a lot of chits on this, you guys, so don't make me look bad."

"You tell that asshole Mark Lester that Sy couldn't find his way around a police station even if his dick was in their lost and found," I said hotly to Rob. Behind me, I heard Ken choke down a laugh.

"McPhee," Rob warned, giving me a hard look, "don't make me sorry, either."

"You know you won't be sorry," I answered bravely, knowing Rob would have as much riding on this as Ken and I would. "You definitely won't be sorry."

But as I went back to my desk to get my purse and go home, I wondered. This might be the biggest police story of the year; for me, it might be the biggest story ever. And already I had managed, without even knowing how I had done it, to piss off the man who would have all the information on the case. And then there was that other thing, that feeling of knowing him. I had ruled out any possibility that I did, but the feeling persisted—and had me thinking about Lansing in a way that didn't come close to being professional. In reality, I was hoping even more than Rob was that he wouldn't regret fighting to keep me on this story.

Three

Home, finally. A chance to stop for a little while—stop the running around, stop the verbal fencing, stop the effort to be two steps ahead of everyone around me, stop looking over my shoulder to see who was gaining on me.

It always feels this way when I open the door to my apartment in Alexandria's West End, known by the long-timers (i.e., anyone who has lived in the area for more than two years) as "Condo Canyon." I live on the fourteenth floor of one of the neighborhood's dozen or so high-rises, and my westward-facing balcony and living room windows give me a spectacular view not only of the sunset each day but also of the surrounding Northern Virginia foothills. Because I live there alone, walking through the door always feels like entering a refuge—no newsroom racket or bustle, no frantic pace.

Once inside, I put my things on the small ebony Chinese chest that stands against the wall in what passes for a tiny foyer and walked across the living room to look out the windows at the world I had just left. At this height I could see the lights of homes and offices and high-rises for two or three miles. The constant humming swish of six lanes of traffic on I-395 reached me from three blocks away, and I could see the bright white headlights and softly glowing red taillights of cars moving rapidly in each direction. Immediately below me, a handful of cars circled the building's parking lot, looking for parking spaces, and a man and a woman walked up toward the front door, arm in arm. All of it is part of a huge metropolis that sprawls out from the corridors of power in the District of Columbia, for at least forty miles in any direction—and a very long way from the small Georgia town where I grew up.

With the night outside pressing against the windows like the backing on a mirror, I also could see myself, a thirty-four-year-old woman looking out at the world in bemusement. I studied the reflection in front of me. Somewhat tall. Five-eight, to be exact. A decent body (although no model), the result of nightly sessions on a ski machine and yoga lessons twice a week. Black hair that I usually wore in a thick French braid. A nice mouth, the bottom lip fuller than the top. Brown eyes, dark and large—and tired. Even in the dim reflection of the window, I could see that my eyes looked tired.

Too many deaths to have to chase in one day, I thought. And an editor from page one who wants to take away my story.

And don't forget the handsome cop who doesn't like you, my little voice added.

"Shut up," I told it. That little voice, which had made its opinions about my behavior known throughout most of my life, was my compass and my nemesis. It kept me sane and drove me crazy. It told me that I wasn't so bad and that I wasn't so good. Right now I didn't want to hear it.

I turned from the window and went to my small galley kitchen to find something to eat. From the freezer, I took a boring but convenient frozen dinner—sliced turkey, carrots, and green beans—and put it in the microwave to heat. While that mainstay of the overworked single professional was warming, I went down the short hall to the larger of the two bedrooms to change into a set of the gray sweat clothes I use for pajamas. I ducked into my bathroom long enough to clean the makeup off my face and then went back to the kitchen to pour myself a glass of Burgundy. To hell with white wines with fowl, I thought. I prefer a decent dry red just about anytime.

The microwave dinged behind me as I put the wine bottle back on the counter. I took out my dinner, peeled off the cover, set the little plastic tray on a real plate, grabbed a knife and fork from the drawer, and took all of it and my glass of Burgundy out to the teak dining table that I had inherited from my mother. The table seats six and takes up most of the dining ''area'' off to the right of the living room. I pulled out two chairs, side by side, one for my butt, one for my feet, and sat down to eat and look out through the expanse of windows that continues from the living room across the dining area. Ordinarily, I would have put on some music or moved my portable TV from the kitchen counter to the table to watch a sitcom or the news. Not tonight, though. Tonight, I didn't want to have to think at all.

Which was, of course, exactly what I couldn't stop doing. First I thought about Ann Kane and what could have happened to her. An accidental drug mix-up on her part? Deliberate on someone else's part? What about the two men? The medical examiner said all the semen had been deposited at about the same time. This was a young woman who didn't even have a boyfriend, according to coworkers and her boss. A twenty-nine-year-old woman from a devout Catholic family, who attended Mass regularly, who worked at a food kitchen for the homeless on weekends. How likely was she to have agreed to some sort of seamy interlude with two guys at once?

From there my thoughts went on to Janet Taylor, another doer of good works. What in her life could possibly have called such a fate down on her? Everyone who knew her loved her. Was it a passing killer, who somehow went unnoticed in that swank neighborhood and who found Janet Taylor at home alone? Was it someone she knew or a stranger? Who on earth would have wanted her dead?

And from Janet Taylor, it wasn't very far to Noah Lansing. Why was I thinking about him again?

Because he took an instant dislike to you, my voice said, *and you took an instant like to him.*

Oh, no, are you back? Don't you ever sleep?

The voice went on: *And you aren't used to having people dislike you for no apparent reason. You work hard at ingratiating yourself so they'll tell you what they know. People usually like you, at least at the beginning. Even Jack liked you at the beginning.*

Jack is Jack Brooks, my ex-husband, who still lives in Tallahassee. Our marriage had lasted two years, until he said he was tired of having a wife who spent all her time in the gutter and who was never home. Then he walked out and filed for divorce. What he was really tired of, I had told myself—and him, in one memorable argument—was my refusal to be his mother and to be at his beck and call all the time. I sure didn't need to dredge up that pain right now.

"Get lost," I told my voice.

No way, it answered. *You know how you reacted to Detective Lansing. You'd like to get to know him. You think you do know him. And he wants nothing to do with you. He saw right through you, McPhee. Saw all the warts you try to cover up. And now you think he won't like you no matter what you do. Or maybe you're just afraid you'll never get any information out of him.*

"Okay, that's it," I said loudly into the quiet room, throwing my fork down on the plate. I stood up and gathered the remains of my dinner, eaten mostly unconsciously. Back to the kitchen I went, tossing the disposable tray into the garbage and putting my glass, plate, and utensils into the sink. I was angry, at Noah Lansing for judging me so swiftly and finding me wanting, and at my voice for its efforts at what it called refusing to let me live in ignorance of my real feelings and motives. Yes, Lansing had been unfair. But it was more than that. I didn't want him screwing up my story. Or disliking me.

Way to go, McPhee, the voice chimed in. *You met the guy this afternoon and already he doesn't like you. And on top of that, you've got the hots for him and you haven't even had a conversation with him. And you call yourself a grown-up!*

Disgusted, I turned off the lights and went to the bedroom, where I eyed the ski machine balefully, said screw it, and climbed under the covers.

Thursday

Four

At seven o'clock the next morning, I was at the Massey Building on Chain Bridge Road, which houses the Fairfax County Police Department's criminal investigations bureau. I had my no-regrets reporter persona firmly reaffixed and planned to try to get a moment alone with Noah Lansing. The police day shift begins at 7:00 A.M., and it can be tricky, particularly with investigators who often work well before or after their shift, to catch them before they get out on the road. And I was hoping, despite the wrong foot on which things had begun, to talk to Lansing without any other reporters around, not because I really thought he could or would tell me anything new at this point, but just to try to get a better reading of who he was and to establish some kind of rapport that would ensure access to him when I needed it. Of course, being able to look at him wouldn't be unpleasant either.

Lansing, it turned out, was working temporarily out of an office at the Great Falls Government Center's police substation while some offices in the Massey Building were being renovated. That district government center also housed a satellite office for the Great Falls county supervisor, Hub Taylor. Well, that's convenient anyway, I told myself as I went back out to my car to make the fifteen-minute drive to Great Falls.

Jimmy Turner, the officer at the front duty desk, told me Lansing was in the morning briefing with the rest of the shift and would be done any minute. I knew better than to ask to wait in Lansing's office. The detective would suspect the worst if he found me there alone and probably would blame Jimmy for letting me in. Instead I stood next to the door that led from the small glassed-in lobby into the rest of the station. The briefing room was down the hall to my right, and I would be able to see the cops as they came out to start their rounds.

Two minutes later the door to the briefing room opened and uniformed officers spilled out into the hall, bringing their cups of coffee and their conversations with them. Eventually, Noah Lansing, accompanied by Bill Russell, whose office was in the Massey Building, brought up the rear, coming in my direction. As they approached I knocked on the glass door to get their attention. Seeing me, Bill walked up to the door and signaled to Jimmy that I was kosher, for today at least. A loud buzzer sounded, and Bill reached down to open the door for me.

"Come on back, McPhee," he said, his expression serious, but friendship lurking in his eyes. "I told Noah that if I knew you, you'd be here lying in wait for him at the crack of dawn. But he just couldn't get away in time."

Noah Lansing just looked at me, not overtly hostile like the day before, but certainly not warming up to me. I saw no way around it but head-on.

"Detective Lansing, could I have a few minutes before you leave?"

Lansing flashed a look to Bill, who nodded, obviously having told Lansing that the quickest way to get rid of me

with a minimum of fuss was to humor me, or at least to
appear to. Lansing looked back at me, then turned to walk
down the hall to the left. Not hearing an outright refusal, I
chose to interpret this as an enthusiastic invitation to his
office. I followed him quickly, hearing Bill chuckle to himself behind me. Him I ignored.

Lansing led me into a tiny private office almost completely filled by a gray metal desk with a black vinyl swivel
chair behind it, two guest chairs with oak arms and blue
woven upholstery, a couple of tan four-drawer metal filing
cabinets, a wooden coat tree with a black nylon raincoat
hanging on it, and a small computer table against the back
wall, on which sat a computer whose blank blue monitor
screen showed only a small white cursor blinking in the
top left corner. The office's starkness and cramped size
were relieved by a window, on the wall opposite the door,
that looked out on a stretch of green grass and the police-
cruiser parking lot. On the wall facing the desk was a large
color photograph of a sailboat with a navy-blue hull and a
very small boy standing on deck, waving to the camera.

I stood in the doorway a moment, watching as Lansing
removed his suit jacket, this one a deep heather blue with
pinstripes, and stepped in front of the desk to hang it on
the coat tree. I was noticing a trend here, I thought to myself. Lansing certainly seemed to be a sharper dresser than
most of the plainclothes cops I had met. Of course, he did
share one ugly piece of attire with all the others, the leather
hip holster, his dark brown and well-worn and holding an
ominous-looking automatic pistol. He moved behind the
desk, with the easy grace of the physically fit, I noted, sat
in the swivel chair, crossed his right ankle over his left
knee, leaned back, and looked up at me with a neutral gaze.

"Why thank you, I'd love to have a seat," I said, closing
the door on Bill, who had sat down in one of the gray metal
chairs in the hall to look at some notes. I deposited myself
in Lansing's guest chair, bending to lay my purse at my

feet, then put my notebook and pen in my lap, unopened but available should Detective Lansing decide to be forthcoming with hot tips. I looked up again to find him still studying me with the same steady, unrevealing look in his intense blue eyes. We watched each other in silence. I felt like a virus under a microscope. Finally, Lansing took pity on me or just got impatient.

"What did you want to ask me, Ms. McPhee? I can't believe you're suddenly at a loss for words."

That pissed me off, but it kicked my brain, which seemed to keep going on vacation around this guy, back into gear.

"Never," I assured him, smiling. "I'd be out of business."

"Mmm," he responded. I had a strong suspicion that the idea appealed to him.

I plunged ahead.

"Are you going to be questioning Hub Taylor further?"

"Yes."

"Can you tell me when?"

"Probably later today."

"Any autopsy results yet?"

"No."

"Well, when do you expect them? I'm sure the medical examiner has put a rush on them, considering who the victim was."

Lansing's tone remained unchanged: cool, inflectionless. "I expect the first batch sometime today or tomorrow. Some of the blood work and toxicology reports will take longer."

"Any suspects or motives yet?"

"I can't tell you any more than I said yesterday." It was clear that he hadn't changed his mind about me since then, either.

"Look," I said, deciding to take a chance on honesty. "I really just wanted to introduce myself sort of formally and to say that I don't want yesterday to give you the wrong idea about me. That was just the latest skirmish in some good-natured ribbing between Bill and me. Neither of us was serious.'' I paused, waiting for a response.

I got none, just the look.

''Anyway,'' I went on, less encouraged by the second, ''what I am serious about is my job. I'm good at it, but to do it, I need information. The Janet Taylor murder is a big story. I . . . ah . . . what I'm trying to say is that I hope you'll be up front with me. Tell me what you can tell me. If you can't tell me something, just say so. But don't bullshit me. And if you tell me something off the record, I promise you won't see your name connected with it in print.''

His look was unwavering—and silent. I felt like an ass.

Finally, Lansing blinked. I thought, So he's not in a coma after all.

''Ms. McPhee, I don't give a damn whether you're serious about your job or not,'' he said. Yes, there definitely was life there, but it wasn't a friendly form.

''I just—'' I began.

''Can it,'' he snapped. He uncrossed his leg and, with both feet now firmly on the floor, leaned forward, forearms on the desk, and laced his fingers—none of which wore a wedding ring, I noticed—together. His eyes had lost their neutral expression. They were definitely hostile again.

''You want honesty? You've got it. I don't like you, Ms. McPhee, and I don't like what you do for a living. I have to go out there and deal with people getting killed, up close and personal, while you . . . well, you're a voyeur. Even worse, you think all this is funny. I'll give you information, but only when it isn't going to jeopardize my investigation and only when I give it to the rest of the press. Don't expect favors from me. You won't get them. Now, if you'll excuse me, I have real work to do so no one else gets killed, if I can prevent it. Good-bye, Ms. McPhee.''

I snapped my jaw shut. It must have been hanging open

during his entire outburst. I grabbed the notebook and pen out of my lap, picked my purse up off the floor, gathered what was left of my dignity, and marched to the door. Lansing might set off all my hormones, but the reporter in me was still in control when it came to having the last word. I stopped and turned toward him.

"I don't know what your problem is, Detective, but it isn't nice to piss off the press. Sometimes we know things you'd like to know, too. But don't worry, I'll be back, so tell me what you know, or don't tell me. But whatever you do, don't lie to me. Oh, and a couple of other things. One, if you knew anything about me at all, you would know I don't find anything about murder funny. And second my name isn't Ms. It's Sutton."

With that, I left—some might say fled—and nearly fell over Bill, still sitting in the hall. Without a word he stood up, took my arm, and steered me down the hall to the small lunchroom at the opposite end, next to the briefing room.

I was practically sputtering in frustration. This wasn't going well. Something about me pushed all of Noah Lansing's buttons, but I had no idea what. I knew plenty of cops who didn't care much for reporters, but they usually weren't hostile for no reason. I hoped Bill could give me a reading on Lansing that would help me get a handle on this thing before it got completely out of control. Who knew how often I would have to cover a case he was working?

Five

In the lunchroom, empty at the moment, Bill left me at the last of the four tables, walked over to a coffee vending machine, put in some coins, pressed a few buttons, and got two cups of black coffee in return. A lot of cops these days are into fitness and healthier foods and turn their noses up at overcooked vending-machine coffee. But Bill said once that he had been drinking coffee that could stand on its own two feet too long to change his ways now. He walked back over and put down the cups, a grin on his face. I could have slugged him.

"Is round one over?" he asked smugly, sitting down across the table.

"What an asshole," I huffed, dropping into the chair next to me. "What is his problem, anyway?"

"What's the matter, McPhee? Finally met someone who's a match for you in the sharp-tongue department?" Bill was enjoying this far too much.

"Boy, he just flayed me alive in there, and I don't even know the guy! And for that matter, he doesn't know me.

What's with him? And would you stop laughing at me?''

Bill sobered, a little.

"I'm sorry, Sutton. I just don't get to see you bested very often. I would have warned you if I'd had a chance, but there hasn't been time. He just came on board a couple of weeks ago, and this is his first big case. I knew you and Lansing would be like oil and water.''

"What are you, some kind of psychic?''

"No, but I know you, and I know his story. Any idiot could figure out you wouldn't get along.''

"And just why not, pray tell, oh wiseass . . . excuse me, wise one?''

"Because of his wife.''

So much for the wedding-ring observation . . . and my hormones.

"His wife? What's the matter? She doesn't like him working with female reporters? Is she the jealous type?'' My sarcasm was in full force by now, mostly because I was so angry at myself for letting Lansing make me lose my cool.

"No, the dead type. And Lansing blames a smart-ass woman newspaper reporter like you for it.'' For all his easygoing manner, Bill knew how to go for the jugular when he thought it was called for.

"Aw, shit,'' I said, sitting back in the chair as muddied waters cleared. "Well, you sure let me get blindsided with that one. What happened?''

Bill no longer looked amused. "It was in Virginia Beach, where Lansing worked before coming here. Maybe five years ago,'' he said.

"Lansing was working undercover on a drug case. One night he was in a bar with some hard-core coke-dealer types and ran into a reporter who had worked at the paper in Charlottesville when Lansing was in graduate school at UVA and worked for the campus police. She had dealt with him two or three times on stories, so when she moved to the Norfolk paper and saw him in the bar, she recognized him. Lansing apparently had to hint around at what he was doing to shut her up before she gave him away. She seemed to think it was pretty funny, and said it would make great headlines. She didn't let on that night in the bar that he was a cop, but two weeks later the paper ran a series by another reporter about drug trafficking in the whole Hampton Roads area and pretty much said that the police had managed to plant at least one undercover cop in the drug ring's inner circle. Lansing wasn't named, but his superiors immediately pulled him out, and I guess someone put it all together. A few days later his wife was abducted from the parking lot of a grocery store. They found her body three days later. She had been beaten, raped repeatedly, and then shot. Her body was thrown out in a park, where it was meant to be found easily, obviously as a message.''

I felt ill.

''She and Lansing had a baby, a little boy, and he's been raising the kid alone ever since. From what I hear from Virginia Beach, he was crazy about his wife, and what happened nearly killed him with grief. Apparently he blamed himself. I guess it was the kid who kept him going.''

That explained the little boy on the sailboat, I supposed, and Noah Lansing's reaction to me. It also underscored why my mother always told me I was far too quick to sit in judgment of people. She was right, as usual, and now I felt like something that had crawled out from under a rock—or one of the supermarket tabloids. But I didn't have the luxury of sitting around feeling sorry for myself.

''Okay,'' I asked Bill, ''how do I begin to repair this? I have to have access to this guy.''

''Just be straightforward,'' Bill advised, standing up and crumpling his empty coffee cup, ''and maybe cool the smart mouth a little, at least around him. I'll do some smoothing of the waters behind the scene. I can't guarantee you'll get anything special, but you won't be shut out. Lan-

sing is a professional, too, and I really don't think he wants
you out for his blood. Nobody in their right mind would.''

Nor did I want to be. In spite of my urge to strangle him
a few minutes earlier, there was something about Noah
Lansing that made me want him to see me in a halfway
positive light.

"Something" as in hormones, maybe? I ignored my im-
pertinent questioner.

"And Sutton," Bill said, "there's one more thing I'd
better tell you."

I groaned, knowing I wasn't going to want to hear this
either.

"Tom Coster has moved over to our special-operations
unit," he went on. Coster was the detective who was handling the Ann Kane case.

"So who's going to cover Ann Kane?" I asked, and then
I knew the answer. "No, please don't tell me. Not him."

"Right, Noah Lansing has that one, too."

"Well, that's great," I muttered, having visions of Rob
Perry berating me over a blank computer screen, uninter-
ested in my explanation for why I had no stories for him.
"Just great!" It looked like I would be running into Noah
Lansing every way I turned. This was quickly becoming an
untenable situation. I had to at least make an effort to fix
things.

I walked over to the coffee machine, put in some coins,
and got a second cup of coffee. I picked up my things from
the table and followed Bill back out into the hall. At the
door into the lobby, he reached to open it for me.

"Hold on just one minute," I said, and went down the
hall instead, back to Lansing's office.

"Sutton," Bill called after me, exasperated, "what are
you doing?"

I stepped inside Lansing's door. He was standing, his back
to me, looking out the window, his suit jacket in his right

hand and thrown over his shoulder. I could tell his mind was someplace far away, so I cleared my throat.

He turned, dropping the jacket down to his side, his eyes cutting like a knife through the space between us, either because his thoughts had been interrupted or because he realized it was me, or both. I didn't give him time to say anything. I put the coffee cup on his desk.

"A peace offering," I explained quickly. "I really don't want to have to fight with you just to do my job."

For just a fraction of a second the anger in his eyes turned into something else, a look that I could have sworn was pain. He opened his mouth to speak, but I was already going back out the door and down the hall. Bill, who was still standing there, swept open the lobby door, ushered me through it, on through the lobby, and out the front door, where he stopped.

"You're incorrigible, you know," he said, shaking a finger at me.

"It's why you love me so," I responded, waving airily as I walked off to my car, asking myself why Lansing had to be so damned good-looking and intelligent, too. Graduate school, no less!

Six

Ken Hale and Rob Perry were deep in conversation up at the news desk when I walked into the newsroom. Ken, who was facing my way, motioned me over. I went ahead to my desk to put away my things and saw that my voice-mail light was blinking frantically, its usual state. It'll have to wait, I thought, and went over to join Rob and Ken.

"Anything from the cops?" Rob asked, knowing I usually was up and out early to talk with Bill Russell and to put in an appearance at one or two police stations. It helped me find out what had happened overnight and also helped me develop sources. Familiarity can breed loose lips as well as contempt.

"Lansing says they'll have the autopsy results sometime today or tomorrow," I answered. "I'll have them about as fast as he does."

Ken raised an eyebrow in question, but I just smiled confidently. I had learned long ago and the hard way not to reveal how I got information, even to another reporter, except under very exceptional circumstances. It was about the same time I learned that the most important people to cultivate in any office are usually the worker bees—the secretaries, the clerks, the people who answer the phones or open the mail. These people usually are the least appreciated in any office and often are the ones who know as much as or more about what goes on than the bosses do. I make every effort to be friendly, to treat them with respect, and occasionally to do favors for them. I have sources everywhere—the courthouses, the phone company, the local hospitals. My respect for the people who really make the world work makes any number of them more than happy to tell me what they know when I need to know it. Like I did now.

Cheryl Wiggins was a good example. A transcriptionist in the Northern Virginia Medical Examiner's Office, Cheryl had a boss she didn't like. She also had a college-age daughter who would be working as a summer intern at our rival, the *Post,* in part because I had put in a good word for her with their assistant vice-president for human resources. He had been the personnel director at the *Democrat* in Tallahassee, back when I was a reporter there and back when people's job titles actually told you what they did. Cheryl had become my best pipeline into the world of medical examining, not only for timely updates on causes of death, but also on frequently interesting tidbits about other things found during an autopsy, things that didn't necessarily contribute to the death but that were important pieces in the picture of how and why someone died. I made a mental note to call her.

"Oh, yeah," I added, looking back at Ken. "They're also going to be bringing Hub Taylor in for some more questioning sometime today."

"That's what I heard, too," Ken replied. From a lot of other reporters, a comment like that would require a tiring little round of "I Can Top You." Ken was a solid reporter, who didn't play those kinds of games because he didn't have to.

"I called Mannie Sims to try to get an interview with Taylor," he went on to explain. "He said Taylor is staying at Ed Lloyd's house until after the funeral and that he won't be available today because he has to go in to talk with the police."

"When's the funeral?" Rob asked.

"Tomorrow, if the medical examiner gets done in time. The Taylors go to a Methodist church in McLean. Willow Hill Methodist, I think. They're having the funeral there. Mannie said they're letting only the family and close friends in, no press. But I suppose I'd better go anyway, even if it's just to stand around outside."

Rob nodded in agreement. "So what will I have coming from the two of you for tomorrow morning's paper?" he asked. Just as reporters have to, Rob always is thinking at least twenty-four hours ahead in addition to whatever moment he's actually in. His job—and ours—require it, but it sometimes makes for rather schizophrenic thinking. At any one time you're dealing with the fallout from your story in this morning's paper, you're trying to be in four places at once to cover what's going on today, and you're worrying about what kind of story you'll have for the next day's edition and whether your competition will have your tomorrow story in their pages today. It's no wonder Rob has three ex-wives and he dresses funny. And he isn't the only one in the newsroom who fits that description.

"Well, I'll have the autopsy results," I told him, "and anything I can get on Hub Taylor's police interrogation."

"And I'm doing a profile of both the Taylors," Ken added. "I've gotten quotes from a couple of fund-raiser types about how much Janet Taylor's death will hurt their efforts. She could talk money out of a stone, and some of these charities were pretty dependent on what she brought in, and what she contributed herself. Somehow, I suspect

Hub may not be as generous with the money as his late wife was.''

Rob looked down at his shoes, put his right hand on his hip, and used his left hand to squeeze his forehead into a giant wrinkle in the middle. It was Rob's classic I'm-thinking-about-what-you-said-but-you-could-make-me-happier stance.

''Okay,'' he said finally, dropping his hand from his face and looking back up at us. ''I'll put them in the lineup. But I gotta tell you, they don't sound real exciting. If you come up with something better, let me know ASAP.'' What went without saying was that he shortly had a noon editors' meeting in Mack Thompson's office, where he would have to lay on the table his stories for tomorrow's issue, including any we were contributing to page one, and he probably would have to take a lot of heat from Mark Lester, who was chomping at the bit to take the Janet Taylor murder away from us. Editors sometimes have to fight for space for stories they aren't writing and haven't seen. And editors like nothing better than congenially ripping each other to shreds. So when your editor puts his (or her) gonads on the chopping block for your upcoming story, you had damned well better produce.

Rob turned and walked to the back of the newsroom, probably to go to the cafeteria for coffee to fortify himself for the editors' meeting. A lot of reporters and editors over-indulge in alcohol: They have to find some way to counteract all the caffeine they consume during the day.

Ken and I went back to our respective desks, where I knew the voice-mail light on my phone was still waiting.

It was the usual cast of clowns with no perspective on reality. A guy from Springfield wanted me to investigate why the police were out to get him. He knew they were because they gave him three speeding tickets in a month. A real-estate agent in Mount Vernon was upset that the police had an officer assigned full-time to the high school there, which she worried would bring down property values. I wondered if I should call her and tell her about the undercover officers posing as students and staff. Then I got to the third message.

The beep was followed by a hesitant male voice.

"Ms. McPhee, I really need to talk with you in person. I . . . uh, I think I may know something about Ann Kane." He paused for several beats. "But I don't want to say any more to a recording. I'll call you back." I hit the button to listen to the message again. He sounded rational enough, the voice crisp, cultivated, but reluctant, maybe even a little afraid. I went on through the voice mail, only to hear two more calls that were hang-ups without messages. Probably the same guy, I thought. It was frustrating, but since he had left no name or number, all I could do was wait for him to call again. In the meantime I still needed to reach Cheryl Wiggins about Janet Taylor's autopsy.

Cheryl was in. We had agreed on a pseudonym for me to use when I was calling to get information from her. I identified myself to the receptionist as Miss Lane (as in Lois Lane, my little private joke) and Cheryl came on the line immediately.

"I'll bet I know why you're calling," she said in greeting.

"It's pretty obvious," I agreed. "I need Janet Taylor's results as soon as you can call me with them."

"No problem. They're finishing up now, and I'll be getting the tape to transcribe into the computer. In a case like this, Dr. Riner usually calls the police with the results as soon as the autopsy is done, but I can call you when I go out to lunch and let you know what the report said."

"Thanks, Cheryl. I owe you one. And if I'm not here for any reason, leave it on my voice mail. Nobody can access it but me. You've got my direct number?"

"I do."

"Talk to you later. And thanks again." We hung up, and

the instant I replaced the receiver, the phone rang.

"Sutton McPhee," I answered, snatching it back up.

"Ms. McPhee?" I recognized the caller as the mystery voice from my message. It wasn't difficult. On the police beat, I don't deal with many people who speak with the sounds of a Boston Brahmin background.

"Yes, hi. I'm glad you called back. Who are you?"

"I'll tell you that when I see you, Ms. McPhee. Could we meet? I really need to talk to somebody about this, and I don't think I can go to the police."

"Where and when? I can meet you right now." If this guy really did know something about how or why Ann Kane died, I didn't want to take a chance on his getting spooked and disappearing or calling another reporter. This could be the first and only break I—or anyone else—might get in her death. And while Rob had told us to forget any stories other than Janet Taylor's murder, I knew better than to let this chance pass. I would just neglect to mention it to him until I had something I could nail down and that he couldn't be mad at me for.

"I think my office might actually be the best place," the caller said. "We close from twelve-thirty until two, and my staff is going out today for a birthday party for my office manager. I'll be here alone."

"That's fine. What's the name of your company and where do I find you?"

"It's in Vienna . . . Maple Avenue. Do you know it?"

"I know where Maple Avenue is."

"Okay, the office is at 397 Maple Avenue West, Suite 104. Come at twelve forty-five. That will give my staff time to leave. The office door will be locked, but just knock and I'll let you in."

Driving out to Vienna meant I would miss Cheryl's call, but I knew she would leave the information as I had asked her to.

"I'll be there at twelve forty-five. Thanks for—"

The click in my ear told me he had hung up.

The curiosity devil had me full in his grip now. The caller's voice said he really did know something—or thought he did—and it wasn't something he was at all happy about knowing. I decided to go on out to Vienna and scope out the address. Knowing in advance who I was dealing with might give me an edge in knowing what to ask this guy once I met him.

Seven

Vienna is one of the older Virginia suburbs of Washington. It sits south and west of the Potomac, a couple or so miles west of the Capital Beltway, that eight-lane circle of asphalt around the capital that acts as a barrier to any logic or common sense penetrating from the rest of the country. Maple Avenue is one of Vienna's main streets, lined with countless small businesses and office buildings. Three-ninety-seven was par for the course, a two-story office building of white painted brick and green wood trim. I drove into the parking lot, looking for Suite 104.

It proved to be on the back right corner of the building, facing the parking lot. As I drove slowly by, I could see the name on the bronze plate next to the door: PETER MOR-RIS, M.D., INTERNAL MEDICINE.

Peter Morris. Dr. Peter Morris. This was sounding less like a nutcase and more like the real thing. My watch said it was 11:45, and the three cars parked around the door of Suite 104 told me Dr. Morris was probably pretty busy right now, so I didn't see any point in hanging around. Instead

I decided to find someplace to grab a quick lunch and to try to learn a little more about the good doctor.

I pulled back out onto Maple Avenue and, within a couple more blocks, found a Wendy's fast-food restaurant. I used the drive-through window to get a grilled chicken sandwich, some coleslaw, and a diet Coke and drove around the back to one of several empty parking spaces.

I picked up my cellular phone and called the information operator to get the number for Fairfax Hospital, the largest hospital in the area, the closest to downtown Vienna, and the one where Dr. Peter Morris most likely would have staff privileges. I dialed the hospital and asked the switchboard operator for the office that would have information on physicians. She quickly put me through to something the secretary who answered identified as Medical Staff Services.

"Hi," I told her. "I'm new to the area and I'm looking for a doctor who uses your hospital. A friend recommended Dr. Peter Morris to me, and I wondered if you could tell me whether he has staff privileges there."

"Yes he does," she answered without hesitation. "In fact, Dr. Morris is the chief of internal medicine here."

"I see." I thought for a moment. "I suppose that means he's good at what he does?"

"Well, we're not allowed to make physician recommendations," she said in a well-rehearsed voice, "but I think it's safe to say he's well thought of by the other physicians and he's well-known in the community."

"Listen, thanks a lot for your help. Sounds like my friend was right about him."

Curiouser and curiouser, I thought as I hung up and reached for my lunch. What would a prominent physician out in Virginia know about the death of a woman who lived on Capitol Hill and whose body was found twenty-five miles away in a forest? And what would make him risk his solid-gold reputation by telling a reporter about it?

At 12:15, I put the scraps of my lunch back into their

takeout bag and called in to my voice mail at the newspaper. Immediately I heard Cheryl Wiggins.

"Hi, Sutton," her recorded voice said without identifying herself. "I think I have something you'll find interesting, although I don't know what it means. It seems Janet Taylor wasn't strangled to death. There was a scarf cinched around her neck, but that wasn't what killed her. In fact, it looks like the scarf was put there after she was already dead. Dr. Riner says she actually died from a closed head wound, a skull fracture, and that she didn't die right away. The blow was to the left side of her head, probably from the front. She could have been unconscious for an hour or two before she died, and he put her time of death at between two-thirty and three-thirty P.M. Also, she wasn't raped and there were no signs of her trying to fight anyone off, no skin under the fingernails or any other injuries except the blow to the head and the phony strangulation. Well, I hope this helps. 'Bye."

Interesting was right. And while I couldn't say for sure what it meant either, I did have some ideas. It could very well mean that Janet Taylor didn't put up a struggle because she knew the person in the room with her and she never expected that person to harm her. And it significantly changed the time when everyone had mistakenly assumed the attack occurred.

I really wanted to get over to the police station where Hub Taylor was to be questioned, maybe even was being questioned right now. But I also had to meet with Dr. Morris to find out what he knew about Ann Kane. Now I had two dead women, at least one of them a murder victim, whose faces floated in front of me, asking for someone to learn how they died, to expose the evil that had found each of them. I knew neither was going to leave me alone until I had those answers.

• • •

Back at Dr. Morris's office, I parked my car several spots away, next to cars for another office, but close enough to watch people going in and out of his door. At 12:35, I saw a group of three women come out, chatting and laughing, to pile into a black Jeep Wagoneer across the parking lot and leave, followed a couple of minutes later by two more women, who left in a blue Ford Escort.

At 12:45 exactly, when no one else had put in an appearance, I got out and walked over to the office, where I knocked sharply on the door. It opened in seconds, held by a green-eyed, blond-haired man of about forty-five, whose six-foot-or-so frame was covered in a knee-length white coat over a crisp white shirt, a navy-and-red-striped tie, and black suit pants. He would have been handsome, but the dark circles under his eyes and the generally exhausted look about him weren't flattering and told me I was seeing someone who was dealing with a lot of internal conflict and not handling it well.

"Ms. McPhee?" he asked, just as I said, "Dr. Morris?"

"Please, come in," he answered quickly, stepping back to open the door fully, then closing it behind me. The waiting area of his office was done in soft tasteful shades of plum and pale rose, with expensively upholstered armchairs and love seats, and what appeared to be signed, numbered lithographs on the wall. This was the office of a very successful doctor, I thought, wondering again what could be driving him to talk to me.

"Sit down, won't you?" He gestured to one of the armchairs in the far corner, by a window. "Could I get you some coffee?"

"No, no thanks," I answered, taking the chair he indicated. "I just had lunch, and I have a feeling you'd like to do this quickly, before your staff comes back and sees me here."

He took the companion armchair, which was positioned

to let him see out into the parking lot and from which he looked me over thoughtfully.

"I . . . I've never really dealt with a reporter before," he began hesitantly. "Is it true that if I ask you to, you will keep anything I tell you in confidence?"

"It's true that if I agree this is off the record, I won't attribute it to you unless you tell me I can. I'll try to corroborate what you say some other way so that I can report it without identifying you as the original source of the information. You have my word on that, Dr. Morris. Keeping a source confidential when I've promised to do so is a basic part of my job. My credibility is the only currency I have, with my sources and my readers. Plenty of reporters have gone to jail rather than violate the confidence of a source, and I feel pretty strongly about it, too."

Dr. Morris was sitting at an angle in the chair, his legs crossed and his hands clasped in his lap. As he looked down at those hands it was clear to me from his body language that this was a man who was used to being in charge of the situation and who now found himself at the mercy of events. I decided I would get more out of him by letting him take the lead than by prodding. So I held my tongue—a monumental feat—and waited for him to begin. After a minute or so he looked up and I knew he would tell me what he so obviously needed to tell someone.

"I suppose we're somewhat alike in that way, Ms. McPhee."

"What way is that? And please, call me Sutton."

"We're both keepers of confidences, Sutton. Just as I'm sure you are, I'm frequently told very personal things about my patients' lives, with the expectation that what they tell me will go no further. In fact, I'm under legal and ethical restrictions to keep their secrets, and I could be punished for what I tell."

I nodded silently.

"This is very difficult for me, you see. Telling you what

I'm afraid I know goes against all my training and experience. But I also was trained to save lives, to do everything in my power to save lives. Ever since I read the stories about Ann Kane, I've been torn over what to do. I'm afraid I may know what happened to her, and if I do, I might be the only person who can keep it from happening again.''

"Then why not go to the police, Dr. Morris?"

"Because I could be wrong. So very wrong. And if I am, the person I believe was involved is in a position to destroy me. If I go to the police, I would have no control over what they say to whom or how their investigation is conducted. I was hoping that if I told you what I know, you might be able to get at the truth without sacrificing my career.''

"I'll do the best I can."

Again he looked down at his hands in thought. When he made his decision to tell me the rest, I could see it in the squaring of his shoulders as he looked back up.

"I think Senator Ed Lloyd may have had something to do with Ann Kane's death."

Although I'm not a gasper, I came pretty close to it at the magnitude of his blunt statement. Senator Ed Lloyd, senior Virginia statesman and mentor of the recently widowed Hubbard Taylor, was one of the most powerful men in the country. He had the money and influence to buy and sell anybody I knew ten times over, and the political clout to make even the president tremble. But I tamped down my shock for fear a strong reaction on my part would frighten Morris back into silence.

"That's a pretty strong statement, Dr. Morris," I said finally. "What makes you think so?"

"Because I helped him cover up an earlier situation that could have killed another young woman like Ann Kane."

Peter Morris was watching me closely, his eyes asking me not to judge him too harshly. I could see that whatever it was he thought he knew had been tearing him apart, and his self-respect was in shreds.

"Go on," I prodded him.

"It was several weeks, maybe a month, before Ann Kane died. A Sunday night. I was home alone at my house in McLean. I'm divorced, you see, and my ex-wife has moved back to Boston, so I live in our house. I got a phone call from Senator Lloyd, who's been a patient of mine for about ten years. It was late, almost eleven. I know because I looked at the clock when the phone rang so late. Ed told me he had a problem that he needed my help with, and he asked me to meet him here at my office. I asked what kind of problem. He said his date had gotten ill and needed to see a doctor right away. Of course, I recommended he get her to an emergency room or call an ambulance. He said he couldn't do that, that she was ill because of something she had taken at his house and he needed help from someone who could be discreet about it. I thought they must have been doing some drugs together or something. I'd never known Ed to have any sort of drug habit, but you know how older men can be around much younger women."

That was true. Ed Lloyd certainly wouldn't have been the first fifty-five- or sixty-year-old politician to make a fool of himself over a pretty young thing. And he already had a reputation to prove it. Dr. Morris went on.

"I tried to reason with him that I might not be able to do what was needed in my office, but Ed insisted that this was the only place he could take her, that I was the only person he could trust. So I agreed. I was afraid to delay him any longer, you see, because I knew the woman had to get to some kind of help soon, and Ed is a very influential and well-connected man who has referred some important patients to me over the years. I was concerned about her, and I didn't want to offend him."

"So you met him here?"

"Yes. I know I shouldn't have. I could have put the woman's life as much at risk as he had. I should have forced him to take her for emergency treatment, but Ed Lloyd can be very . . . persuasive, very forceful. So I met him."

"What happened then?"

"When I got here, his car was parked outside, right in front of the door. He rolled down the window and said for me to come help him. I walked over to his side of the car and then I could see a woman lying down in the backseat with a coat over her. He told me to get her out of his car and inside, but I refused until I knew she was still alive. I told him to unlock the back door, and I opened it and reached in to check her pulse. She had one, but it was thready. Her skin was clammy and her breathing was shallow. She was moaning something and seemed to be at least semiconscious. I gave Lloyd the key to the office door and told him to get it unlocked and turn on a light while I got her out of the car."

"Did you know the woman?"

"No. I couldn't really see her well in the car, but once I got her inside and on an examination table, I could see she wasn't anyone I knew."

"Did Senator Lloyd tell you who she was?"

"No. He never used even her first name. In fact, at one point I asked him who she was, and he told me it was better if I didn't know."

"Okay, so then what happened?"

"As I said, I took her into one of my exam rooms and began to check her over, and I asked Lloyd what had happened, what she had taken. He told me she had taken Demerol."

"The same thing that helped kill Ann Kane," I said.

"Yes," Dr. Morris agreed. "At first I assumed it was this woman's own medication. I asked Ed if she had been drinking along with it. He said she had had a couple of cocktails. I asked him how long after the drinks and the Demerol before she had gotten ill and what kind of symptoms she'd had. He said it took twenty or thirty minutes and that she had gotten very drowsy but also very agitated, and she kept falling down. That was when he called me.''

''Were you able to help her?''

''Yes, fortunately for all of us. A doctor's office has to keep certain equipment and supplies on hand in case a patient has a bad reaction to medication they've taken in the office. In a few minutes I was able to pump her stomach and do some other things to make her more comfortable. She responded well to it, and finally dropped off to sleep. I monitored her vitals for a couple of hours, long enough to see that she would be all right. I told Lloyd he should take her home and put her to bed. I told him she'd feel like hell for a day or so, but that she should be okay. He said, 'Of course she will. I knew I could count on you to take care of her.' But he said it in this cold, unemotional voice. I realized that he had shown very little concern for the woman the entire time she was in my office, other than to make sure she would be well enough so no one would know what had happened. That was when I remembered.''

''Remembered what?''

''That I had prescribed Demerol for Ed Lloyd after some office surgery. Maybe nine months before. It was a onetime prescription, but he probably didn't need the full amount. The conviction began to grow on me that Ed had given her the Demerol. When I started asking myself why he would have done such a thing, I didn't like the answers I came up with. That was when I began to be afraid.''

''So you think Ed Lloyd risked this woman's health by drugging her, maybe in order to have sex with her?'' I had heard the stories of Ed Lloyd over the years, as had every other reporter who had spent any time in or around Washington: his womanizing, his drinking, his divorce when his wife of decades couldn't stomach it any longer, and his vindictiveness when a woman he wanted turned him down. But this allegation that he had drugged a woman to have sex with her was a new and outrageous low.

"I knew he did," Morris answered, his shoulders slumping down into the chair. "I looked at him, and in that moment I knew he did, and he saw that I knew it. That was when he threatened me."

"In what way?"

"Not blatantly, you understand. He's too experienced a politician for that. He helped the woman out to the car and came back inside. He said, 'Doctor, I need to be sure that this little incident will stay just between you and me.' He said, 'I can't afford for this story to get out . . . and neither can you. She's just a piece of ass I found up on the Hill, and she's not worth our careers.' I knew he meant what he said, that if I told anyone, reported it to anyone, he'd do his best to ruin me."

"How could he do that?"

"At the very least I was guilty of poor medical judgment. I shouldn't have let him bring her to my office instead of an emergency room, knowing she was having a reaction to some kind of drug. When I found out what it was, I should have called an ambulance immediately. She could have had permanent neurological damage. She could have died. And when I realized he had drugged her deliberately, I was afraid I might be guilty of helping him cover up a crime of some sort. So I let him take her home, and I assumed she was okay when I never heard any more about it. Until they found Ann Kane."

Now we were getting down to it, to what had convinced Morris that Ed Lloyd was involved in Ann Kane's death and had driven him to call me.

"Dr. Morris, was this woman Ann Kane?"

"No, no. I'm sure of that. This woman had black hair, and she looked very different from the picture of Ann Kane that the papers ran."

"Then I don't understand, Doctor," I said, trying to keep impatience out of my voice. "What is it about all this that makes you think Ed Lloyd had anything to do with Kane's death?"

"Like Ann Kane, this woman worked on Capitol Hill. That's what he called her, a piece of ass he found up on the Hill. Someone he could have met there but who wasn't at a level to have any power over him. Someone very much like Ann Kane."

My hopes were dashed. Was this all he had?

"Is that it?" I asked, sitting forward in the chair. "You're accusing Ed Lloyd of having a role in Ann Kane's death because you think he drugged another woman who also probably works on the Hill? That could be nothing more than coincidence, Doctor."

"No, there's more," Morris answered tiredly. "There's the fact that Ann Kane also had been given Demerol, something the police don't believe she would have taken herself because she was on an MOA. And there's the sperm. The police said that based on the sperm they found in her, one of the men who'd been with Ann Kane had AB-negative blood. That's a rare blood type, Sutton. But Ed Lloyd is AB-negative. I know none of this is proof, but you tell me, how far can coincidence stretch?"

I let it sink in. Peter Morris was right. None of it, not even the blood type, was proof, not by a long shot. But it was a connection—and one that all my instincts told me was real. I saw Ann Kane's body again, lying naked in the woods at Mason Neck, surrounded by yellow police tape and a cadre of patrol cops and homicide detectives, her blue lips, the thin trail of blood and vomit dried down the side of her chin, her chestnut hair a tangled mess, her hazel eyes staring sightlessly into the spring morning.

I sagged back in the chair, my posture echoing Morris's. He was right. I knew he was right. It's a feeling that good cops and reporters alike get when, even though a trail of solid evidence doesn't yet exist, something in a part of the brain that operates outside logic and fact sits up and says, "Pay attention. This has the imprint of truth."

Ed Lloyd. No, damn it, *Senator* Edward Lloyd! What a story. I could hear the fame sirens singing. The kind of story that makes a career, they sang. If you can nail it down, if you can prove it without getting eaten alive in the process. What a nightmare it would be to prove, though. What a slimy son of a bitch! I felt the adrenaline. And then I felt a brush of air moving across my forearms, raising the hairs, like a wispy tendril of fear.

Eight

I studied Peter Morris for a minute or so as the hamsters that turned the wheels in my brain went into wind sprints, sorting through the possibilities, looking for the most productive way to go after this story.

"So what do you think of all this, Sutton?" Morris asked me finally.

"I think that it's very possible you could be right about this. I think that Ed Lloyd certainly has one of the busiest zippers on the hill. But this—this is absolutely creepy. And if you are right, that he drugged the woman you met and that Ann Kane might have been another victim of his, it's going to take some hard, and very careful work to prove it. Ed Lloyd isn't somebody to take lightly."

"I know," he answered, "all too well."

"Dr. Morris, I need to know everything you can tell me about the woman Lloyd brought to your office, anything you can remember about her that might help me track her down. She may be the key to this whole thing and the only way to corroborate what you've already told me. Tell me everything, no matter how trivial.''

Morris's gaze focused on the plate-glass window facing the parking lot as he went back again to the night Ed Lloyd had called him.

''I remember how she looked,'' he said eventually, his voice in that faraway near monotone of someone concentrating hard on a memory. ''She looked terrible, of course, but I could tell she actually was very lovely. Long, dark hair, down just below her shoulders. Full red lips. Pale skin, naturally pale, not just from being ill, with a beautiful texture, very fine pores. And when she finally was recovering, she opened her eyes and I could see that they were a striking violet color. Almost like Elizabeth Taylor's.''

I was jotting it all down in my mental notebook, not wanting anything on paper to connect Peter Morris with any story I might eventually do. It was an added risk for me and for the paper, should someone decide they had grounds to sue, but one I was willing to take to protect a source.

''And she was tall,'' he went on. ''Maybe five-eight or five-nine, and slim. Very nice figure. And, as I said, well dressed. She was wearing a deep magenta woven dress, like a sweater. Cashmere. It was a mess, of course, but expensive and ordinarily very lovely.''

''Did she say anything, to you or to Lloyd, anything that might give us a clue?'' I hesitated to interrupt his thoughts, but a surreptitious glance at my watch told me we were running out of time.

''Not really,'' Morris answered, focusing on me again. ''After I got the Demerol out of her, she roused somewhat, became more aware of what was going on. That was when she opened her eyes. She looked terrified and confused. I quickly told her I was a doctor, that she was sick and was in my office. She began to cry, and I realized Ed had walked up behind me. She started to cry when she saw him.

He reached around me to pat her arm and said, 'There, there, my dear, you'll be just fine. But I think it's better if you don't try to talk now.' You should have seen the way she flinched when he touched her. Maybe that was what set off the first alarms in my mind. I could see she was afraid of Ed.''

"But she never said anything to you, anything at all?''

"Nothing. She was exhausted, of course, and I told her just to close her eyes and sleep, that I would sit there with her for a while to make certain she was okay. She actually reached out and took my hand and held on to it until she drifted off.''

Dr. Morris looked as if the thought that she had trusted him just made him feel worse instead of better.

I could see that Morris was giving me everything he could remember. I decided he probably wasn't going to remember anything else at the moment, even if there was more to remember. Sometimes thinking hard about something is the least productive way to get at it. Morris thought then to look at his own watch.

"Oh my,'' he said, "it's getting late, and my staff could be back anytime. I'm sorry, but I think you'd better go now.'' He stood up and so did I.

"That's fine, Dr. Morris,'' I told him. "I've got to go anyhow. But thank you for telling me all this. I'll do the best I can with it, and I promise to keep your name out of it.''

"Thank you, Sutton,'' he said, standing up straighter, as if a weight had been partially lifted from his shoulders. "I don't want to think about the consequences should Ed Lloyd find out what I've told you. I don't want to think about the medical ethics I've violated. I don't want to think about Ann Kane either, but I keep doing so. I finally decided I had to tell someone, someone who might be able to do something about it.''

I reached the door and put my hand on the knob. I looked at Morris hard.

"We know for a fact that Ed Lloyd has risked at least one woman's health for whatever sick reasons of his own," I said sternly. "We suspect he may have killed a second, even if he didn't intend to. No one else, including the police, seems to have any idea that he may be connected to Ann Kane. Until someone puts it all together and stops him, he's free to do it again. And he will. He's a man who wields tremendous power, and I think somewhere in his mind, that power has pushed him over a line. Screw the ethics, Dr. Morris. You did the right thing."

Morris's face colored and he looked down at the floor momentarily. When he raised his face again, his eyes looked clearer than at any time since I had walked in the door.

"Yes," he said, nodding. "I think it was the right thing."

I smiled at him and opened the door.

"Call me if you remember anything else—anything—no matter what time of day or night. You have my office number, and I'm in the phone book," I told him as I stepped outside.

"I will," he agreed, "and thank you, again."

I turned and headed over to my car, hearing him close the office door behind me. Once inside, I just sat behind the wheel, trying to absorb what Dr. Morris had told me. It wasn't until the black Jeep Wagoneer pulled up beside me and three of Morris's office staff got out to go back to work that I remembered I still needed to go down to the police station to find out what had happened with Hubbard Taylor. The possibility that Ann Kane might have died at the hands of a U.S. senator threatened to put Janet Taylor's death farther down my list of story priorities.

And either way, you'll still have to deal with the cute detective who doesn't like you.

Thanks a lot for the news bulletin, I thought back. Now tell me something I don't already know.

Nine

Driving from Vienna to Great Falls, I tried to put my conversation with Peter Morris in the back of my mind, to clear my head for another conversation with Noah Lansing about Janet Taylor. I was no longer under any illusion that I would be able to charm my way into his good graces. Even if I had known about his wife's death when I met him, it still would have meant I would have been going in with one or two strikes against me. But his first impression of me—as a smart-ass reporter who found other people's pain amusing—pretty much sealed my fate as far as he was concerned. It was doubtful if I ever would be able to redeem myself in his eyes. Add to that the fact that he was the lead investigator on my biggest story—whichever of my two murder stories that turned out to be—and the fact that I found myself drawn to him as a man, and it was clear . . . well, it was clear that my friend Bill Russell was going to be highly amused at my expense for quite a while. And it also was clear that I didn't like the position into which I had put myself. It looked like I was going to have to endure a lot more lectures from my little voice.

At the moment the thing that kept going through my mind was what Cheryl had said the autopsy had shown: Janet Taylor hadn't died right away, but in fact had died of a skull fracture, not strangulation. That meant she had been attacked earlier than everyone first thought. And she hadn't tried to defend herself. Which probably meant she had felt safe with the person who killed her. Hubbard Taylor was at a board meeting when she died. That was beyond question. But where was he when she was attacked, possibly as early as 12:30? At the government center? At home? Elsewhere? Did he have an alibi for that time? Relatives, particularly spouses, and significant others are, after all, usually the first people police look at in a murder like this one.

But why would Taylor kill his wife? She had gone far beyond the call of love or duty to support him. She apparently loved him. He apparently loved her. Could their marriage have been less sound than it had seemed on the surface?

A lot of questions for which I had no answers. But I knew Ken Hale might very well have some of them, or could get them. I swung into a gas-station parking lot and used the pay phone to page Ken, dialing in the pay-phone number for his return call. While cellular phones are a wonderful invention, the transmissions also can be picked out of the air, both inadvertently and, if you have the right technology, deliberately. I try never to pass along sensitive information on the car phone.

Three minutes later the pay phone rang. I answered it quickly.

"Ken?"

"Sutton, is that you? I didn't recognize this number."

"It's a pay phone. Listen, I got my hands on the autopsy results for Janet Taylor, and I think there's something there for you to follow up on." I told him what the medical examiner had found and the way my mind was working. "I'm almost at the police station now to find out what Hub Taylor has said, if anything, and to confirm the autopsy results with them."

"Way to go, Sutton," Ken said, with what I could trust was genuine admiration. I could hear excitement rising in his voice. "The board meeting yesterday didn't start again after lunch until two. I'll see what I can find out about where Taylor was until then. And I have a couple of secretaries here who know more about these guys' personal lives than the supervisors themselves do. If there was anything going on with the Taylor marriage, they'll know. I'll see you back at the paper."

"Thanks, Ken," I said, hanging up and turning back to my car.

Ken had great sources at the county government center, I reassured myself as I turned onto Route 7. I could stop worrying about that part of the puzzle for the moment.

Instead I had to figure out how I was going to get anything worthwhile out of Noah Lansing, especially considering the number of other reporters I saw outside the Great Falls substation when I drove into the parking lot. I shouldn't have been surprised. The police interrogation of a county supervisor in his wife's murder is news, whether he's a suspect or not.

No sooner had I gotten out of my car than several people appeared inside the building at the glass front door, and the reporters and photographers all began to move in closer. The door opened, held, I noticed, by Bill Russell. Hubbard Taylor, these days carrying a couple of dozen pounds too many on his middle-aged frame, his face grim and red-eyed, walked out uncertainly and accompanied by a very well-dressed older man with silver hair and pale blue eyes, who carried an expensive leather briefcase. Taylor had seen the pack of reporters and looked like he wanted to turn around and go back inside. His elegant companion—probably his attorney, I realized—stopped, took Taylor by the arm, and turned to face the wolves.

"Ladies and gentlemen," he said, in a deep, courtroom-polished voice, "while we understand your interest in the death of Mrs. Taylor, there is very little we can tell you. My client has spent the better part of two hours with the police, telling them everything he knows that might be of assistance in finding the animal who did this to his wife. But because her death is an open police investigation, we really can't say more than that at this time. Thank you very much." With that, he skillfully slipped through the surrounding reporters, guiding Taylor out to a black limousine now waiting at the curb. Although several reporters continued to call out questions, Mr. *GQ* just smiled at them and got into the limo with Taylor. The closing door cut off the questions, and the limo moved smoothly out onto Crimmons Avenue and into the flow of traffic.

Although Bill Russell had remained inside the station while Taylor and his attorney negotiated their path to the limo, he knew he wouldn't get off as easily as Taylor had. He stood watching in the lobby, waiting for the reporters to turn their attention to him. As soon as the press pack lost Taylor as a source of answers, their heads and cameras swung back to the police. I watched, amused, as Bill quickly stepped outside to intercept them before they could enter the station and irritate anyone inside. I also listened to what he had to say, but I knew it would be perfunctory, almost a replay of the comments of Taylor's attorney. I would have to wait awhile to get anything of value, until the rest of the reporters had gone, and I could talk with Bill and, I hoped, Noah Lansing in private.

"No," Bill was saying, in answer to a question, "Mr. Taylor was here for routine questioning, in hopes that he might have seen or heard or remembered something that would help us in the investigation.''

"Is he a suspect? Do you have any suspects?'' That was Hugh Granham of the *Fairfax Record,* one of a chain of small suburban daily papers. They tried to cover the local suburbs in ways the larger papers couldn't, but their smaller circulations—and thus, their smaller advertising base—meant less money and often a very young and inexperienced staff. Hugh Granham was no exception. Early twenties, new on the *Record* staff after a year at a small daily in Pennsylvania, Hugh had good intentions, but he still frequently was at a loss about how to find out what he needed to know.

Bill, in spite of whatever private doubts he might have about the savvy of certain members of the press corps, publicly accorded all of us the same treatment, except, of course, when he was giving me a hard time.

"Let's just say that while we don't expect to make any arrests today, we are following several important avenues in the investigation,'' he told Granham. I knew that meant they probably had very little, if anything, in the way of evidence or suspects and were hoping someone somewhere would remember something suspicious or get nervous and make a mistake. Or it meant that even if they had a suspect, they couldn't prove anything yet. Hugh, bless his heart, busily scribbled down Bill's every word.

"What about the autopsy report?'' I asked, knowing already what it said. The other reporters tensed for the answer.

Bill looked at me sharply, realizing I probably knew something about those results, but he smoothly did his usual masterful job of giving the police as much investigating space as possible without lying.

"We are still waiting for the official report,'' he answered. Translated, that meant the written report. A phone call wasn't official. We smiled at each other thinly, and two more reporters called out questions. You're quite a dancer, Bill, I thought to myself in admiration.

"I'm sorry," Bill was saying. "That's really all I can tell you at this point. The Fairfax County police are taking this case very seriously, and we are investigating it with every resource we have. But there's just nothing more specific I can say right now. Thank you." He quickly turned and was back inside the station and through the inner door. Knowing they wouldn't get past Jimmy the Desk Officer, the reporters shrugged and began to pack up their equipment and notebooks, some of them muttering about how closemouthed the police could be. I slowly walked back to my own car and got in as if I were leaving, too, but when the last of them had driven away, I got out again and went inside, where I asked Jimmy to call back to Bill and Noah Lansing and ask if they could spare a few minutes for me.

Ten

Jimmy hung up the phone and reached for the buzzer to open the door to the inner sanctum.

"They're in Lansing's office," he said, grinning. "You know the way." Obviously, the word of my little set-to with Lansing that morning was making its way around the station grapevine.

I opened the door and turned left down the hall, hearing the low tones of Bill and Lansing talking through Lansing's open door, but unable to make out their words. As they heard my approaching footsteps on the tiled floor, their conversation halted.

At the doorway I stopped just for a moment to try to tune my instincts' antenna to whatever vibes were floating on the air inside the small office. I had found over the years that I often seemed to be able to pick up on people's emotions even when I had no idea what they meant. More than once this ability had told me when someone was lying or avoiding the truth. More than once it had warned me to keep digging even though appearances said there was nothing there.

Right now, as I looked at Lansing sitting at his desk and Bill leaning against the windowsill, my antenna was picking up a lot of frustration. I just hoped it was with the investigation and not with me.

"Come in, Ms. McPhee," Lansing said, looking at me steadily. Obviously, my earlier hint about my name had fallen on deaf or disinterested ears.

"Hi, Sutton," Bill said, smiling at least.

I walked on into the office and took the blue chair again, but moved it into the corner closest to the door and turned it at an angle to face both men. I sat down, looked up brightly, and said, "So, gentlemen, the plot thickens."

Their look at each other told me they thought it had, too, but they were wondering how I knew it.

"In what way?" Lansing asked coolly.

I smiled at him, having decided he needed an object lesson. It was Lesson Number 1: Never Underestimate Sutton McPhee.

"For starters, I understand you not only have heard from the medical examiner but that the autopsy shows Janet Taylor really died from a blow on the head and that the scarf around her neck either was a smoke screen or possibly a bungled attempt to strangle her when the skull fracture didn't kill her immediately."

Bill looked down at his feet. He had known from my earlier question outside that I had something. He just hadn't realized I had so much.

Noah Lansing looked at me in cold fury.

"Exactly where did you get that information?" he asked, pronouncing each word distinctly.

"Now, now, Detective Lansing," I chided, "you know a good reporter never reveals her sources, especially not the really accurate sources—which this one is, I would guess, judging from your reaction. It's like I told you yesterday. Sometimes reporters know things, too.''

"There's no official medical examiner's report yet," Lansing said. "You can't use—"

"Noah," Bill said softly, "it won't work with her." He stepped in front of the desk and closed the door to the office, then turned to face us and leaned against the door frame. "She obviously has another source."

"I can use anything I can get, Detective," I told Lansing, "but if you'll confirm what I've been told, I won't attribute the information in my story to police sources." I was hoping the implied threat of pointing the source finger at Lansing and the corresponding offer of a compromise would both motivate and placate him.

Lansing looked at Bill, who nodded.

"All right," he agreed. "What have you been told?"

"That, although she appeared to have been strangled, Janet Taylor actually died from a skull fracture. That she didn't die right away. That she might have lain there alive but unconscious for an hour or more before she died. That that little tidbit adds a whole new dimension to who might have had the opportunity to kill her."

"I can confirm the cause of death. It was the skull fracture," Lansing answered, the words apparently leaving a sour taste. "No, she did not die immediately. As to opportunity, I have no comment. You can draw your own conclusions there, Ms. McPhee, but I'd be careful which of them I printed if I were you."

"Don't worry," I said. "I'm intimately familiar with the libel laws."

"No doubt," Lansing answered.

I wasn't going to let him get the best of me. I laughed.

"Okay, point number two," I went on, wanting to keep him off balance, "I also understand that there were no signs of a struggle, other than her overturned wheelchair, and no defensive wounds or anything like skin or blood under her fingernails.''

"Meaning?"

"Meaning either that she was taken totally by surprise, which would be kind of hard considering she was hit on the side of the head, probably from the front, or that she knew the person who killed her and had no reason to think she was in danger.''

"Possibly.'' Lansing wasn't going to admit anything he didn't absolutely have to, at least not to me.

"Well?'' I prodded.

"Well what, Sutton?'' Bill interjected, trying to defuse the tension he could see was building again.

"Well, Bill, doesn't that raise some interesting questions about who could have gotten that close to her without making her suspicious? Certainly not some random killer she didn't know.''

"Sutton, that's speculation on your part,'' Bill answered. "How can we confirm that?''

"Okay,'' I conceded. "Then how about this? She didn't die right away. She probably died between two and three o'clock, but she could have been attacked as early as twelve-thirty, at least according to the medical examiner. Where was Hubbard Taylor at twelve-thirty? Or one-thirty? I'm sure you must have asked him that? What did he say?''

"This is an ongoing police investigation,'' Lansing said. "What we asked the subject of an interrogation and what that subject said are not part of the public record.''

"Very good, Detective,'' I said, unable to keep sarcasm completely out of my voice. "Check for your side. But not checkmate. Fortunately for me, you aren't the only source of information I have. Now, if that's all you can tell me about Janet Taylor, let's move onto another case you're handling.''

"And what case is that?''

"Ann Kane.''

"What about it?"

"Are you making any progress? Do you have any suspects there, yet?"

"As I believe Bill told you yesterday, at least according to your story in this morning's paper, we have no leads and no suspects. Any further questions?"

At least he was reading my stories. I considered that progress of some kind. Still, I thought, it was time to play my ace, to mix a few game metaphors.

"What if I told you, Detective Lansing, that Ann Kane wasn't the first woman who worked on Capitol Hill to find herself the victim of an overdose of Demerol, that she was just the first one who died from it?"

Bill Russell was looking at me with surprise and something approaching admiration. Noah Lansing, however, was glaring.

"What are you talking about?" he demanded. "We've turned up no information to that effect."

"Guess you'd better do your homework a little better from now on," I told him. "There's a good chance Ann Kane didn't do herself in, either on purpose or by mistake. She probably didn't even know she was taking the Demerol until it was too late to do her any good. And she wasn't the only one. Makes you wonder whether she really had sex with two guys or whether she was gang-raped."

Lansing slammed his fist down on the top of his desk, making Bill and me both jump and scaring the smile off my face.

"Damn it, McPhee," he yelled, dropping the more formal Ms., "if I find out you have information on the Ann Kane case and you're withholding it, I swear I'll charge you with impeding a police investigation."

"Noah," Bill cautioned, surprised at Lansing's threat.

"Don't worry, Detective," I went on, "what I have right now is hearsay. If I turn up concrete evidence, why of course, as a concerned citizen, I would report it to the police. But I do seem to be ahead of you guys. It's really too bad we all have to stand on correct procedures, so we can't tell each other what we know."

"I'm warning you," Lansing answered, ignoring Bill, "don't let me find out you're withholding evidence. If you have any knowledge of how Ann Kane died, you'd better report it!"

I stood up and moved toward the door.

"Guys," I said, my smile firmly back in place, "it's been real. Sorry I have to run, but I have stories to write and deadlines to meet. You'll understand if I can't stay."

Bill stepped aside, openly shaking his head this time, and I opened the door.

"Thanks again for all your help," I said, looking back at Lansing, his arresting blue eyes full of anger—directed, unfortunately, at me. Then another thought prompted me to say one last thing.

"Oh, and if you're thinking about screwing me and my exclusive over by giving the autopsy results to anyone else from the press the minute I leave here, you should think about it some more. I suspect Chief Fielding would hate to have to explain to Supervisor Taylor why the police were volunteering such information. At least if I'm the only one with the story, I can make it clear I didn't get it from you."

"Get the hell out of my office," Lansing replied, apparently never having read Emily Post.

Damn Noah Lansing to hell, I thought as I drove away from the police station to go back to the paper in D.C.

Once I sat down in my car, I had realized how tense my whole body was, from the effort of trying to make him think I was way ahead of him and that I didn't care what he thought of me. Only when I had taken some slow, deep yoga breaths and felt the muscles relax could I calm my mind enough to admit that I did care—much more than I should, considering how things had gone between us and considering what I did for a living.

I had started the Beetle, backed out of the parking space, pulled out of the parking lot onto Crimmons Avenue, and drove west, pondering the effect this man had on me and what I was going to do about it.

It wasn't that I had sworn off relationships after Jack. There had been a handful, but none that I ever had expected, or even hoped, would go past the lovers stage. The closest had been Chris Wiley, who had been scared off by my emotional neediness after my sister was murdered. With the others, it often had come back to a choice between my job and the guy. The couple of guys I had known who were mature enough to want commitment and to think about things like marriage and children also wanted a commitment from me that my reporting career wasn't going to take away time from what they expected family life to be. I was honest enough—with them and with myself—about the demands of my job to know better than to promise any such thing. Reporting and, for that matter, most jobs on the news side of a paper, are never an eight-hour, punch-the-clock kind of work. Covering cops is even less so. Crimes and accidents don't show me the courtesy of happening only between 9:00 A.M. and 5:00 P.M. Frequently, the very best stories on the police beat happen at the most inconvenient times. I work hard to convince the police I cover to keep me informed, but a midnight call from the cops to invite me to a drug bust does little to improve the mood of the man I leave behind in bed.

And there was another problem here that went beyond the demands on my time. Noah Lansing was not only a good-looking, intelligent guy who stirred my blood, but he was also one of the cops I covered. After one unpleasant dating experience with an assistant high-school principal while I covered education at my first newspaper job in Georgia, I had made it a strict rule not to date the people

I wrote about. It just made things way too complicated when I had to do a less-than-positive story about something involving them.

In Albany, Georgia, I had investigated a story about football coaches who were pocketing some of the money they raised selling advertising space in the game programs. The assistant principal, my lover, was one of the people I had to question about what the higher-ups knew. He had a fit. I refused to give my story to another reporter to cover. I refused to tell him what I knew and what I was writing. Naively, I expected him to understand that this was my job, that it was nothing personal. Of course, he had taken it all very personally, had forced a very ugly scene between us, and then had precipitated another at the paper when he went in to complain to my editor. The upshot was that he had ended up hating me, my editor had given me a chewing-out on conflicts of interest, and I had decided it was time to start looking for my next job. But it definitely had been a "learning experience" for me, and the painful lessons had become a permanent part of my psyche.

Until now, anyway. But here I was, actually wondering what it would be like to spend time with Lansing under some other set of circumstances, to be someone he liked, to see him smile. Damn it, I had yet to see the man smile!

You idiot, this man doesn't even smile around you, and you're wondering if he'll go out with you?

Guess who.

Come on, Sutton, get a clue! He wants nothing to do with you under any circumstances whatsoever—not social, not work, not anything. The only thing about you that might make him smile is if he heard he never had to see you again.

But slapping myself around made no difference. Noah Lansing attracted me—a lot. Whether it was the way he looked, or the pain I saw in his eyes, or something else, or everything else, I continued to think about him, to wonder about him. And there was that feeling that there was something between us already, something from some other time. Where was that coming from?

Are you really this desperate? It was my little friend again. *You've only known the guy twenty-four hours and here you are acting like those silly women you despise who can't live without a man. Worse than that, you know what a mess it would make of your job, and yet you still would even entertain the possibility? What a dolt!*

I couldn't even muster up the ire to argue. My voice was right. Getting involved with Noah Lansing would make a mess of my personal life and add to the problems he already was causing with my job. I decided I was going to have to find some solution to the Noah Lansing problem and find it fast. But throughout the entire drive into D.C. from Great Falls, I couldn't come up with one. I didn't like this at all.

Eleven

I parked in the garage a block away from the office, where the *News* leases parking for its staff, and walked across to the eight-story glass-and-metal building that had become the paper's new headquarters ten years ago. As I went through the revolving glass door and said hi to George, the daytime security guard, I pushed my frustrations aside. I was on my way up to the city room on the third floor to check in with Rob and Ken and to get my copy written for Friday's paper. I couldn't do that with my mind in turmoil.

When the elevator opened to deposit me across from the glass-topped wall of the city newsroom, I could see through the bank of windows that Ken was there and already had Rob's ear. I went into the newsroom, where most of the reporters now were at their desks, writing stories for the approaching deadlines, and as I walked over to Rob and Ken, I thought about all the thousands of times I had walked into a newsroom over the years and how, each time, I knew all over again that this was where I belonged.

The warehouselike openness, broken up in places by

chest-high movable dividers, the clicking of fingers on computer keys, the phones ringing, the constant movement and conversation, the sense of urgency imposed by daily deadlines, the sense of doing something that mattered, that changed lives or even history, still spoke to me. I knew far better than our readers how imperfect newspapers—and their reporters—could be, but that never tarnished the job for me.

"Hi, Sutton," Ken said. "I have gossip."

"Which he was just about to tell me," Rob added. "Let's go into my office and talk about this." Rob led the way into his office. Like the newsroom's hallway wall, it was all windows from the waist up. Editors like to see what's going on, even when they're forced out of the newsroom and into their roles as administrators. While Rob used his office for private meetings and phone calls, and occasionally to get necessary paperwork done, he preferred spending his time out at the city desk, where he also kept a computer and a seat and where he could more easily be involved in the minute-by-minute of putting out the paper, as well as monitoring the output and interactions of his assistant metro editors and reporters.

"Good work on the autopsy," Rob said to me as he dropped into his well-worn "executive" chair. Ken and I took the two black vinyl chairs in front of the desk. "Ken's been filling me in on what you found out."

"Thanks," I said, pleased, knowing Rob handed out praise only when he really meant it. And for all our sarcastic back-and-forth, his opinion meant a lot to me. "The best part is, I think—knock on wood—we may be the only ones who have it."

"Even better," Rob said. "Sy Berkowitz was in here earlier, making his own pitch for putting him on the story. This ought to be enough to get him and Lester off my back once and for all." He turned back to Ken. "Okay, go ahead with what you were telling me."

"Wait'll you hear this, Sutton," Ken said, including me in the story he had begun telling Rob. "I talked to one of the secretaries for—well, let's just say for another supervisor who has very little use for Hub Taylor—and she told me some interesting things. It seems that while their bosses don't get along, she's good friends with Taylor's secretary, who says Taylor's been acting very strange the last month or so."

"Strange how?" I asked.

"She says he's gotten paranoid. She also says he's even been arguing with his wife on the phone, and in all the time she's worked for him, including at his car business, she's never heard him raise his voice to his wife until now. Says he's real touchy about things, and his mind seems to be somewhere else half the time. And she says he disappears sometimes for several hours and she has no idea where he is. At least that's what she told the secretary I got it from."

"What about yesterday?" Rob asked. He understood the possible implications of the autopsy results as well as Ken and I had.

"Interesting that you should ask," Ken said, smiling like the proverbial canary-eating cat. "The morning part of the meeting adjourned at eleven because a couple of the supervisors had to go to a lunch meeting downtown. Taylor was in his office when his wife called about eleven-fifteen. His secretary said his wife was really upset on the phone, very angry. She said she'd never heard Mrs. Taylor sound like that. The secretary put the call through to Taylor, and she could hear him trying to calm his wife down. He finally hung up and went out the door in a hurry, saying he was going home for lunch. And he didn't get back into the office until about fifteen minutes before the afternoon meeting started. The secretary doesn't know whether he might have been someplace else in the building, but she didn't see him until one forty-five."

"Did anyone else see him?"

"No one I could find. The other supervisors' secretaries say he wasn't in any of their offices. Of course there are lots of places in that building he could have been, but he wasn't in the most likely ones."

"Well, I guess that doesn't mean he didn't do it, but it doesn't mean he did either," Rob said. He turned to me. "What did he tell the police about where he was?"

"I don't know yet," I admitted. "They're being real closemouthed about it. They've got a new guy there who's in charge of the case, and I haven't been able to get much out of him yet." The understatement of the year. "But I'll find out one way or another." I had to.

"And Taylor's still not talking to anybody," Ken added. "I tried again this afternoon to get to him, but he's over at Ed Lloyd's house, and you can't get within five hundred yards of that place. It's like a fortress, with fences and gates and stuff. Between Lloyd's staff and Taylor's, they're isolating him pretty effectively from reporters. Mannie Sims says Taylor doesn't plan to go back to his house until after the funeral. I think they're having the wake there."

Rob looked thoughtful.

"Okay," he said. "We'll go with what we've got for tomorrow. Sutton, your autopsy news will give us some ammunition. Ken's got his profiles of Mrs. Taylor and the honorable supervisor. It's a start. But you two really need to corner Taylor or lean on the cops and find out what kind of alibi Taylor's got." Rob looked up at the large round clock on the opposite wall of the newsroom, which said our deadline was an hour away. "Let's get to it."

We did.

I had turned in my story, said good night to Ken and Rob, and was on my way home, when I got off the elevator in the lobby at the same time as Sy Berkowitz exited the one next to it.

"Well, well," he said, moving to cut me off. "If it isn't Sutton McPhee, star reporter."

"What?" I asked bluntly, trying to move around him. There was no love lost here. Sy Berkowitz is uniformly disliked by most of the other reporters at the *News*. He's a smug bastard with a raging superiority complex and a powerful protector in Mark Lester. No one denies that he has done some good stories, both in Philadelphia and here, but that never seems to be enough for him. He wants all the good stories for himself and never feels his own work looks good enough until he's torn everyone else's work to shreds.

"I hear you and Kenny aren't making much headway figuring out who killed Janet Taylor," Sy said sneeringly, his New Jersey accent grating harshly in my ears. "I hear they're thinking of shipping the both of you and Rob Perry out to the Maryland bureau, where the stories won't be too taxing for you to handle."

My frustrations from a long day got the best of me. I turned on him.

"Sy," I said, my voice in that low register it takes on when I've gone past anger and into fury, "get out of my way. If you were any kind of reporter, you'd have too many things of your own going on to worry about what I'm doing. Ken and I are doing just fine on this story. We certainly don't need any help from you. Our work speaks for itself. We aren't the ones who have to kiss our editor's ass three times a day to keep our jobs or take stories away from other reporters because we don't have the brains to find any for ourselves. You're the only one who has to do that. So leave me the hell alone." I was so angry, I actually pushed him aside and stomped off through the lobby toward the front door. Shawn, the evening security guard, had been watching our little display wide-eyed, probably wondering if he was going to have to intervene and separate us. When I steamed past him, he grinned weakly at me in apparent relief that he wasn't going to have to go save Sy.

"We'll see who has to kiss whose ass, McPhee," Sy called out loudly from behind me, his voice echoing across the marble floors and walls. I went through the outer door.

Friday

Twelve

Friday morning, the morning Janet Taylor would be buried, dawned red. From my bedroom window on the eastern side of my end-unit apartment, I watched the sun come up behind a low bank of clouds that hugged the horizon, turning them into gorgeous and yet ominous fluffs of rose and blood, and I remembered the old sailor's poem that warned about red skies in the morning. How appropriate for today, I thought.

The funeral was scheduled for 10:30, and when I went to the county building to look for Bill and to the Great Falls police station to look for Lansing, neither was in, both apparently on their way to the church. It wasn't a wasted trip, however. Jimmy Turner at the front duty desk proved quite helpful.

"Hey, Sutton," he said, when I walked into the police-station lobby. "How's it going?"

"Could be better, Jimmy," I told him. "Is Noah Lansing around this morning?"

"Nope, not till sometime after Mrs. Taylor's funeral.

You wanna leave a message for him—that I can repeat publicly?''

I laughed.

''No, I'll just see him there. I might as well go nose around and see who shows up. Don't the police always look around at the funerals to try to spot the murderer?''

''Shouldn't be too hard in this case,'' Jimmy answered darkly, and I sobered up instantly. Jimmy knew just about everything that went on at the Great Falls station. It was how he compensated for the fact that he no longer was out on patrol, not since eighteen months ago when he had responded to a report of screaming in an abandoned house, had interrupted a man who was raping a ten-year-old girl, and had taken a bullet in the left hip in the process. He had shot the rapist in the chest and called for more police and three ambulances before passing out, the little girl sobbing next to him on the pavement beside his cruiser. The rapist had gone to prison for life. The little girl lived, unlike the two other children the police learned the man had raped previously. Jimmy had a torn-up pelvis that put him on permanent desk duty and turned him into an alcoholic. My story about what his selfless act had done to his life and about his struggles to put things back together had resulted in several heroism citations for him and a couple of awards for me. Jimmy told me at the time that reading my story about himself was what finally helped him stick with AA and kick the booze for good. He didn't mind telling me things when he could.

''Why's that?'' I asked.

Jimmy looked around the quiet station to make certain no one else was nearby to hear us.

''You want to put money on whether her husband bumped her off?'' he asked.

''But everyone says they were the perfect couple. He was crazy about her. Why would he want to kill someone like his wife?''

"Beats the hell out of me," Jimmy said, warming to the subject. "But it wouldn't be the first time one half of a perfect couple did in the other half, usually for some reason that makes no sense. Besides, her husband was the last one to see her alive, and he's got no alibi."

There it was, the lodestone I needed to point me in the right direction.

"You . . . ah, want to elaborate on that?" I asked, now looking around as carefully as Jimmy had.

"Don't let this come back to my doorstep, Sutton, but Hub Taylor's in deep shit. He says he went home for lunch with his wife and left by twelve-thirty, at which time, he says, she was fine. But he didn't show back up at the county building until nearly two for that meeting that was on TV. And the best he can come up with is that he was driving around thinking about 'things' during that time."

"No kidding," I said. "He told them this during the interrogation?"

"It was what he told 'em at the house the day she was killed. Of course, then it looked like she was attacked while he was at the board meeting. But by the time he came in yesterday, they'd gotten the autopsy results. You should've heard the buzzing going on around here when the medical examiner called with that bit of news. Bill Russell had the chief on the phone, and Lansing was looking real grim. You have to be careful how you suspect a county supervisor of killing his wife."

"I'll just bet you do," I said.

"Of course, when Taylor got here yesterday he had John Aldritch, that fancy-shmancy lawyer of Ed Lloyd's, with him. Lansing and his guys tried six ways to Sunday to nail Taylor down, but Aldritch kept saying, 'My client doesn't have to answer that.' Taylor couldn't deny what he told them at the scene, but they sure didn't get much else out of him."

As I was absorbing what Jimmy had said another cop

came up to the inner-hallway side of the desk to ask a question. I knew what to do.

"Well, listen, if Lansing shows up before the funeral, would you tell him I'm looking for him?" I said, without missing a beat.

"Oh yeah, sure," Jimmy answered, taking my cue. "I'll tell him."

"Thanks. A lot."

Jimmy winked at me. I went back outside to my car.

On my way to Willow Hill Methodist Church, I stopped at a Mobil station to get some gas and then pulled over to the side of the parking lot to use the pay phone. I wanted to check my voice mail, and considering the stories I had going on, I vetoed the car phone again. The first voice I heard was Cheryl Wiggins.

"Sutton, hi. I saw your article about the autopsy results in the paper this morning. Thanks for keeping me out of it. It looked good. I hope your boss thought so, too. Talk to you later. 'Bye."

The next one was from Bill Russell.

"McPhee, what am I going to do with you? It took me an hour to calm Lansing down after you left yesterday. Do you have to go to such pains to bait him? Anyway, I had a long talk with him. I gave him a little lecture on police-press relationships and how we don't threaten to prosecute reporters just because they found out something we didn't. I also talked to him about you. I think I made some headway. Now, if you'll just behave, too, maybe he'll at least be civil. We'll talk." He hung up. I would have to thank him if I saw him later this morning.

The third message was from Peter Morris, M.D.

"Ms. McPhee . . . uh, sorry . . . Sutton . . . it's Peter Morris. I'm sorry you're not there. I remembered something that might help. But I'd rather you didn't call me at the office." He paused, then resumed speaking. "I suppose it will be all right to leave it on your voice mail. Anyway, I remembered that when I first brought the woman into the exam room, she had a coat over her. I took it and hung it on a coat hook on the door. This was when I thought she had taken the Demerol on her own, so I checked the pockets to see if the bottle was there, to make certain that was really what it was. I didn't find a bottle, but I did pull out a business card. I just glanced at it, long enough to see that it had a senator's name on it, a man. I didn't think it was important and stuck it back in the coat pocket. Last night, after we talked, I was racking my brain for anything I might have forgotten. I was going back over that night in my mind and I remembered the card. It occurred to me that the senator on the card might be someone she knows, someone who could tell you who she is. I wish now I had kept the card, but I wasn't thinking this clearly at that time. As I say, I just glanced at it, but I'm pretty sure the name on it was a Senator Black." He paused again. "Well, that's all. I hope this helps."

The cutoff tone sounded and the voice-mail recording told me that was the last of the messages. I stood at the pay phone, digesting Peter Morris's latest tidbit.

Paul Black, I knew, was the other senator from Florida. Junior senator to Rita Wills, Ann Kane's boss. So I knew the following: that a woman who knew, or perhaps worked for, Senator Paul Black had an experience at the hands of Ed Lloyd that sounded disturbingly similar to what might have happened to Ann Kane, an aide to Black's Florida colleague, Rita Wills. Might the two women have known each other? Possibly. Probably, if the mystery woman worked for Black. If I found Morris's unknown patient, would she know anything about what happened to Ann Kane, or whether Ed Lloyd also knew Ann Kane? Would she know who the second guy with Ann Kane could have been? Might it have been Black?

I walked back to my car and got in.

It looked like Ann Kane definitely wasn't going to take any kind of back burner to Janet Taylor. It also looked as if I might have to make a trip over to the Hill to a certain Florida senator's office. In the meantime Ed Lloyd most certainly would be at Janet Taylor's funeral and interment. What were my chances of getting to him with some questions? As usual, I would just have to make the most of whatever opportunities arose.

Back into traffic I went. Shortly, I turned onto Willow Hill Road, and up ahead I could see where the police had blocked the street off at the church, detouring traffic around a couple of blocks and back onto Willow on the other side. Inside the barriers, the church was surrounded by black limousines and other upscale cars. Outside, there was the usual flurry of reporters and cameras, all waiting for the funeral to end—which should be almost anytime now—and for the mourners to reemerge. I saw Ken in one group, although he didn't see me. Instead of stopping, I decided to drive on over to Potomac Memorial Gardens, where the obituary had said Mrs. Taylor would be buried.

Thirteen

As I drove between the large white brick pillars that held the entry gates to the cemetery and looked out across the acres of softly rolling green, I noticed that the sky was becoming more threatening by the minute. Apparently, the red dawn's promise was going to be fulfilled shortly.

I didn't know where Janet Taylor's grave site was, so I drove around until I found a digging crew at a newly excavated grave, covered by a large tent from the funeral home that had cared for Mrs. Taylor's body. When I stopped and called out my question to them, the grave diggers told me that was the place. I put the car in gear and drove farther along the road until I rounded a curve that put my car out of immediate sight. I had no idea what the security arrangements were going to be, but I saw no point in calling early attention—from the police or the rest of the press—to the fact that I was there. I put on the raincoat and hat I had brought, black to blend in and the hat brimmed to delay recognition. From my car I walked at an angle across the lush green lawn to stand by a group of trees that looked across the hillock back toward the Taylor grave site. I hoped to stay unnoticed until people were converging on the site. I didn't want to get lumped in with the rest of the press and completely isolated from the mourners if I could prevent it.

From my spot under the tree, I couldn't see the gates, but after another thirty minutes of watching the clouds build overhead, I saw the flashing lights of the police-escort cars come slowly around the bend closest to the grave site, followed by a long line of black limousines and private cars. As I watched, the funeral procession snaked to a halt before going as far as my car. Uniformed police, mourners, and the funeral-home staff all began to empty out of their cars for the walk up to the grave.

The pallbearers, who rode in the first limo immediately behind the hearse, moved as a group to the hearse's rear, to take charge of Mrs. Taylor's coffin and carry it up to the waiting hole in the earth. From the next limo came Hub Taylor with an elderly couple I took to be his in-laws, as well as a clergyman easily distinguished by his telltale white collar, and Ed Lloyd. They all fell into step behind the coffin and trudged up the hill, Janet Taylor's parents leaning on each other's arm for support in their grief.

As they made their way they were followed by other members of the board of supervisors, by county officials, who included the chief of police (accompanied, I noticed, by Bill Russell) and the county executive, and by others I assumed were family friends and acquaintances from Janet Taylor's charitable causes.

With a start, I recognized one of the mourners as Dr. Morris. Was he Janet Taylor's physician? I wondered. It would make sense, of course. Very possibly Ed Lloyd even had introduced them. Morris said Lloyd had sent some influential patients his way. The Taylors might well have been among that group. Fortunately, Morris didn't see me. His eyes were on the flower-covered coffin that was being lowered onto wide straps to hover above the darkness of the open grave. I didn't want my presence to startle him into giving our acquaintance away to Ed Lloyd.

My eyes resumed their scan of the crowd. I watched Hub Taylor most closely. His face was mottled and bloated, his eyes red-rimmed, even from my vantage point. His slumped shoulders and shell-shocked face certainly gave the appearance of a man in deepest mourning over the loss of his beloved wife. Could he possibly have killed someone whose absence he felt so heavily? Of course he could, the cynic in me thought. People kill people they love every day. Love is not necessarily a shield against violence and anger.

But if that was what had happened—that he had killed in anger—what could that gentle, loving woman possibly have done to make him that mad? She was the one who had been angry, according to his secretary. Perhaps he killed her—if he killed her—for some other reason. So what other motives usually led people to murder?

Actually, the list is quite short. Besides anger (which includes what are usually known as crimes of passion), there is money. But Hub Taylor had more money than he knew what to do with. Then there's power, control. But Janet had been his wife and had done more than most women would have to support him. And there is fear. But what could Janet Taylor have done to instill the kind of unreasoning fear in her husband that would have led him to kill her? It was definitely a maze, I thought, a maze of human emotions and motivations, and a quagmire for anyone trying to navigate it.

As the first of the mourners reached the grave site, they began to take the rows of folding chairs lined up along the side of the grave, with Taylor, the in-laws, and Lloyd in the first row. I turned my attention to the senator, a tanned, fit-looking, broad-shouldered man of fifty-seven or fifty-eight, his once-black hair now on the silver side of salt-and-pepper. Taller than Hub Taylor, he exuded the kind of strength and power that comes from those who know no self-doubt. Ed Lloyd had been wielding power in Washington, D.C., first as a representative and then as a senator, for more than twenty-five years. He had belonged to a variety of powerful committees, currently chaired Foreign Affairs, and was considered the heir to the throne of the Senate Appropriations Committee.

If Hub Taylor's motives for killing his wife were a puzzle, it was even more puzzling to imagine someone of Ed Lloyd's stature risking it all by drugging a woman to have sex. Stranger still to see these two men here together when I suspected each of them of having a hand in someone's death. How truly bizarre, I thought. Two men in powerful positions, two friends, each of them possibly hiding his own terrible and separate secret.

By this time the end of the line of mourners was reaching the grave, where the last of the chairs long since had been occupied and the rest of the group of probably three hundred or more had fanned out to encircle the grave. Several uniformed policemen had arranged themselves as a barrier between those surrounding the grave and the reporters, who were allowed to come only so far and no farther. Because I was on the opposite side of the crowd, I decided to approach and, I hoped, blend into the edges of the group around the grave.

As I slowly made my way from under the tree and over to the grave site, I noticed that among the people off to the right was Noah Lansing, talking softly to a second man I assumed was probably another detective working with him on Mrs. Taylor's murder. As they talked their eyes constantly moved over the crowd, watching, searching, measured gazes sizing everyone up as a potential murderer. Even if Taylor was at the top of the suspects list, the police weren't taking chances on missing a less obvious suspect.

When Lansing's head turned in my direction and watched me approach, I felt a jolt of electricity that told me he somehow knew it was me, in spite of the rain hat. But he made no move to intercept me, probably not believing that even I would be so lacking in manners as to interrupt the graveside services.

To get out of Lansing's line of sight and to avoid giving myself away to anyone else, I moved to the side, behind a cluster of a half-dozen people. I hoped that in my black coat and hat, I would just look like one more of the grieving.

My goal wasn't to hear what was being said by the minister. How different could it be from what got said at most burials? Probably no more reassuring either. The graveside services certainly had given me little solace when I had buried Cara one sunny spring morning in south Georgia. Or at my parents' funeral several years before. Formulaic words never could have contained the essence of who they were. In fact, I thought, the only place I had ever been where they knew the proper way to bury the dead, the way I would want to go out, was New Orleans, where your final send-off could include a parade and music and dancing and a wild party or two. We certainly wouldn't see that here today. What I really wanted was to position myself to be near Hub Taylor and Ed Lloyd when the graveside rituals ended.

As the minister's voice dropped, followed by amens from the crowd, the rustle and stirring near the grave halted my reverie about death and told me the exodus was about to begin. As quickly but unobtrusively as I could, I moved to a point where I was in a direct line from the grave to the parked cars. As the crowd parted to let the family descend and enter the waiting cars first, I moved down the edges of the crowd toward the limo that had brought Hub Taylor and his group.

Taylor, his wife's parents, Ed Lloyd, and the minister came back down the hill as they had climbed it, with the others closest to the grave falling in behind them. By the time they reached the road and the cars, I had worked my way down to the road as well. I decided as I went that trying to talk to Taylor would be a useless exercise in this setting.

But Ed Lloyd was another story. I was certain that, at this point, he had no idea he was at any risk of exposure. Why should he? No one but Peter Morris could connect him to the mystery woman, and even Lloyd didn't know that Dr. Morris wanted to tie him to Ann Kane. All Morris had was a logical mind, some inside information as Lloyd's physician, and a lot of supposition. As far as Lloyd knew, Morris hadn't even made the connection between the woman he helped and what happened to Ann Kane.

The police literally had nothing on Lloyd. He wasn't even in their ken as a possible suspect. As long as he didn't make a stupid mistake, there might never be anything to connect him. I decided it could be interesting to apply a little unexpected pressure to see how susceptible to such mistakes he might be.

But I couldn't do it too openly. Other members of the press also were moving forward in the disorganized dispersal that usually follows a graveside service, and I wasn't about to let them in on the suspicions I harbored about either of these men. Nor did I want to surprise Peter Morris with my presence, although he seemed to be staying as far away from Lloyd as possible.

By this time the family had reached the limos, and Ed Lloyd stopped to help first Taylor, then Janet's parents and the minister into theirs. Quickly, I decided what I was going to do.

I stepped around another couple who were between me and the family's limo and put a hand on Lloyd's arm. He straightened and turned from the open limo door to see who wanted his attention.

"Senator Lloyd," I said, counting on my appearance to delay any suspicion of me.

"Yes?" He looked at me questioningly, apparently thinking I was another mourner expressing condolences.

"I'm Sutton McPhee from the *Washington News*. I have a question I'd like to ask you."

Irritation sparked in his eyes, but still he saw me as only one of the more morbidly curious of the press.

"I'm sorry," he said, beginning to turn toward the car again. "Not now."

But I held my grasp of his arm and leaned toward him, to whisper in his ear, where only he could hear my question.

"How well did you know Ann Kane, Senator?" I said, then stood back for his reaction.

He straightened again, this time slowly, and fixed me with a hard look, as if memorizing my face.

"I don't know what you're talking about," he said evenly, and climbed into the limo, pulling the door closed as he went.

But he did. He knew exactly what I was talking about. I had seen no sign of question or confusion in his look. What I had seen was cold anger and warning.

The solid thud of the closing limo door apparently was some sort of signal to the sky to let go the clouds it had been collecting since before dawn, and it began to rain, suddenly and heavily. Around me, everyone started running for their cars, hoping to avoid a drenching. But I stood, the rain pouring down around me, transfixed by what I had seen in Ed Lloyd's eyes, watching as the limo carried him off to the wake at the Taylor home. Until a hand grabbed my own arm in a firm grasp and I heard Noah Lansing say, "We have to talk."

I didn't know he was behind me. I jumped.

"Damn it," I said, before I had time to remember my promise to Bill to be nice, "you scared the shit out of me!"

That was when Noah Lansing smiled at me for the first

time, standing there in the pouring rain, both of us getting soaked. He liked the idea of scaring the shit out of me. I was sorry I hadn't seen him smile sooner. It did wonderful things around his eyes.

"Do you have a car?" he asked.

"This way," I said, and started walking fast across the edge of the hill to where the VW was waiting. Lansing caught up with me in three strides, and we hurried together around the curve to get to my car and out of the rain.

"It's unlocked," I said to him as I jogged around the back bumper to the driver's side. He opened the passenger door and got in, deftly folding his tall frame into the small seat and closing the door. I was doing the same thing— well, maybe not the deftly part—on the other side.

No sooner had I gotten in than the sky redoubled its efforts to wash us away, pounding on the fabric roof of my little car in fury at our escape. In the tiny interior of the VW, I was immediately wrapped in the steamy warmth coming off both our damp bodies and the smell of whatever soap and cologne Lansing had used that morning. Combined with the fact that the entire length of his body was only inches away from mine, it made me nervy—as in, every nerve was on edge—and eager to distract my mind with talk.

"Where to?" I asked, fishing my keys out of my raincoat pocket and looking over at him as I reached up to put them in the ignition, being very careful not to brush his leg in the process.

"Nowhere," he answered, looking out through the windshield, now smeared with rain. "I've got a car back there. But I'd just as soon have this conversation privately rather than at the station."

Oh God, I thought, not another chewing-out. I knew this guy didn't like me, but really, how much was I expected to endure?

"Look," I said, thinking to head off another confrontation, "you don't have to yell at me again. I know you don't like anything about me, including how I do my job, but I'm really not trying to cause you problems. How about if I just stay out of your way as much as possible. We'll talk on the phone, if necessary. Can we just call a truce—at least for today?" The weather and a funeral had left me in no mood for sparring with him. Memories of burying my sister had seen to that.

Something in my voice must have echoed my funk. He turned to look at me sharply. I braced myself.

"I was thinking more along the lines of some sort of peace accord rather than a truce," he said, completely surprising me. I opened my mouth to respond and then closed it again. I didn't know what to say. I was prepared for another fight, not a cessation of hostilities.

Then, for the second time in two minutes, he smiled, no doubt at the idea of me speechless. This guy in a good mood could grow on you, I thought. He propped his right elbow on the top curve of the door and leaned his head against his hand, giving me a look I couldn't interpret.

"Bill Russell really gave me a dressing-down yesterday after I threw you out of my office. I won't go into what he said, about either of us, but the bottom line was he told me I was acting like a prick, and I decided he was probably right. He said you're as good as your word, and I saw that when I read your article in this morning's paper. At least when the chief called, he didn't think the details of Janet Taylor's autopsy came from me. I'm not saying you're not a pain in the ass, you understand. I think you have some genuine talent in that direction. I just haven't known you long enough to really say it from personal experience." He paused, and a shadow seemed to pass across his face as his thoughts ran ahead.

"Let's just say there are a lot of reasons why I reacted badly," he went on, "only some of which had anything to do with you." I knew the shadow I had seen was the memory of his wife, but I stayed quiet. If Bill hadn't told him I knew about her, I certainly wasn't going to tell him I did—at least not yet.

"Anyway," he said, mentally clearing the memories with an effort I could see, "what I wanted to say was that I'd like to start over here, put things on a professional basis. Bill says you're a lot easier to tolerate if you're not mad all the time."

That smile again. And a sense of humor, too. And even something that felt like an apology. I wasn't encouraged by the feeling in the pit of my stomach. I should have been thinking, Great, this will make it easier to do my job. But doing my job wasn't what I was thinking about at all. Sutton, you are in deep, deep trouble here, I told myself, hoping he couldn't see on my face any of what was going through my mind. I was beginning to find this scary.

Back off, I told myself, back away, now, before he has any idea you're attracted to him. Before you screw up your job. Before you start to care. Before another man sees the real you and walks away. Before anybody gets hurt—especially you.

I realized how long I had been silent when I saw his smile falter and fade away. I jumped into the breach.

"You're right," I told him, knowing his sobering expression probably was a reaction to my own grim one. "There's no reason we can't each do our jobs; we don't have to be friends. And that's all I want, just to do my job. It's like I said before, just be up-front with me about what you can and can't say. And if you can tell me something helpful, great. So thanks for the fresh start."

That wasn't what he had expected, obviously. He had been pleasant; I had responded coldly. He had no way of knowing why. I saw a flash of irritation in his eyes again, but in the new spirit of the times, he quickly squelched it.

"Well, that's all," he said, his voice now as distant and professional as my own. "If you'll just drop me back around the curve at my car, I won't take up any more of your time.''

"No problem,'' I answered, turning on the engine and putting the car into gear. The VW easily made the U-turn on the small road and in a few seconds we were at the unmarked car Lansing had driven to the cemetery, now the only other car in sight except for the truck of the grave diggers who had returned to close the last chapter on Janet Taylor's life. I braked to a stop beside Lansing's car. He reached for the VW door handle and turned to look at me.

"Thanks . . . McPhee,'' he said, paying me the courtesy of officially promoting me from Ms.

"Sure,'' I responded, my voice thick with the effort I was making, my eyes having a hard time meeting his. He opened the door and got out. Immediately, I put the Beetle in gear and drove away, seeing in my rearview mirror that he stood beside his own car, just watching through the now-slowing rain as I left.

Fourteen

I didn't bother going to the Taylor home to try to crash the wake. I figured Ken would have a much better chance at getting in than I would, especially after my recent conversation with Ed Lloyd and my article in today's paper, which made it clear that Hub Taylor wasn't out of the woods in his wife's death.

Instead, I decided to go to Capitol Hill, to see if there was anything to learn from Senator Paul Black about Dr. Morris's mystery woman, who had carried Black's business card around in her coat pocket.

All the way in to the District I replayed the mental tape of my latest encounter with Noah Lansing. What a bitch he must think I am, I told myself. Here he was, just trying to apologize for misjudging me, letting his guard down a little to show the man under that tough-cop skin, and I come across as the ice queen. He couldn't know the thoughts I had been having about him, couldn't know that my lack of a warm response to his overture was out of fear of the way he affected me. I could imagine the report he would make back to Bill.

Goddamn it, I thought, honking at a cab that cut in front of me and nearly took off my left front fender, why did Noah Lansing have to be the one who affected me this way? Why couldn't it have been someone who wasn't on my beat? Why couldn't it have been someone who might be affected the same way? Instead it had to be a cop who was investigating my two biggest stories and who blames someone like me for the death of the person he loved most. No way he was going to return the interest.

I went 'round and 'round with myself as I drove across Memorial Bridge and took a right around the Lincoln Memorial to follow Independence Avenue to the Hill. Finally, I had to push it all aside to concentrate on finding a parking space—always a challenge in the District—near the Senate Office Buildings and on searching out Paul Black's office. I knew my dilemma over Noah Lansing still would be there waiting me for once I had time to think about it again.

Black's office was on the second floor of the Russell Building. It took me a few minutes to find it. I rarely spend any time on Capitol Hill. Not because there aren't any criminals there, but because the *News* has a whole staff of other reporters who cover the Hill and because the type of crime I follow generally confines itself to Northern Virginia. In fact, if anyone at the *News* had any idea of the lead I was chasing now, Mark Lester would be right back in the city room, demanding I turn over the Ann Kane story as well, and this time with some justification, since his congressional reporters had much better sources here than I did—which were none at all. But I wasn't turning this story over to anyone, and I was determined to make up for my lack of sources through sheer, cussed stubbornness. Something I do really well.

On the second floor I left the elevator and turned down the corridor to the right. Black's office was several doors down, again on the right. I went through the door and found myself in the reception area of what I could see actually was a suite of offices. A smartly dressed blonde of about thirty was working the reception desk behind a name placard that said SUSAN BARRETT.

"Hi," she said, smiling with practiced professional warmth. "May I help you?"

"I'm Sutton McPhee," I told her. "I'm a reporter with the *Washington News*."

"How do you do?" she asked, standing gracefully and holding out a slim hand for me to shake. "I'm Susan Barrett."

"Hi, Susan," I responded, shaking hands. "Is Senator Black in, by any chance?"

"No, I'm sorry, he's not," Susan told me, using her hands to smooth the full skirt of her green silk dress underneath her as she took her seat again.

"Will he be back anytime soon?"

"I don't think so. He's down on the Senate floor right now and will be in committee hearings all afternoon. Could I help you with something?"

"Possibly," I told her. "I'm working on the Ann Kane story for the paper, and I thought that since she worked for the other Florida senator, the people in your office probably knew her."

"Oh, yes, we all knew Ann, although I only knew her to speak to. What a terrible, terrible thing." Her expression now was suitably somber. "She didn't really socialize with the Senate crowd, you understand. We often deal with Senator Wills's staff on legislative issues, but outside working hours, Ann didn't spend a lot of time with the people around here."

"So I was told. So you really didn't know much about her personal life, then? What about Senator Black? Do you think there might be anything he could tell me?''

"I'd be surprised," Susan said. "He doesn't hang around a lot after hours either. His wife and kids stay up here most of the year, and he's a real family man. But you know, the person you really ought to talk to is Maggie. She used to work for Rita Wills back when Rita was the Florida attorney general. I don't know that she and Ann were close friends, but she knew Ann longer than any of us.''

"Maggie?''

"Yes, Maggie Padgett. She's Paul's secretary.''

"Is she here?''

"Not today. She's been out sick all week, but she said she planned to come in tomorrow, even though it's Saturday, to catch up. You could call her or come back then. She usually gets in about eight.''

"Okay, maybe I'll do that. Well, listen, Susan, thanks for your help.''

"Certainly," she said, and walked me to the outer door. I left the office wondering if this Maggie Padgett would be of any more help than Susan Barrett had been. I decided I would have to make the trip back regardless, just on the off chance that she might know more about the people in Ann Kane's life than I had learned so far.

Although it was doubtful. From the sound of it, Ann Kane wasn't much of a social butterfly. She spent most of her free time among the less affluent, apparently. Still, the Capitol Hill connection—and Ed Lloyd—were worth pursuing. While the crowd one meets in soup kitchens might be less than savory, few of them would have had either the means or the opportunity to slip Kane a lethal drink or to transport her body twenty-five miles away to dump it.

It was always possible, I supposed, that she had been done in by some nutcase priest or soup kitchen volunteer who spent his spare time doing good works for the homeless and killing young women on the side. But I didn't think it was very probable. No, her death stank of some other kind of ego at work, someone who thought the rules didn't apply to him, someone who would drug her for sex, either because she wouldn't go to bed with him willingly or because he got off on having her helpless. Someone who also had an accomplice he trusted enough to share his murderous little escapade with.

None of which left me with anything for a story for Saturday's paper. Back in my car, I picked up the phone and called Rob to tell him to cross me off the story lineup.

"Too bad," he said, when I told him there was nothing new on Janet Taylor from the investigation end. "Woulda been nice to have a story on the police arresting someone for it, to go along with Ken's piece on the funeral."

"That'll take a little longer," I replied. "But I'm working on it."

"Do you think he did it?" By *he,* I knew Rob meant Hub Taylor.

"Just between us girls, he could have," I told Rob. "But what I can't figure out is why."

"Don't you hate it when that happens?"

I laughed. " 'Bye, Rob," I said, and hung up.

He was right. I did hate it when I couldn't figure out why. Why Hub Taylor? Why Ed Lloyd? Why Noah Lansing? Today had been one big question mark. I decided to pack it in, take some well-deserved comp time, and go home.

Fifteen

I struggled up out of the forest through which I was running after a receding light, to discover that I had been dreaming and that the loud noise I was hearing was the telephone on my kitchen wall. I realized I had fallen asleep on the sofa just as the sun was going down, and now it was full dark outside.

The phone kept ringing insistently. Apparently, I had left the answering machine turned off. I pulled myself up, groggy from the depth of sleep I had reached, and stumbled over to the kitchen. I snatched the phone off the hook in mid-ring and forced out a "Hello" in a voice that sounded like mud.

"Sutton McPhee?"

"Yes?" I swallowed deeply, trying to clear my throat to the point of intelligibility. My brain would take a little longer.

"Sutton, it's Peter Morris."

"Oh, Dr. Morris. Sorry I'm a little groggy here. I was asleep." The effort of putting words together helped clear the mental decks. I was rapidly coming back to the present. The digital clock on my oven said it was 8:15 P.M. I wondered why Morris was calling.

"Oh, I do apologize for waking you up," he said quickly.

"That's okay," I told him. "I was having a very frustrating dream anyway."

"Listen, Sutton, I need to talk to you right away."

"Did you remember something else?"

"No. Nothing. But something very disturbing just happened."

"What?"

"I . . . I really don't want to discuss it on the phone. Do you have plans for the evening? Is there any way we could talk in person?"

I looked around at the wild party that wasn't going on in my living room. No one there seemed to object to my leaving.

"Sure," I agreed. "Where are you?"

"I'm at home in McLean. Would you just come here? I would rather no one saw us talking, especially now."

"Fine. What's your address?"

"Twenty-seven-nineteen Cedarbrook. It's just off Georgetown Pike and Great Oaks Terrace."

"Okay, give me a few minutes to wash my face and throw on some clothes. I'll be there by"—I estimated the distance in my head—"oh, let's say nine-thirty. Is that too late?"

"No, no. That's fine. Just come as soon as you can."

Then, my brain fog clearing a little more, I thought to ask the question that had occurred to me earlier.

"By the way, Dr. Morris," I said, "I saw you at Janet Taylor's funeral today."

"Were you there?"

"I was, but I was trying to be unobtrusive." Well, as far

as most of the people there were concerned. "Was she a patient of yours?"

"Yes," he answered, sadly. "Ed Lloyd sent the Taylors to me after her accident. I've been their internist ever since."

"Interesting," I told him. "All right, I'll be over soon." We hung up.

What, other than a jog in his memory, could have prompted his call? I wondered as I went back to my bedroom. I splashed my face with cold water, brushed my hair out and rebraided it, slipped on a lightweight, tweedy blue sweater and jeans, and stuck my feet into a pair of cordovan loafers.

In the foyer, I took my wallet and keys out of my purse, turned off all but the kitchen light, and went out into the night to talk to Peter Morris.

Needless to say, Dr. Peter Morris, internist to movers and shakers, lived in a very upscale neighborhood in McLean. Large, expensive lots that maintained privacy. Looming, center-hall Colonials covered in heavy red brick, a favorite way in the nation's capital to say "I have arrived." Extensive landscaping and outdoor accent lighting. Twenty-seven-nineteen Cedarbrook fit the mold.

Lights were on in the house when I pulled into the driveway behind a black Lexus. The double garage door was in the up position, showing a white Porsche 911 and a red 1960s-vintage Jaguar XKE taking up the two bays. Admiring the doctor's taste in cars, I went up the bricked walk to the front door and rang the doorbell.

No one came to the door in response, so I rang it a second and, eventually, a third time. Still no Peter Morris. I was puzzled. Even if he had been in the bathroom when I rang the doorbell the first time, I had waited long enough between rings for him to hear it. I pulled out the brass door knocker and rapped loudly. Still no response. I tried the door, but it was locked. I backed out onto the walk to look through the lighted dining-room windows to my left. No sign of movement. To the right, behind what I assumed were the living-room windows, there was only darkness.

Where could he be? I wondered. His car was in the driveway. He had asked me to come over, so he was expecting me. It was 9:32, so I was right on time. Maybe he was out on a deck or in the backyard and hadn't heard me.

I had seen when I drove up that a wooden fence jutted out from the sides of the house, enclosing the backyard. I walked around to the outside of the garage and up to the fence, but there was no gate on that side.

"Dr. Morris?" I called, thinking he might hear me if he were in the backyard. "Are you there? It's Sutton." No answer. Now I was becoming concerned.

I went back around the front corner of the garage and walked between the Porsche and the XKE to look for another way into the house. A connecting door was in the back right corner. The window in that door was dark, but I went over to it anyway and grasped the knob, which turned easily in my hand, opening the door. I stopped.

"Dr. Morris?" No answer. What there was, however, was a palpable feeling in the air that something was wrong inside this house. The hair stood up on the back of my neck.

Through a window on the wall to my left, the reflected glow of a security light in the backyard showed me that I was in a largish laundry room. A white washer-dryer pair sat beneath the window. Next to them was a laundry sink, where a faucet dripped with clocklike precision. Beyond the sink were shelves on which sat bottles and boxes of laundry supplies and some unidentifiable stacks of folded laundry. I brushed a hand against the wall next to the door and found a double light switch, which I flipped up. Simultaneously, lights came on overhead in the garage and in the laundry room.

Ahead of me was a closed, solid wood door, which I guessed led into the kitchen. Again, the door opened easily, into another darkened room. Again, the flick of a switch in a bank of switches on the left-hand wall turned on a couple of small, recessed lights in the ceiling, this time to show me a spotless, modern kitchen with oak cabinets and white Corian countertops running down either wall, a cooking island in the middle, and white appliances breaking up the oak here and there. Terra-cotta tiles on the floor felt hard under my loafers.

I called out Morris's name, again without any response. Something was badly wrong here. I could feel it. I wanted nothing more than to turn around, run to my car, and go home. But that desire lost out to an even stronger need to know what was wrong—as it always did. Jack used to get really angry with me when, having heard an odd noise in the middle of the night, I would get up and go to see what it was instead of waking him. But I always had been that way, figuring that if a killer or monster waited for me in the dark, it would be over quickly and was preferable to the long minutes or hours of heart-pounding fear I would endure if I just lay in bed listening. This was just the same. What I didn't know was always more frightening than what I did.

On the right-hand wall of the kitchen, a swinging door showed a strip of light at the bottom. I pushed it open slowly to see the dining room, with its elegant set of Chippendale chairs around an oval mahogany table large enough to seat ten easily. The wall to my right was completely taken up with a built-in china display cabinet that went from floor to ceiling and was filled with what I knew was an expensive china in blue and gold. On the floor was a luxurious cream-colored carpeting overlaid with an expensive-looking Oriental rug on which the dining table sat. Overhead, a crystal chandelier, that probably cost two months of my salary or more, glittered brightly. The decor, I suspected, was the legacy of the ex-wife who had moved back to Boston.

Still there was no sign of Dr. Morris. By this time fear had silenced my calls to him.

On the dining-room wall to the left, a doorless archway led into a darkened hall. I crossed the room slowly, almost holding my breath from the tension that enveloped me. In the hallway, carpeted stairs to my left led up to the second floor. On the right was the front door. Opposite where I stood, another archway led into a lightless room I thought most likely was the living room.

I crossed the hall, trying not to notice the darkened top of the stairs. One terror at a time, I thought. At the entryway into the living room, I stopped and felt the wall beside me again for a light switch. This time it turned on several lamps on small tables around the room. My subconscious mind and my peripheral vision noted glassed-in bookcases against walls, a large elaborate mantel above a fireplace to the left, and several tall green plants in corners. But my conscious attention and my eyes immediately went to the grouping of an overstuffed navy-blue sofa facing the fire-place from the center of the room, flanked by two navy, burgundy, and cream-striped upholstered chairs. In the chair opposite me, sat Dr. Peter Morris. His eyes were open, but the small round hole on the left side of his forehead and the blood all over his shirt and the chair behind him told me he wasn't seeing me or anything else.

For several seconds I thought my heart would stop. Then, when it not only didn't stop, but in fact beat louder and faster, I thought I might faint. I've seen plenty of dead bodies in my time. It's hard to avoid them when you're a police reporter. But I was usually prepared to see those. Even viewing my sister's body in the morgue, as horrible as that experience had been, was something I first had a chance to steel myself to see. This was the first time I had had the experience of being the person to actually find the body. Nor was this some anonymous victim. This was someone I knew. I dropped my keys on the floor and bent over at the waist to let my own blood go back to my brain. Finally, I straightened up slowly. There wasn't a doubt in my mind that Morris was dead, but I knew I would have to make certain.

I went over to the right side of the chair so that I didn't have to keep looking at the vacancy of his eyes. There was no chest movement that I could see. Carefully, I reached down to his left wrist, not wanting to touch his blood-drenched neck or to disturb the revolver with the grained wood handle in his hand. There was no detectable pulse either. His skin was still quite warm to the touch, so he hadn't been dead long. But dead he unquestionably was.

I walked over to a Parsons table behind the sofa, to the cream-colored telephone that sat there. I knew I had to call the police. I could have left the house altogether and called it in anonymously, I supposed, but who knew how many neighbors had seen my car in the driveway by now. The first time any of the cops who knew me heard "white VW Beetle convertible," I probably would come to mind immediately. Then I would have a real problem. And, come to think of it, once the police arrived, I was going to have to have a story ready for them, one that was the truth, but not enough of the truth to tie my hands in finding out where Ed Lloyd stood in all this. I was afraid I knew the whole truth—that Peter Morris hadn't committed suicide. On the phone, he hadn't sounded depressed or self-destructive. What I had heard in his voice was fear. No, I thought, someone else killed him. And it suddenly occurred to me that for all I knew, that someone was still in the house.

Quickly, I went back to the doorway, picked up my keys, and let myself out the front door. Once inside my car, I locked the doors and used my cellular phone to call nine-one-one. At least if someone came out of the house after me, I could always drive away.

The 911 dispatcher answered. There was no way around it; I was in for a bad night here. I identified myself to the dispatcher, told her briefly what I had found, gave her the address, and asked her to have someone call Bill Russell and send him out as well. More than likely I was going to need to call in whatever remaining chips I had left with him. I figured the hassle factor from the cops at the scene would be minimized with Bill there to vouch for me. He would be called eventually anyway, but I wanted him there from the beginning to run interference for me.

In the driveway, I waited for the police, working out my story about how I came to be here. I thought back to what Peter Morris had said on the phone and wondered what it was he had wanted so urgently to tell me.

Sixteen

I still had seen no signs of anyone else in the house by the time the police began to arrive eight or ten minutes later. Nothing had moved, no lights had gone on or off, no one had entered or left, at least not through the doors I could see from my car. Whoever had murdered Peter Morris probably was long gone.

Behind me, the first squad car, colored lights flashing but siren silent, pulled up behind me in the driveway. The driver, who looked like he hadn't seen thirty yet, turned his spotlight onto my car and, over his loudspeaker, ordered me to get out and stand away from the car, hands in the air. Which I promptly did. I knew they would have it figured out in a moment. In the meantime I wasn't fooling around with nervous policemen with loaded guns.

Once I was out on the driveway, the cops slowly got out, their guns pointed at me, and began walking toward me.

"I'm a newspaper reporter," I told them. "I made the call to nine-one-one." Some other time the idea of being

frisked by a twenty-eight-year-old cop might have its ap-
peal. Tonight, I wasn't in the mood.

"You have some ID?" the officer who had been driving
asked.

"Yes, it's in my wallet on the passenger's seat of my
car. You'll have to get it from this side. The other door is
locked."

The driver nodded to his partner, who holstered his own
gun and came up to the driver's door of the VW to reach
in and bring out my wallet. He took his heavy cop's flashlight out of his belt and flicked it on to examine my driver's
license and my press ID, the two things I kept easily visible
in the little plastic windows just for anxious moments like
this.

"Sutton McPhee," he said, looking up at his partner. "It
says she works for the *News*. I've seen her name on stories." He closed the wallet and turned off the flashlight.
His partner reholstered his gun as well.

"You can put your hands down," the driver said just as
a second and third squad car and an ambulance rounded
the curve a couple of houses away and drove up to park
against the curb on either side of the driveway. Gratefully,
I complied.

"You found the body?" he asked as other police got out
of the newly arrived cars.

"Yes, in the living room. I went in because he called me
to come over, and then I couldn't get him to answer the
door."

"Any sign of anyone else in the house?"

"Not that I saw, but I didn't go through the whole
house."

"Okay, we'd better search it. Would you go over and sit
in one of the other cars while we go through the house,
please?" As I walked toward the rear police car he called
out instructions to the other officers, who quickly and expertly began a search of the yards, front and back, the ga-

rage, and then inside the house. The ambulance crew, a man and a woman, waited patiently until they could go inside and confirm that the victim was beyond their help. I watched as more lights inside the house came on one by one, first in the hallway and then throughout the second floor. By the time three of the four cops who had gone into the house came back out, two more cars were pulling in behind the one in which I sat. Both cars were unmarked, and when I turned around to look out the rear window, I saw Bill Russell getting out of the first one and Noah Lansing walking up from the second.

Well, I thought, my luck is holding. Snake eyes, start to finish. Lansing already had me at the top of his list of people not to trust. If he didn't like anything about the scene or my explanation, the night was going to be very long indeed.

Lansing said something to Bill, and they stopped to talk to each other for a moment by Bill's car. I heard Lansing say, "Shit!" I guessed that Bill had told him I was involved. They turned to come up to the house, and I got out of the cruiser in front of them.

"McPhee," Bill said, sounding as if he were trying to decide whether to be mystified or exasperated, "what the hell is this? How come you called this in?"

"I found the body," I replied simply, my eyes going of their own accord not to Bill but to Lansing. Unlike Bill, there wasn't much question of his mood. He looked pretty aggravated.

"Can you be trusted to stay here while we go inside for a few minutes?" Lansing asked, his voice rife with irritation.

"Sure," I said, trying not to get defensive in return. He was going to be even angrier with me before the night was over. I didn't want to push any more of his buttons any sooner than necessary. I sat back down in the car. Lansing turned and started toward the house.

Bill put his left arm on the top of the open door and his right on the roof, bending down to look inside.

"This had better be good," he said. "I can bail you out with him only so many times." Apparently Bill had decided he wasn't entirely happy with me either. But him I could needle.

"Bless me, Father, for I have sinned," I told him sarcastically, "but I'll make a good and honest confession."

"Yeah, right!" He shook his head, straightened up, and walked up to the house, where Lansing was talking with the cops who had driven up in the first car. When Bill got to them, they went into the house as a group.

As for me, well, for all my bravado with Bill, I was trying to get my legs to stop trembling. What had happened was just beginning to hit me. Finding Morris dead was bad enough, but it finally occurred to me that he might be dead because of what I had said to Ed Lloyd at the cemetery this morning. I was beginning to worry that I might have dangerously underestimated Senator Lloyd's deductive abilities. The shock of finding Morris's body, the strain of dealing with the police, and the growing fear that I somehow had gotten Morris killed were unnerving me. As I leaned back against the seat and closed my eyes to do some yoga breathing, I realized my teeth were clamped together and chattering as well.

Some fifteen minutes later I had managed to calm my mind and body back to a manageable point, and neighbors, several sporting dogs in the current fashionable breeds, had gathered along the street to find out what was going on. Two of the policemen had cordoned off the yard with yellow crime-scene tape and were keeping the neighbors back from the property and responding to their worried questions with vague answers to the effect that there wasn't anything anyone could tell them yet.

I stood up next to the cruiser to test my legs—much

steadier now—and saw Bill and Lansing coming down the front steps. Coming, unfortunately, right in my direction.

"Okay," Lansing said once they reached me, "you've got a lot to talk about. Get in."

Once more I sat down in the backseat of the cruiser, this time scooting over to the passenger's side when Lansing made a move to climb in beside me. Bill opened the driver's door and got into the front seat, where he closed the door and turned sideways to listen to whatever it was I was going to tell them.

Lansing closed his door as well, sealing us off from the murmuring voices of the neighbors and the chatter of the rest of the police radios. Bill reached down to turn off the radio in the car we occupied and to turn on the dome light over our heads. He looked at Lansing. Lansing looked at him. They both looked at me.

"Okay, McPhee," Lansing said, "I want the whole story, and you're the one who had better not bullshit me. I've got a dead doctor in there who appears to have killed himself, and I don't have time for any crap about reporters' rights. You can start with why you're here in the first place." Bill, I noticed, wasn't jumping to my defense.

"He called and asked me to come over," I said, thinking to myself, Keep it simple, keep it simple.

"You knew him?"

"Yes."

"How well?"

"Not very."

"So you didn't know him very well," Lansing echoed, the disbelief evident in his voice, "but when he decided to kill himself, he called you? He didn't call a close friend. He didn't call his family. He called you."

I shrugged, the picture of innocence.

"Okay," Lansing continued, incredulity written all over his face, "go on. So he called and asked you to come over. What happened when you got here?"

"The garage door was open and the dining-room light was on, but I couldn't get him to answer the door. Finally, I got worried. When I checked the side door from the garage, it was unlocked, so I went in through it. I . . . I found him in the living room. He was already dead."

"Yeah, we could see that much," Lansing responded sarcastically. "He also has what looks like a self-inflicted gunshot wound to the temple, and there's a pistol in his hand. What did you do when you found him? Did you touch him, move him at all? Touch anything in the room?"

"I went over and looked to see if he was alive, but I couldn't see any signs of it. I felt his wrist for a pulse."

"What else did you touch besides the body?"

I rethought my movements. "Just doorknobs and light switches. In the garage, the kitchen, and the living room. And the front door. I called nine-one-one from my car."

Up until this moment Bill had been quiet, just watching us. Now he decided to stir the pot and show me I wasn't fooling him.

"McPhee," he said, "were you doing some kind of story with this guy?"

Well, here it was. Did I tell him or not? It would have been easy just to spill everything I knew or guessed and let the police handle it. Especially given what had happened to Peter Morris. But when the moment came, I couldn't do it. Like Morris, I knew that telling the cops everything meant I would lose any control over how this thing played out, any chance at exclusivity. I wanted this story badly, wanted to nail it myself. Especially after finding Morris's body. If Ed Lloyd had anything to do with Morris being dead because of what I had said, there was now a personal score to settle between us. I wanted more than ever to find a way to lay Ann Kane's death—and now Morris's, too—at Lloyd's doorstep.

"I can't tell you that," I answered flatly.

"Sutton, be sensible," Bill cautioned. "You have to tell us what you know."

"He's right," Lansing said. I could see he was making an effort not to start yelling. "If you know more about this than you're saying, it could help explain why he killed himself."

"That's just it," I told him. "I don't know anything. Morris had a theory about something I was interested in. But it was supposition on his part and guesswork on my part. I don't have anything concrete."

"Morris is dead. Isn't that concrete enough for you?" Lansing asked nastily, his temper beginning to fray. "Nothing you tell us can hurt him anymore, that's for sure."

"It's more complicated than that," I said. I knew that the angrier he got, the calmer I would have to stay, or we could be here all night.

Bill was still thinking, trying to read between my lines.

"Do you think it was a suicide, Sutton?" he asked quietly.

Lansing turned to look at Bill. Immediately, I could see the night getting longer as Bill's question sent a whole new train of thought along the track of Lansing's mind.

"It certainly looks like one," I told Bill. Well, that much was true. It did look like a suicide.

"Forget what it looks like," Lansing interjected. "Tell us what you know. It won't help your friend in there, but it might help you."

"What does that mean?" I asked in irritation, getting a little tired of being bullied.

"Just what it sounded like," he answered. "If you know why Morris is dead and you're withholding that information, you could be making big problems for yourself. For all we know, you could have killed him and made it look like a suicide."

He had done it again. He had pulled the big-bad-cop routine and pissed me off.

"Detective," I snapped, "don't be an ass. And let's get something straight here once and for all. I've been doing this for a long time, and you're not the first cop to threaten me. But you don't scare me any more than they did. So unless you've got something you can make stick, drop the idle threats of bringing charges against me!"

"Believe me, I'd like nothing more right now!" he said angrily. "A night in a holding cell could do you a world of good!"

"Noah . . ." Bill started to warn him. A horn blew loudly beside us. It was a group of crime-scene investigators who needed to talk with Lansing. He got out of the car and walked around to speak briefly with them through the driver's open window.

Looking out at him and then out the windshield in front of us, I realized that while we had been having our little chat the crowd had grown in size by several reporters, including Will Anderson, my coworker at the *News* who covered the police on the weekends. If they hadn't recognized my car already or heard that I somehow was involved in this, they would know it as soon as I got out and tried to drive away.

Lansing came back around, opened the door, and looked at me.

"You can go," he said. "Go get your car and get the hell out of here. We'll let you know when we need to talk with you again. And don't worry, we will be talking about this a lot more!"

"So what are you going to say to the rest of the press about my finding the body?"

"I don't see that you've left us very much to tell them," said Bill, showing his own displeasure with me. "Morris is dead. It looks like he killed himself. You knew him. He called you to come over. When you got here, he was dead. You called the police. Is that about right?"

Lansing and I both thought it over. No self-respecting

reporter would be satisfied with that, but they sure as hell weren't going to get anything more from me, and the police didn't know any more.

"It'll do for now," I told Bill.

"Like hell," Lansing gruffed. He gave me another hard look and then slammed the car door and walked up to the house.

Bill and I exited the car together.

"You know a lot more than you're saying, don't you, Sutton?" he asked me as we stood out in the cool night air once again.

"I have suspicions, Bill, but I don't know anything."

"Well, I know you, Sutton. If there's a chance this is more than what it looks like, you had better think hard about keeping Lansing in the dark."

"Come on, Bill. What's he going to do to me? Charge me with failing to do his job for him?"

"Sutton, be careful."

"Oh, for . . . He doesn't scare me, Bill."

"I didn't mean Lansing," he answered, and started walking toward the house.

I walked in his wake to the driveway. As I got into my car I heard the reporters' exclamations as they recognized me and realized I was behind the police tape, where they couldn't go. I started the car, and as I waited for one of the cops to move the cruiser parked behind me so I could get out, I saw Bill going over to soothe their fears of my getting preferential treatment and to answer their questions. I decided there was no point in hanging around.

What I would have to do was to warn Rob Perry. If I let him get hit with this without an advisory from me, shit creek would look like a resort. It would be bad enough if he heard from Will Anderson first that I had found the body. It would be even worse if he started getting calls from angry cops without hearing my side of it. It was

11:30 on Friday night. I knew Rob still would be at the paper for at least another hour, until the presses were running without any problems.

As soon as I got out of the subdivision where Dr. Morris had lived and into traffic, I called the city room. For once, I was too tired to care whether someone could listen in to my call.

"Perry," Rob answered, rarely standing on ceremonies such as "hello."

"Rob, it's Sutton."

"McPhee, what's up?"

"I've got a little problem, Rob, and I think it's about to be your problem as well, so I thought I had better warn you."

"Who's mad at you now?" he asked.

"Most of the Fairfax County police, for starters."

"So tell me something surprising. Okay, let's hear it."

Quickly, I told him that I had gone to visit a source and had found him dead, apparently a suicide, that it was a doctor in McLean, that I had called the police, that Will had been there to cover it.

"Is this about Janet Taylor?"

"No, but it's just as big, if not bigger."

"You mind telling me what, exactly?"

"Listen, Rob," I said, "don't ask. I'm on my cellular phone. And besides, it would be just like this detective to try to muscle you into making me talk to them about what I'm working on. What you don't know, you can't be forced to tell. You know I know what I'm doing. Just trust me for a little while, won't you?"

"McPhee, if you don't—"

I interrupted. "I just need a little time, Rob. A few days. If the cops call, help me stall them until I can nail this thing down. Okay?"

"But what about the Taylor murder? Who's gonna be

covering that with Ken if you're off on whatever wild hair this is?''

"I will. I will," I tried to reassure him. "Don't worry, I'm not letting that one slide. Help me out here, Rob. Please."

"Okay, okay, stop. You know I hate it when you beg. But, Sutton . . ."

"Yes?"

"You had better make this worth it."

" 'Bye, Rob . . . and thanks," I said. I hung up. I knew he would back me up.

As traffic flowed around me I decided the best thing to do at this point was to go home and get some sleep. I would turn off my phone so anyone trying to call me would get the answering machine. It was almost midnight, so I probably could avoid any potential visitors until tomorrow morning. By then I already would be gone.

I was planning to show up at Hub Taylor's house first thing, in hopes of finding him at home. I not only needed to grill him about his wife's death—a story that I knew better than to neglect just because I had another big one going on—but he was also a crony and protégé of Ed Lloyd. Maybe I could get a better reading of Ed Lloyd and his potential as a sleazeball killer from Taylor.

That was when it occurred to me. What I should have seen from the beginning when Peter Morris told me he thought Lloyd might be connected to Ann Kane's death. What I hadn't seen because I had been looking at the two things as separate. Before Ann Kane died, she had had sex with—or had been raped by—two men, not one. One man had AB-negative blood, like Ed Lloyd. The other had O-positive. It was possible that the two men had sex with Ann at two separate times, but the medical examiner had said that the condition of the sperm made him think all of it had been deposited at approximately the same time. If that were true and if Ed Lloyd was Mr. AB-negative, who was his partner? Who did Ed Lloyd trust enough to initiate into his nasty little game, enough to let that person know such a damaging secret about him?

I didn't know all Ed Lloyd's friends, but I could have smacked myself for not seeing, until now, one very obvious candidate for Mr. O-positive—Hub Taylor. Jesus!

The honk of a horn to my left brought me back to my driving, and I saw that I was drifting over into the next lane. I also saw that my exit onto Duke Street was coming up quickly. I put on my turn signal and moved onto the exit ramp. As I merged into the Duke Street traffic my conscious brain noted what my subconscious had been recording ever since I left Morris's McLean neighborhood—a set of distinctive headlights on a large dark sedan that had stayed one to two cars behind me through McLean, onto the Beltway, and again onto I-395. Now it was directly behind me, about three car lengths back. As Duke Street went past Landmark Center and curved down to Reynolds Street, I gradually moved across the traffic to the left lane. So did the sedan. At Paxton Street, I moved into the left-turn lane, to go the last block to my building. So did the sedan. But just as I pulled into the building's front parking lot and decided I was being followed, the sedan glided past, on up Holmes Run Parkway, toward Van Dorn.

You're getting paranoid, McPhee, I told myself. It's just a coincidence. There are four other high-rises between my building and Van Dorn Street. If the sedan were going from McLean to any of those buildings or to several other nearby town-house and apartment complexes, the driver might easily have chosen the same route I took, to get there. I put it out of my mind and circled my building looking for a parking space, finally finding one at the far end.

What I couldn't put out of my mind as I walked up to the front entrance was my brainstorm about Hub Taylor. The implications were mind-boggling. I didn't know how I ever would get to sleep with them going through my head.

Saturday

Seventeen

Go to sleep was exactly what I did, however, almost as soon as I lay down. I was exhausted, and my body outvoted my brain, sending me so far into the depths that I don't think I even turned over until my alarm clock went off at six the next morning.

When I came back into the bedroom from my shower, finally able to think, I noticed that my answering machine said I had three messages. I ticked off the likely suspects: Rob, Bill Russell, Noah Lansing, other reporters wanting me to comment on Morris's death. No, I didn't think I wanted to hear what any of them had to say. I ignored the phone, went about dressing in tan slacks and a navy blouse, and walked into the kitchen for a quick breakfast. I took a look at Will's story in the morning's paper. He had done a good job, considering I wasn't talking. He had included a quote from me, obviously dictated to him by Rob, saying that Morris was an acquaintance, that I had gone over at his request, found the body, and had no idea why he would want to kill himself. A couple of Sara Lee frozen croissants later I headed out to Great Falls, to the big white house where Janet Taylor had died. I was hoping that if I got there by eight, I could catch Hub Taylor at home.

A middle-aged man in green work khakis was on his knees in one of Hub Taylor's flower beds when I came up the drive and parked in the paved circle outside the front door. The groundsman nodded a good morning as I walked up the steps. I smiled an acknowledgment and rang the door-bell. Within thirty seconds the door was opened by a maid who said, in heavily accented English that I guessed meant she was from someplace in Central or South America, "Yes? May I help you?"

I took a business card out of my pocket and gave it to her, explaining that it was very important that I speak with Mr. Taylor about his wife. I was counting on him to know, as an experienced politician, that he couldn't avoid report-ers forever and that he might as well let me in and get it over with.

The maid stepped back and said, "Come in, please." I went inside the marble-floored foyer and unashamedly gog-gled at the elegance around me. The house said Janet Tay-lor—graceful, tasteful, expensive. To my left was a large, formal living room, done in whites, beiges, and accents of lavender. On the walls was a series of Impressionists that I wouldn't know from Adam but that I was sure were orig-inals. To my right was a partially opened door through which I could see a sliver of a room lined with books and furnished in darker woods, an office or library, I assumed. Through the door I could see a full-length oil portrait of Mrs. Taylor in informal riding clothes, apparently in her prewheelchair days. Directly ahead of me was a wide stair-case going to the second floor. Behind it, on either side, I could see an expanse of floor-to-ceiling glass that looked out on a very green backyard that I guessed dropped off toward the Potomac.

"Wait here, please," the maid said, and turned to wander off toward the back of the house. I sat down on one of a matching pair of beige upholstered benches that stood along the walls on either side of the foyer, between tall, basketed palms. I wondered how Taylor was handling the reminders of his wife everywhere he turned.

A couple of minutes went by before the maid returned.

"Mr. Taylor will see you for five minutes," she said. "Please follow." I stood up and walked behind her through the house. The glass wall I had seen extended all the way across the back of a family room and looked out over a flagstone patio that ran between the house and an in-ground pool. The pool was perpendicular to the house and heated, judging by the steam rising from it in the early-morning chill.

In the L created by the pool and the south-facing house, Hub Taylor sat at a black wrought-iron table, the remains of breakfast in front of him. He looked up as the maid opened the exterior door and let me out onto the patio, and I was struck once again by how blasted his face looked in the wake of his wife's death.

"Thank you for seeing me," I said, walking over to the table and offering my hand to shake. He made no move to return the gesture or to offer me a seat. Too many questions from reporters already, I figured. I dropped my hand, pulled out a chair opposite him, and sat down anyway, while Taylor just looked at me.

"I'm sorry about your wife," I told him. "She was an exceptional person."

"What is it you want?" Taylor asked bluntly.

"Mr. Taylor, do you know of any reason why someone would want to kill your wife?"

"No, none."

"The police say she wasn't sexually assaulted and that apparently nothing was taken from the house."

"Meaning?"

"Meaning that it sounds as if someone came in specifically to kill her."

"I don't know." Taylor looked away from me and out across the yard. His attention seemed to drift away as well. I decided I needed to get it back.

"Was your wife involved in something that would have been enough to kill her for?" I asked.

Taylor jerked back around, his faraway look replaced with a glare.

"What are you implying?" he asked angrily.

"Maybe she knew something, or saw something, that was threatening to someone, threatening enough that they felt they needed to silence her," I said, working through the possibilities in my own mind even as I asked the question.

"She never told me if she did."

I decided to put my finger a little deeper into the wound.

"Mr. Taylor, the police say your wife was attacked sometime before she actually died, perhaps even as early as twelve-thirty. You told the police you left the house about then and that she was fine when you left. But they also say you have no alibi for the next hour or more, until you showed back up at the county building a few minutes before the meeting started at two o'clock. Where were you?"

"It's like I told the police," Taylor said angrily. "I was just out driving around. I had a lot on my mind and I didn't want to go back to the county building any sooner than necessary."

"But you have no one who can vouch for that, no one who saw you at a gas station or someplace else where you might have stopped?"

"I didn't stop. I drove around the whole time."

"I also was told that you came home at lunch that

day because your wife called your office and was very angry. Did you have an argument with her when you got here? What was she so angry about?''

"That is absolutely none of your business!"

"Mr. Taylor, did you kill your wife?"

Taylor stood up abruptly, bumping the table and turning over cups and glasses. I stood up, too, to avoid the resulting spills and to take flight, if necessary.

"Get out," he shouted, his face reddening. He held both hands, clenched into fists, at his sides. "Get out and don't come back."

"I'll go, but I need to ask you one more thing," I said, standing my ground for a moment. "Were you with Ed Lloyd when Ann Kane died?" It was a question that I hadn't even been planning to ask a moment before. Now it just popped out of my mouth.

"Maria!" Taylor shouted, looking into the house. Maria appeared instantly at the door, this time accompanied by John Aldritch, the attorney. Taylor saw him and started shouting.

"John, get this bitch out of here, right now! I want her out!"

Without waiting for them to throw me out, I walked quickly up to the door. The maid opened it and Aldritch stepped out onto the patio.

"Who are you?" he asked, his eyes hostile.

"I'm out of here," I replied, and stepped around him and through the door. Maria already was walking ahead of me to get the front door. I paused for a second to look back and saw that Aldritch and Taylor were now arguing with each other. I went on, past Maria and out the front door. My VW was dwarfed by the looming silver Mercedes that had pulled up in the drive behind it, owned by John Aldritch, I was sure.

I climbed in and started the car. Once again an interesting response to a question about Ann Kane—no confusion about who she was, no denial, just anger. Now that I had stirred up that anthill, it was time to go into the District to see if Maggie Padgett was in her office.

Eighteen

This time I knew my way to Senator Black's office. I walked in, not knowing how many staffers might be in. As it turned out, it was just Maggie. The receptionist's desk was empty, as were the two offices into which I could see from the reception area.

"Hello," I called out. "Ms. Padgett?"

I heard a muffled response from somewhere in the back of the office, and a moment later a young woman with luxurious black hair down to her shoulders, porcelain skin, and incredibly violet eyes came around the corner.

"Yes?" she said, smiling vaguely. "May I help you?"

All my bells were going off.

"Are you Maggie Padgett?"

"Yes, I am." She was also lovely. I could see how Peter Morris had been struck by her beauty, even in the circumstances under which he had met her. I also could see why a predator like Ed Lloyd would want her, perhaps enough to do something incredibly stupid in an effort to have her.

"Ms. Padgett, my name is Sutton McPhee. I'm a reporter

with the *Washington News*. Susan Barrett told me I should
talk to you about a story I'm working on. Did she mention
that I would be coming by today?''

''No, she didn't. What was it you wanted to speak with
me about?''

''Could we sit down?'' I asked, motioning to the sofa
across from the receptionist's desk, hoping that getting her
seated would make her less likely to bolt when I told her
why I was there.

''Oh, yes, certainly,'' she said, her face coloring as she
became flustered. ''I'm so sorry. Please forgive my manners. I've been out for a week, and I'm rather distracted by
all the work that has piled up.''

We moved over to the sofa and sat down facing each
other. She laid her long-fingered hands in her lap and
looked at me again. Her eyes were a truly arresting color.
Combined with the guileless expression in them and with
all the rest of her, I expected she probably turned men's
heads regularly without any effort on her part. If this was
the woman Dr. Morris had treated, her experience with Ed
Lloyd must have been a nightmare for her. God, I thought,
another innocent. One more face to add to the line that
paraded in front of my sleepless eyes on bad nights, and I
was going to have to cause this one some more pain myself.
I could bait slimebags like Ed Lloyd without batting an eye.
But hurting someone like Maggie Padgett was not a part
of my job I particularly enjoyed. Still, she was alive after
her encounter with Lloyd. Ann Kane—and possibly Peter
Morris—weren't so lucky. If some pain on her part could
pin their deaths on Lloyd, then I would find a way to live
with my conscience.

''Susan told me you knew Ann Kane,'' I said.

''Yes, I did,'' she replied, looking a little puzzled. ''I
used to work for Senator Wills when she was a state official
in Florida. I know everyone in her office.''

''How well did you know Ann?''

"Somewhat. I was already in Washington, working for the Democratic National Committee, when Rita ran for the Senate. She brought Ann and a couple of other people on her Florida staff with her. I got this job with Senator Black two years ago. The two staffs work closely together on several projects. I also see most of them from time to time at various committee hearings or receptions. And Ann and I have gone out to lunch a couple of times. But I don't think you could have called us close friends. We really didn't move in the same circles outside work at all."

"Would you know enough about her social life to have any ideas about who might have been with her when she died?"

Something happened in her eyes at that. Not a flinch, but something in her look changed slightly. I had touched a nerve. She looked away from me toward the outer door.

"No, I don't. I don't know the people she spent her time with after work."

"People at church and at charities like soup kitchens, apparently. And yet, somehow, she ended up in a situation where she took or was given a prescription drug that was dangerous for her. And had sex with two men. It doesn't sound like the Ann Kane people keep describing to me."

Maggie looked down at her hands, then back up.

"I'm sorry I can't be of more help," she said, thinking— or hoping—I was done.

"Actually, I think you still can. If I could just have a few more minutes . . . ?" My voice trailed off in a question.

"Yes?" she asked, and her expression changed again, this time to a wary one. She knew, on some level, that something bad was coming. She knew there was going to be no way around it.

"I was wondering if you, by any chance, know a doctor out in Vienna named Peter Morris, an internist."

"No . . ." She paused, doing her best impression of someone searching their mind for information they didn't have. "No, I don't think so." She shook her head from side to side.

"So you didn't know that he was found dead last night under some rather suspicious circumstances?"

Then she did flinch.

"No," she said. "I haven't read this morning's papers yet."

"What about Ed Lloyd? Do you know him very well?"

"The senator?" she asked. I could see the panic beginning to build in her eyes and in the tension of her body. I knew I was on the right track, that she was Dr. Morris's mystery woman, and Ed Lloyd's earlier, luckier victim. "Of course I know him to see him. I probably know all the members of the Senate by sight, and he's a very important senator." Her eyes were asking me to stop, to leave it, but I had no choice.

"But you didn't socialize with him? Go out with him?"

"No," she said, an undertone of anger appearing in her voice. "I didn't."

"Did he ever ask you out, or make a pass at you?"

"Excuse me," she said, standing up suddenly, "but you'll have to go now. I don't think I want to answer any more of these questions, and I have a lot of work I need to do."

But I wasn't letting her go so easily. This might be my last chance to make the connection.

"I don't mean to offend you," I said, standing, too. "I really don't. But this is important. At least two people have died, and I think you can tell me who killed them."

"What?" she exclaimed, backing away from me.

I knew I had to push. "Maggie, I think you know what happened to Ann Kane. The same thing that almost happened to you. It was Ed Lloyd, wasn't it? He's a lecher and a rapist. If he decides he wants something, he's going to have it, one way or the other. But you weren't interested, were you? And neither was Ann Kane. So he got each of you alone, and he drugged your drinks. You were lucky. It only made you sick, maybe before anything else happened. Lloyd took you to Dr. Morris to clean up his mess. But even then he didn't learn his lesson. He's apparently too far gone for that. Instead he did the same thing to Ann Kane, this time with a second guy there. Only something went far more wrong in her case, and she died. And now Dr. Morris is dead, too, probably because he told me about you. You know it's what happened. I know it's what happened. So why won't you tell me about it and help me nail this bastard before he kills someone else?''

By the time I finished, I realized just how angry the things Ed Lloyd had done made me, and that anger had suddenly focused on Maggie Padgett and all the women like her, who silently suffer the abuses some man heaps on them. Because she had kept quiet, cowed by the threat of Ed Lloyd's power, two other people were dead.

As I talked she had moved to put the receptionist's desk between us, and I had to quash the urge to walk back there and shake some sense into her. It was clear I had frightened her, but when she spoke again, I knew she was far more frightened of Ed Lloyd than of me.

"You'll really have to leave now, please," she said, breathing rapidly, her voice almost gaspy. "I don't know what you're talking about. None of that is true. So please, just go. Please. If you don't, I'll have to call security."

It was no use, I knew. There was no way past the fear of Ed Lloyd. At least not here and now. The anger went out of me, leaving me tired. I reached into my pocket for one of my business cards. I put it on the desk in front of her.

"All right," I said, quietly now. "I'll go. But everything I said is the truth. I know you were the woman Lloyd brought to Dr. Morris's office that night. So, if you think about it and decide you want to tell someone, would you please call me? You'll be helping me, but I can help you, too. At least I can still help you. All I can do for Ann Kane and Dr. Morris at this point is to find out the truth of what happened to them.''

I turned and walked out of the office, leaving her standing there, her eyes wide and frightened, her body rigid, a woman who had been a victim, probably through no fault of her own, and whom I had just victimized again. Riding the elevator down to the lobby, I felt about as low as dirt. I hated what I had just done up there, but I hadn't seen any alternative. Nor would I let it end here; I would have to make another run at Maggie Padgett. Someone had to stop Lloyd, and she probably was the only one who could, now that Morris was dead.

And the only one who can nail down your story, said my voice.

I gave it a mental punch in the nose, and the elevator opened to deposit me in the lobby.

Nineteen

The drive back out to my apartment was shitty. I didn't know where to go from here. Maggie Padgett wouldn't talk to me. Peter Morris was dead, taking his knowledge with him. I didn't know what results, if any, my questions to Lloyd and Taylor had wrought. They were both politicians. They knew denial was nine-tenths of the law, unless I had solid evidence to raise against them.

At home, I gathered up the week's laundry and took it downstairs to the basement laundry room, where I filled up three washers, stuffed them with a small fortune in quarters, and turned them on. I figured they would take half an hour, just enough time for me to clean my bathroom, which was about as much as I could handle thinking about right now.

Twenty-five minutes later I was putting out fresh towels in the now-sparkling bathroom when the phone on my bedroom nightstand rang. For a moment I hesitated to answer it, thinking of all the people it could be to whom I would rather not talk at the moment. On the other hand, it could be a friend or someone with information I wanted. I relented and went to pick it up. It turned out to be a sales-person, whom I quickly dispatched back to telemarketing limbo, but the flashing message light reminded me I prob-ably should listen to the messages that had come in last night and that I had chosen to ignore this morning. In fact, according to the counter, I had received two more since then. I sat down on my bed and pressed the play button.

"Sutton, it's Bill," Bill Russell said. "I don't know what you've gotten into the middle of, but I don't like the sound of it. Would you be careful? And would you please use your common sense and bring us in on whatever it is? I know we're only the police, but we might actually be able to help." The machine said he had called at 1:00 A.M.

Bill's message was followed, just as I had suspected, by calls from reporters at the *Post* and two of the local TV stations, all of which had come in during the night. I let them play and erase themselves, having no intention of re-turning the calls.

The next message was a 10:00 A.M. call from Rob Perry.

"It's Rob. I thought I'd better let you know that I just got off the phone with Mack Thompson, who just got chewed out by Jim Todd." Jim Todd was the paper's pub-lisher, who had come up through the business side of news-papers and who the reporters were convinced was more concerned with keeping advertisers happy than with re-porting the news. He hobnobbed with Washington's upper crust and hated, in the worst way, to offend any of them.

"It seems," Rob's voice went on dryly, "that Todd had gotten an earful from John Aldritch, that attorney for Hub Taylor. Aldritch says you went out to Taylor's house bright and early this morning, completely uninvited, finagled your way in, and started accusing Taylor of murdering his wife. Aldritch apparently made lots of noises to Todd about ha-rassment and slander and restraining orders. What Todd knows about reporting wouldn't give a gnat pause, of course, and we all know how he sucks up to anybody with any public clout. So, he apparently kissed Aldritch's ass all over the place and then called Thompson and said he had better not get any more calls over this. Thompson called me, trying to figure out whether to be pissed off at Aldritch, Todd, or you. I told him all three. I also said that it made perfect sense for you to go out there, since you're one of the reporters covering Janet Taylor's death. And I reminded him that Taylor is a public figure, that he isn't off the hook over his wife's death, and that when you get our tails in a crack, it's usually for a good reason. It *was* for a good reason, wasn't it, McPhee?'' He hung up without specifically ordering me to call him, so I decided it wasn't necessary. I wondered which of my questions to Hub Taylor had touched such a nerve. The one about his wife or the one about Ann Kane?

The final message was Ken Hale.

"Sutton, where are you? We need to talk about this Taylor stuff. We are supposed to be working on it together, don't forget. And I'd love to know what the story in this morning's paper was about. Did this Morris guy know something about Janet Taylor? Let's go have a drink. Call me.'' Ken had called at 10:30 this morning.

Him, I rang back immediately.

"Hello,'' he said, picking the phone up on the third ring.

"Ken, it's Sutton.''

"Who?'' he asked archly.

"I'm sorry. I'm sorry. I'm not trying to be the Lone Ranger. I just haven't had anything to tell you. I've got something else going, too, and it sort of got the best of my time.''

"Is this something else the reason you're finding dead doctors out in McLean?''

"That's part of it. But there are also some things we need to discuss about Hub Taylor. I managed to get in to see him this morning. So how about dinner? I'll buy.''

"You don't have a very high opinion of me if you think

my affections can be bought for the price of a dinner, do you?'' he joked.

''Let's just say I've heard from certain sources at work that the only thing required to get your affections is to be female.'' As a single, nice, good-looking guy who liked women, Ken never lacked for ''companionship'' anytime he wanted it. In spite of that, he had never been married, not for lack of wanting to, he had told me once, but because he was still waiting for the woman who would absorb his attention outside the bedroom as much as inside it. I kept telling him he was picking the wrong kind of women as an avoidance mechanism.

''All right, where and when?'' Ken asked, laughing.

''Seven o'clock. Port of Italy.'' I had had no lunch, and I knew that by the time I finished the three o'clock yoga class I planned to get to, I would be ready for something filling. Port of Italy's long menu of pastas and other Italian dishes sounded like what was called for. And it would be halfway between my apartment and Ken's house off Old Keene Mill Road.

''Great. See you then,'' Ken agreed.

I remembered my clothes. I went to the kitchen for another roll of quarters, which I got at the bank by the handfuls just for laundry, and headed downstairs to put my clothes in the dryers. At 2:30, clothes cleaned and dried, I changed into a leotard and tights and headed over to my yoga class.

Teresa, my teacher, was a forty-two-year-old nurse who had gotten interested in yoga after a car wreck had given her a chronically painful back injury. The yoga had worked so well for her that she had gone on to become a certified instructor and eventually turned the entire top floor of her 1930s house in the Rosemont section of Alexandria into a yoga studio, where she held frequent classes. Teresa was one of the most grounded people I had ever met. She gave off such feelings of quiet confidence, such composure and peace with who she was, that I was convinced most of her students came back as much in hopes of awakening those feelings in themselves as for fitness. I always left her classes rested, my thoughts quieted, more aware of my body and how it worked. On a day like today, there was no price I wouldn't pay to let Teresa work her magic on me.

Port of Italy, which sits across Franconia Road from the department-of-motor-vehicles building, was crowded when I got there. I was glad I had had the presence of mind to call a couple of hours before and make reservations. It was one of my favorite restaurants: good food, made from scratch, an imaginative menu with tasty dishes from both northern and southern Italy, a dining room divided into several sections to provide a little more intimate atmosphere, and an attentive staff who were always in motion and smiling.

Anna, a college student with a long, straight, blond ponytail and mischievous blue eyes, was playing hostess and greeted me by name.

"Ms. McPhee, how are you?" she asked, picking up a black grease pencil to make a mark on her seating chart.

"Good, Anna, I'm good," I told her. "Just very busy."

"Is that why we haven't seen you for a while?"

"I know. I know. I've got to do a better job of having a personal life somewhere in all this work."

Grinning, Anna picked up a stack of menus and lifted a couple off the top.

"Two tonight?" she asked.

"Yes, Ken Hale should be coming along any minute. But go ahead and seat me, and I'll wait for him inside. Could we have a booth tonight, please, Anna?" She knew Ken as well. We had had drinks here more than once, and since he didn't live far away, who knew how many times Ken had been here on his own.

"Certainly," Anna answered agreeably, "whatever you'd like. This way, please."

I followed her back past a wall of wine bottles residing inside a see-through cooler that runs from floor to ceiling. On our right was the stairwell down to the restaurant's popular sports bar, from which I could hear a low rumble of conversation and occasional cheers over some sort of televised competition. Anna led me to a corner booth, where I sat down, ordered a gin and tonic from the waitress who appeared immediately, and sat back to wait for Ken. Five minutes later my drink arrived, and so did my coworker. He asked the waitress for a beer and sat down opposite me.

"So, how goes it, Sutton?" Ken asked, smiling. He never called me McPhee, and he was always in a good mood. I thought to myself what a nice guy he really was, amazed that no one had managed to tie him down yet. Tie him down—maybe that was what no one had tried on him. I entertained myself with lascivious thoughts for a second and smiled back at him.

"I have no idea," I finally answered truthfully, getting a grip on my imagination. "I feel like I'm poking around in the dark. Things move, but I still don't know what's in there."

"I might be able to help shed a little light," he said as the waitress came back with his beer. He grabbed it, drank a large swallow, put it down on the table and relaxed against the upholstered seat back. "But before I tell you anything, you have to tell Father Ken what naughty things you've been doing. I understand you've been a very bad girl."

"Fine, your holier-than-thouness, but can we order dinner first? I'm starving."

"I suppose so," he agreed, opening his menu, "although I should confine you to bread and water as punishment for not keeping me filled in."

We studied the offerings for a couple of minutes, by

which time our waitress was back. We each rattled off our preferences—stuffed mushrooms and chicken Marsala for me, minestrone and veal piccata for Ken—and gave the menus back.

"Well?" Ken asked when the waitress left.

So I told him about my visit to Hub Taylor's house, about asking Taylor point-blank if he killed his wife, and about Taylor throwing a fit and then throwing me out.

"And John Aldritch showed up just as Taylor was going ballistic, so he got in on the act and called up Jim Todd. And you know what a wimp Todd is. I'm sure he kissed the telephone receiver all over because that was as close as he could get at that moment to Aldritch's ass. He called Mack Thompson who called Rob Perry who called my answering machine."

"What did Rob say?" Ken asked, knowing that it was what Rob said to us that really mattered in these situations.

"Basically, that I should just make sure I know what I'm doing, cover my ass, and come back with a good story."

"I love that guy," Ken said.

"Don't we all?"

"That's all well and good and quite fascinating, Sutton," Ken went on, "but you haven't told me where Dr. Morris fits in to all this."

I looked at him for at least sixty seconds, my brain calculating the pros and cons of letting him in on the full extent of what I knew and suspected. On the surface, the Ann Kane story was a separate affair that had nothing to do with the Taylor murder I was working on with Ken. And yet, I never had been much of a believer in long strings of coincidence. Some part of my brain was itching with the idea that somehow, somewhere, it was all connected—Ed Lloyd, Ann Kane, Maggie Padgett, Peter Morris, Hub Taylor, Janet Taylor—and no matter how I tried, I just couldn't make the itch stop. I didn't know how they were connected, but every suspicious bone in my body kept feeling that they were.

So what do I do about Ken? I asked myself. Do I keep the Ed Lloyd information from him and keep that story all to myself, or do I bring him in on it, hoping that somewhere down the road he can help me find the thread that ties it all together?

"Sutton?" Ken finally said, beginning to look worried that I suddenly had zoned out on him.

"I'm just trying to decide how far to trust you," I answered.

"You've known me for four years, Sutton. You already know how far you can trust me."

He was right. If and when this whole thing blew up, if my brain itch was right, it would take both of us to cover it. And, once in a while, there were times when common sense dictated that you let someone else know what you were onto, just in case.

"Okay," I agreed finally, "here's what I know, and what I guess."

I took him through all of it: Peter Morris's call; his story about the woman Ed Lloyd brought to him and what he thought had happened to her and to Ann Kane; Lloyd's blood type; my question to Lloyd at the cemetery; Morris's subsequent call that something had happened and he needed to see me; finding his body and my conviction that it wasn't a suicide; my growing suspicion that if Lloyd was responsible for Ann Kane's death, his partner might have been Hub Taylor; the question I had asked Taylor this morning about Ann Kane that actually had gotten me thrown out; my meeting with Maggie Padgett. Ken sat quietly through my story, listening intently, working it through in his own mind.

By the time I finished, we were halfway through our dinners and our second round of drinks. Ken put his fork down.

"That's quite a story, Sutton. If I heard this much supposition from just about any other reporter, I'd say they were crazy. But you're too good for me to pass it off. No," he said, shaking his head and taking his fork to the veal again, "coming from you, I have to think there's something here. Maybe a really big something here."

"So you don't think it's my imagination trying to make a story where none exists?" It actually was almost a relief to be able to bounce my ideas off someone who knew what I knew. It's hard sometimes, when you're working on a big story alone, to know if and when you've lost your perspective on things, to know whether your instincts are good or whether you've just become paranoid.

"Far from it," Ken reassured me. "I think the Peter Morris stuff on Ed Lloyd is sound, especially now that you've met Maggie Padgett, and especially if the police find any evidence that supports your suspicion that Morris was murdered. The idea that Hub Taylor was in on the Ann Kane thing with Lloyd is a lot more tenuous—completely tenuous at this point. But the fact that Janet Taylor is dead and that Hub can't prove he didn't do it isn't tenuous. What we don't know is whether one is connected to the other— yet. But it's an interesting idea, and it's even more interesting in light of what I wanted to tell you."

"Oh?"

"I found a talkative neighbor of the Taylors' this morning. One Elizabeth Van Metre. Seems she was very close to Janet Taylor and disliked Hub Taylor intensely."

"Really."

"Yeah, she called him, if my memory serves, a 'vulgar salesman' and said she didn't know what Janet could possibly have seen in him."

"So did she have gossip?"

"Oh, more than gossip. She had it from the horse's mouth. Janet Taylor had confided in her recently that the marriage was in trouble, that Hub was spending more and more time with Ed Lloyd, who, it turns out, Janet detested. Seems Janet was very worried about Lloyd's influence over her husband.''

My brain was itching in a big way. "Did she say what kind of influence, exactly?'' I asked.

"Not exactly,'' Ken said. "She said she thought Janet probably was more concerned than she was saying, but Mrs. Van Metre was left with the distinct impression that whatever Ed Lloyd was into was 'unsavory,' to quote her again.''

"I would think drugging women for sex would qualify as unsavory,'' I said.

"At least. If not sick and perverted.''

"Certainly not the kind of thing Hub Taylor would want his wife to know about,'' I went on.

"But what if she did find out?'' Ken said, thinking out loud. "Is that really enough to kill her over? Divorce would be a little less extreme.''

"Maybe, if we're talking about a situation where people are thinking rationally. The problem is, though, that Ann Kane went and died. If Taylor was there, it all suddenly became a lot more sinister, with a lot more at stake. Janet Taylor was responsible in a big way for his political success. Having her divorce him wouldn't look very good. And if his wife somehow found out, or even suspected what actually happened, if she confronted him, threatened to expose him in any way, divorce could have been the least of his worries. Maybe she didn't realize until too late that he wasn't rational anymore.''

Ken thought this over, finished the last of his beer, and looked at me.

"This is fucking incredible,'' he said, visible excitement growing in his eyes. "I think you're right. Goddamn it, Sutton, I think you're right.'' He looked up as our waitress materialized again.

"Coffee and dessert?'' she asked as she reached down

to clear away the remains of dinner. We both passed on dessert but ordered black coffee. As soon as the waitress walked away, Ken leaned forward conspiratorially, barely able to contain himself.

"So where do we go from here?" he asked eagerly. "There has to be a way to nail all this down, to find out whether it's all connected. Maggie Padgett seems to be the only real lead to Ed Lloyd right now. What about her?"

"It's clear I'm going to have to try to talk to her again. I know she was the woman Dr. Morris treated. I thought I'd give her the weekend to think about the fact that we're talking about people dying here. Maybe she'll come around. Maybe I'll go back to see her on Monday, try to convince her she has to tell someone what she knows."

"You do realize that if Ed Lloyd figures out you've tracked her down, you and she both could be in danger, too?"

I had realized it hours ago, but I knew Ken was still thinking this thing through, thinking out loud.

"Yes, but I have no reason to think he knows," I told Ken. "After all, Peter Morris never knew who the woman was. Lloyd saw to that. So how could he tell me her identity? As far as Lloyd knows, Maggie is still a mystery woman."

Our coffee arrived. We both fell into silent thought while we sipped it.

"My problem is that I can't figure out a way to put the screws to Lloyd without giving away Maggie Padgett," I said finally. "He's one cool customer. If he killed Peter Morris, it was completely cold and calculated. But if all this is connected, maybe the way in is Hub Taylor. If he killed his wife because she found out somehow, maybe we're talking about a man who's already coming apart at the seams. Ed Lloyd seduced him into something that got completely out of hand, but Taylor was still safe as long as no one knew. Then his wife was killed, and he's under suspicion. So now he's facing the prospect of his whole life going down the drain. And he's got a reporter running around asking him questions not only about how his wife died, but also about another dead woman named Ann Kane.''

"You could be right," Ken said, finishing his coffee. "He can't be sleeping at night if he's really carrying all this around. I'd even be willing to bet he hasn't told Lloyd you asked him about Ann Kane. If not, he's got you after him, he's got the police after him, and now he's afraid he's going to have Ed Lloyd after him, too. Maybe he is the weak link in all this."

We each thought some more while the waitress brought the check and I gave her my American Express card. By the time she brought it back with the credit slip for me to sign, I could tell Ken had an idea.

"How about this?" he said, picking up where we had left off. "You'll never get near Taylor again. But I can. I cover the board of supervisors, so I have access. Unless Taylor has completely lost his mind, he's got to keep up his normal routine just to keep the police from becoming even more suspicious. That means he has to get on with his job as supervisor. So if he shows up for Monday morning's board meeting, how about if I add one more straw to the pile? I'll ask him point-blank if he killed his wife because she found out about Ann Kane. If he thinks there's still another person after him, maybe it will push him into doing something stupid, into giving himself away somehow."

What did we have to lose at this point? The police suspected him in his wife's death, but they had no proof. Even Maggie Padgett couldn't make a connection between Taylor and Ann Kane, because, as far as I knew, Lloyd's disastrous evening with Maggie had been solo.

"Do it." I said, putting the check receipt on the table and standing up. "Go ahead and push all his buttons."

On the way out of the restaurant, we stopped for a minute to tell Anna how much we had enjoyed dinner, and then walked out to the parking lot. Ken was parked a couple of cars beyond mine. He stopped with me beside the Beetle.

"Thanks for dinner, Sutton. And thanks for filling me in," he said. "I know you didn't have to tell me all of it."

"I'm glad I did. My gut knows it's all connected somehow. And I know you won't screw me on it."

"Damn, I love this job," Ken said, grinning broadly. He grabbed me in a bear hug and gave me a big kiss. Then he held me at arm's length, looking me in the eye. "You're good, Sutton." It was one of those pivotal moments, a moment that could go any number of ways. I could have kissed him back. I could have taken him home with me. It certainly wouldn't have been the first time two reporters working together on a good story had gotten the excitement of the story entangled somehow with sex—not even the first time for me. Instead I put my key in the lock of my car door.

"Thanks." I laughed. "So are you. I'll talk to you on Monday, when you get in from the board meeting. Good night, Ken."

"Good night, Sutton," he answered, knowing the moment had passed. "See you Monday."

I liked Ken. I really did. Tonight wasn't the first time I had entertained ideas about him. But somehow I never had gotten around to acting on them, and on the drive home tonight it wasn't Ken's face I kept seeing. It was Noah Lansing.

Damn his blue eyes, I thought as I finally pulled into a parking space at the dark far corner of the lot outside my building. Why do I have to keep seeing them? Even worse, my imagination had them looking at me in a way they probably never would.

But you sure would like for them to, wouldn't you? my

little voice asked as I got out and locked the car door behind me.

I was about to say something choice to it when an arm went tightly around my throat, cutting off my air.

Oh, God, I thought as I struggled to get free, to get the crushing weight off my larynx, not me. Not this.

The arm jerked me even more tightly against the body it belonged to, and I felt a face and hot breath against my ear.

"This is a warning," a voiced hissed. "Keep your nose out of where it doesn't belong, or I'll come back!" Desperately trying to remember anything from the self-defense course I had taken two years ago after I was almost shot while investigating Cara's murder, I raised my right foot, hoping to kick backward and crush a shinbone or a knee. Instead the side of my head exploded in pain and lights and I was gone.

Twenty

I don't know how long I was out—a few minutes. Long enough for the person who attacked me to run away, long enough for someone else driving through the parking lot to find me and call for help, long enough for a crowd to gather and for the ambulance, its siren loud and nearby, to be on its way from the fire station just up the street.

I came to, trying to sit up, not really knowing then what had happened to me, but my instinct for self-preservation having taken over and telling me I had to get up and run. Instead soothing hands and comforting voices forced me back down onto the pavement and told me the ambulance would be there any minute. I groaned, not only because my head felt like a semi was running back and forth over it, but because I was mortified. Losing control is not something I do well. The thought of lying here, completely without dignity and at the mercy of strangers, was too humiliating.

"Do you know what happened to you?" I realized a persistent male voice was asking. I tried to focus and saw that it was Pauli, the night manager for the building, a balding, short, rabbity little man who probably liked working at nights because he didn't actually have to deal with people very often. I had been thinking frantically, ever since my first hint of consciousness, trying to remember what had happened, and it was beginning to come back to me—the arm choking me, the threatening voice in my ear, the blow to my head. As my brain began to work better the ambulance wheeled into the parking lot, its sirens blaring in time to the pounding in my head. I knew I wasn't going to tell anyone here what had really happened. It would mean the police and a report, and a lot of people asking even more pointed questions that I had no intention of answering. Not reporting the attack wasn't putting anyone else in the building in danger. It was very clearly a threat meant solely for me.

"I fell," I told Pauli. "I think I hit my head on the pavement."

The ambulance pulled up to the end of the row of cars where I was laid out and then did a two-point turn to back up to us. Its piercingly bright, flashing lights made me grimace, which sent another wave of pain around my head. From either door of the cab jumped an emergency medical technician in a dark blue uniform, and the one from the passenger's side ran over with his bag of first-aid goodies while the second one opened the back doors of the ambulance and wrestled a stretcher out onto the pavement. He wheeled it over to join his friend, who was gingerly checking me over for broken limbs while Pauli answered his questions about what had happened.

"I'm perfectly okay," I told the first guy, who was still prodding me. I was irritated that he hadn't addressed his question to me. He looked at me sharply.

Number-two hero addressed the crowd. "Okay, folks," he said, "if you don't mind giving us some room, we're going to get this lady onto the stretcher and up into the ambulance so we can check her out better. Everything will be fine. Thanks for your help, but we can take it from here.''

I went to sit up again, but my torturer forced me back down.

"Please lie still," he said. "We just want to make sure you haven't done anything serious to yourself." His companion was back beside me, a long orange board with straps in his hands. The one who had been groping me reached into the bag and pulled out a thick white cervical collar to go around my neck. "If you'll just bear with us, we're going to put this on to hold your head and neck still while we use the backboard to get you up into the bay."

I could see protesting would do no good. They had a job to do and they were implacable. I sighed pointedly and put my head back down. They went to it with a vengeance, putting the collar on me, which felt almost as restricting as the forearm across my throat had, and rolled me up on first one side and then the other to slide the backboard under me. Next, they proceeded to strap me to it, lift me onto the stretcher, strap me to that, and lift me up into the back of the ambulance. They were trying to be gentle, but every movement made my head throb. From my new vantage point I could see, just before the attendants closed the doors for the sake of modesty, that the onlookers had retreated a ways, but few of them had gone back inside. Pauli was still hovering around the ambulance, no doubt worrying about lawsuits.

Inside the ambulance, I started to protest once again that I was okay.

"I just tripped and fell and hit my head," I said, looking from one EMT to the other. "Can't you just let me go home?"

"Lady, look," the driver finally said. "We have to make sure you don't need to go to the hospital or it's our butts on the line. Just let us finish checking you over, and then we can fight about what you're going to do. Okay?''

"Fine," I said huffily. I lay back ill-naturedly and let them shine lights into my eyes and ears and down my throat. They poked up and down my arms and legs and across my ribs. They listened to my heart. They felt my pulse. They took my blood pressure and temperature. They felt around my neck and head, and I winced noticeably when fingers touched what I guessed was a large lump just over my right ear.

"Would you please at least unstrap me and get this collar off?" I asked finally. I wasn't about to tell them my throat was sore where I had been grabbed. "I already sat up once and moved my head around before you got here. There's nothing wrong with my neck."

They looked at each other over my head, silent messages flying back and forth, and came to some sort of agreement about me. Fortunately, not being psychic, I didn't have to hear what it was they agreed to.

"If we told you we thought you ought to go to the emergency room and get this lump on your head checked out, would you go?" the driver asked.

"No, it's just a bump. It's nothing."

"That's what I thought you'd say," he answered. "Okay, here's what we're going to do. We're going to take all this off and let you try sitting up. If you handle that okay, we'll let you go home, but you're doing this against our advice. You're also going to get a lecture on what to watch for in case you have a concussion. And we strongly recommend that you go to the emergency department and have a doctor check you over."

"Thanks, but no thanks. I'll be just fine. I realize you have to say all this, but really, I'll be okay."

They looked at each other again, resigned, and proceeded to free me from my bonds.

"Now sit up slowly," one said as they each took an arm and helped me up. To myself, I could admit that I was feeling a little woozy and light-headed, but I wasn't going to tell them that. They let me sit for a few minutes, until I was feeling steadier. One of them got out his light and made me let him check my pupils one more time. Finally, he picked up his clipboard and did a lot of writing before asking me to confirm my name and address, and to get my telephone number and other vitals. They gave me a detailed discourse on symptoms of concussions and skull fractures, which probably would have frightened some sense into me if it hadn't all been knocked out of me already, and then they helped me out of the ambulance and into the lobby, the curious who were still hanging around parting before us like the Red Sea and Pauli bringing up the rear.

"Listen," I said to the EMTs in the lobby as they turned to leave. "I'm sorry for being so uncooperative. I'm just not much good as a patient. I know you're doing what you're supposed to, and I'm really glad you're around, since it could have been much worse. But I'll be okay."

"It's your call and your head, Ms. McPhee," the driver said.

"Thank you again," I said lamely, deciding belatedly that maybe they weren't so bad after all.

The driver saluted. The other waved, and they went back out to the ambulance. Pauli rushed over solicitously.

"Do you mind if I just escort you upstairs?" he asked, and it occurred to me that he might be genuinely concerned about me, in addition to whatever trepidation he had about the building's possible liability. "I just want to make sure you get there okay."

"Thanks, Pauli, I'd appreciate that." Now that I could go home and not to the hospital, I was able to be magnanimous.

He took my arm delicately, walked me to the elevator, and pushed the button. Upstairs, he handed me my purse, which I only now realized he had been carrying around all this time (maybe I should have agreed to the hospital visit if I was that out of it), and I dug around inside for my keys. I opened the door, thanked Pauli again, closed the door behind me, and headed for the medicine chest and the ibuprofen I kept there. My head felt like hell.

In the bathroom, I turned on the lights, exclaimed at how much they hurt my eyes, grabbed the ibuprofen from the medicine cabinet, and quickly turned the lights back off. I could see well enough from the light that filtered in from the hall and through the bedroom to get two pills from the bottle and fill up a glass of water. I also had seen just enough in the bathroom light to know that not only did I feel like hell, but I also looked like it. I swallowed the pills, went back out to the kitchen to make myself an ice pack for my lump, and returned to the bedroom to ease myself onto the bed, clothes and all.

On the way down to the pillow, I saw the red message light blinking on my answering machine. I lay back, put the ice pack against my skull, and reached over to press the play button. It was Noah Lansing. Even over the tinny machine, I recognized his voice instantly.

"McPhee," he said. "It's Noah Lansing. I was calling to make sure you're okay after Friday night. And to apologize. After thinking about it, I decided I was out of line. I know finding Dr. Morris dead probably wasn't very pleasant. We just always seem to be at cross-purposes. Anyway, the other thing is, I need to talk to you again about him. There are some . . . ah . . . discrepancies that have turned up. If you get back tonight before eleven, call me." He read off a phone number.

I raised my head—through the pain—and looked at the clock: 11:30.

"If not," Lansing's voice continued, "well, I'll be up and out pretty early tomorrow. I've got some work to do on my boat. Is there any chance you could come by and we can talk there? It's down at the Fort Washington Marina in Maryland. You take the Indian Head Road exit off the

Beltway, just over the Wilson Bridge. Go about four miles to Fort Washington Road and take a right. Follow that for just over three miles, to Warburton, and turn left. Stay on Warburton. At the stop sign, it becomes King Charles Terrace, and it goes down to the marina. It's important that we talk. Please call me or come by the boat.'' Quickly I reached up to press the save button: I would need to listen to the directions again if I decided to go see what he wanted.

For now, however, I wasn't going to think about that. My head hurt too much, and I needed desperately to go to sleep. I lay there, calming my breathing, letting the ice pack and the pills begin to work, and eventually I drifted off. It wasn't a restful sleep, however. I woke repeatedly to dreams of a heavy arm pressing on my throat and to the fear that had come with it.

Sunday

Twenty-one

In the morning, things were better. The ice pack had helped the swelling above my ear, and the throbbing pain had mostly receded. My head was still sore to the touch, as was my throat, but I decided I was going to live.

A hot shower added considerably to my improved condition, but I skipped a heavy breakfast and had half a grapefruit instead, eating while pondering whether to answer Noah Lansing's summons. Eventually, I decided that in the interest of future peace, I probably should at least go find out what he wanted to talk about. I went back to my bedroom to dress—jeans and a short-sleeved cotton blouse—and replayed his message in order to write down the phone number and directions he had left.

He did sound somewhat contrite, I thought as I listened again to his apology. Too bad he was right, that we always seemed to be getting on each other's nerves. I wondered how we might have gotten along if we had met under other circumstances, if I did something else for a living. But I didn't and wouldn't.

So deal with it, my voice said.

I was hoping you were dead, I responded, *or at least that the blow on the head had rendered you mute.*

Not a chance. It laughed. *I'm here for the long haul.*

I changed the subject and dialed Lansing's number, thinking I might still catch him at home. It was only eight o'clock.

Apparently, when he said early, he meant early. The phone rang until his answering machine clicked in. I hung up without leaving a message, figuring I would see him long before he got it.

I put on my Keds and grabbed a sweater, in case it was still chilly outside. Halfway out the door I realized I had forgotten to bring the directions, so I ducked back in to get them, then headed downstairs to my car.

Walking across the parking lot, I started flashing back to the attack the night before. The arm across my throat, the way my arms were pinned against me, my struggle to breathe and to get loose. Without warning, it was all there again, almost as real as when it happened. By the time I got into the Beetle, I was sweating and hyperventilating.

"Jesus, McPhee," I lectured myself as I sat there behind the wheel and tried to clear the scary pictures from my brain. "You're okay. It's over. You're safe. You can stop this anytime." But I knew it wasn't over. Before the man who had grabbed me last night had told me it was a warning, I had been afraid I was about to die, the kind of fear that gets imprinted in every cell of your body, that washes back over you unexpectedly and sets off all your alarms all over again. Part of my surliness at the ambulance crew really had been anger, at my attacker and at myself, anger that someone had been able to instill that kind of fear in me.

And it wasn't over, because I knew the warning was sincerely meant. Someone was very unhappy about something I was doing. I didn't think, no matter how much I pissed them off, that it was Noah Lansing or Bill Russell. Which left Ed Lloyd or Hub Taylor—or both of them. At first glance, it might sound farfetched to think that a U.S. senator or even a county supervisor would run the risks involved in making such a threat or in carrying it through. But I knew—and they knew I knew—those risks were small compared with the risk I posed to them, because of the information I had made it clear I had. I would, I decided, have to be a lot more careful from here on out, checking over my shoulder frequently. But no way was I backing off. They might be able to make me afraid, but they weren't going to force me to give in to that fear. All they had done, I vowed, was make me more determined than ever to find out the truth.

My resolve intact, I calmed myself with some yoga breathing, relaxing the muscles and letting the fear drain away, taking the mental pictures with it. Then I drove off to meet Noah Lansing.

This early on a Sunday morning, the Woodrow Wilson Bridge, which carries I-95 across the Potomac at Alexandria and into Maryland, was free of traffic jams, unlike the mess I knew it would be in much later in the day, as every weekend traveler on the eastern seaboard went home. Within fifteen minutes of leaving the apartment, I was taking the exit onto Indian Head Highway. My turn onto Fort Washington Drive led me down through several subdivisions, ranging from modest to the $400,000 range, and down to Warburton, the last street turning off before the entrance to Fort Washington Park. Several more winding blocks of side street took me down to the river, through a cool tunnel of overhanging trees that was laced with the heavy, heady scent of wild honeysuckle and that ended at the Fort Washington Marina. I pulled into the large graveled parking lot and realized I had no idea what kind of car Noah Lansing drove when he was off duty.

At the end of the parking lot was a hulking, gray, wooden-sided building with signs that said things like DELICATESSEN, OFFICE, and SHIPS STORE. A sweeping deck dotted with tables and chairs hugged the water side of the building and looked out on rows of wooden piers along which powerboats and sailboats of various sizes, colors, and styles bobbed gently on the water's surface. It was a beautiful day, I thought. The air was pleasantly warm, with a soft breeze. Except along the water, the marina was surrounded by thick, lush trees, with occasional glimpses of houses clinging to the sides of the bluffs that climbed steeply behind it from the river's edge. It was still early enough and quiet enough for most of the noise to be provided by a variety of birds. There could be worse places to spend a Sunday, I thought.

I walked across the parking lot to the piers. Each one jutted out across the water for two hundred feet or more. At the landward end, they were blocked by a series of locked gates and short sections of wooden fence.

I stopped at the gate to the first pier and looked around for any sign of Lansing or a blue-hulled boat like the one I had seen in the photo in his office. Although there were many boats still in their slips this early in the day, there already was a steady foot traffic of people moving back and forth from cars and trucks and 4X4s to several of the boats, unloading supplies for the outings they were getting ready to take. At the third pier, I finally spotted a boat, its bow pointed in my direction, with a navy hull that looked, to my landlubber's eye, like the one in the picture. I quickly walked along the wooden sidewalk to the third gate, only to find it locked by a push-button combination lock. I fiddled with it for a minute or two, randomly punching in combinations with no success, and was about to walk up to the marina office for help when two beefy guys with a cooler, fishing rods, and sunburned bare chests and backs came up from the parking lot. We exchanged good mornings. One of them entered the right combination and then held the gate open for me to go through first. I thanked them and walked ahead toward the end of the pier where the boat I had seen sat in the last slip. The fishermen stopped halfway along, at an expensive-looking powerboat with a shiny blue, metal-flake paint job and the name NA-DINE in fancy script along the side.

The boat I hoped was Lansing's was called SECOND WIND. It sat gracefully in the water, its mainsail furled and hidden inside a navy sail cover. Its white decks glistened cleanly in the morning sun, made whiter still by the contrast with the navy hull below. A red stripe near the top edge of the hull warmed the color scheme just enough to make the boat look elegant, but not cold. There was no sign of Noah Lansing, but through the open hatch door I could hear a metallic banging followed by some thuds of wood on wood.

"Detective Lansing?" I called. It sounded silly somehow in this setting, but he had never invited me to call him anything else, probably because he was always angry with me. Too bad I liked the sound of Noah so much, I thought.

There was another clank and Noah Lansing stood up in the hatch. He was actually smiling.

"McPhee," he said. "I'm glad you came over. Hold up a foot."

"Excuse me?"

"So I can see what kind of soles your shoes have."

It made no sense to me, but I humored him and held one foot up for him to inspect the white soles of my Keds.

"Okay," he said, "you can come aboard. Shoes with dark soles leave black marks all over the deck. But those are fine." I could see this boat thing was going to be more complicated than I had realized. My experience with boats had consisted of a ten-foot, flat-bottomed aluminum fishing boat that I had paddled around my grandfather's pond, and an occasional ride during high school in a friend's small speedboat that he used for skiing on the nearby lake. Sailboats apparently were more complex creatures.

Intrepid as ever, however, I walked out onto the little finger-shaped pier that ran along the side of the boat, to where I could step across to the boat and through an opening where the lines that encircled the deck had been unhooked. In the U-shaped cockpit, which was molded fiberglass with a bench seat down each side, a large stainless-steel wheel took up much of the space. I sat down on the hard seat, and Lansing climbed up from below and sat on the other side, wiping grease from his hands with an old rag.

"Just doing a little maintenance on the engine," he said, smiling again, the breeze lifting his dark hair slightly. He was dressed in a red knit shirt and khaki shorts. My pulse increased, and I decided I was still feeling the effects of the blow on the head from last night.

"It's a nice boat," I said, my ignorance of sailing terms leaving me inarticulate. "What is it?"

"She."

"What?"

"She. Boats are shes. She's a Sabre. Thirty feet."

"Is that big?" I asked. It was to me.

"As big as I'd want to put on the river," Lansing said. "It's too shallow in too many areas around here, once you leave the boat channel, to get in easily with anything bigger. Plus I sail it by myself quite a bit right now, and I wouldn't want to try single-handing anything larger."

"You must be good to go out alone."

"Actually David, my son, is usually with me, but he's only five, so he's not a lot of help yet."

He had opened the door. I decided to go through it.

"Is he the little boy I saw in the picture in your office?" I asked.

"Yeah, that's him. He's with his grandparents in Richmond for a couple of weeks, or he'd be here supervising." His love for his son was evident in his eyes. How painful it must be to have to raise him alone, I thought.

"I'm a single father," Lansing went on, as if picking up on my thoughts. "My wife died when he was eight months old."

"I'm sorry," I responded simply, not wanting to let on that I already had gotten the whole story from Bill.

"It was a long time ago," he said, dismissing it as a topic of conversation. "Listen, would you like some coffee? I have a Thermos and some mugs."

"Sure," I answered. He went back down below for a moment, then reemerged with a tall, silvered Thermos bottle and a couple of odd-looking, wide-bottomed mugs with pictures of boats on them. As he poured the coffee I leaned back against the side of the cockpit, enjoying the surroundings and the morning, letting myself pretend for a moment that I was here for pleasure, not work, and wondering what that would be like.

"I wanted to talk to you again about how Dr. Morris died," Lansing said, getting down to business and dissolving my fantasy. "We're beginning to think you may be right."

"About what?"

"That it wasn't suicide."

"I never really said that," I told him.

"Bill reads you pretty well. He said you didn't believe it was suicide for a minute."

"Touché, but what makes you think it wasn't?"

"Problems with the scene. Problems with why he would have killed himself."

"Like what?"

"Well, the gun, for one thing. It was still in his hand, but when someone shoots himself, the hand usually opens in reflex and drops the gun. Not always, but most of the time."

"And?"

"The fingerprints for another. The gun was clean of any

prints except the one set. Usually, we'll find the person's prints all over the gun, where they handled it, maybe loaded it, before shooting themselves. Again, not conclusive, but certainly odd. Plus, we can't track down the gun's registration, and Morris's ex-wife says he never would have had one in the house.'' He went into a thoughtful silence for a minute.

"More?" I asked finally, sensing that he wasn't done yet.

"Powder burns."

"Couldn't you find any?" If someone else actually killed Morris, their absence would make sense.

"Plenty on his head, where the gun was fired point-blank. But only some traces of gunpowder on his hands. Not nearly what I would have expected in a suicide."

"Could it have been lost in handling the body?"

"Not likely. His hands were bagged at the scene before he was ever moved, and not uncovered until the autopsy started yesterday afternoon. And then there's the question of a motive."

"Yes?"

"He didn't seem to have one. We've talked to his office staff, his ex-wife in Boston, other doctors, his neighbors. They all swear up and down he never would have killed himself. He was wealthy, he was successful, he was very respected. Stable, down-to-earth guy. They all said he had no reason and that he wasn't the kind of guy to do himself in."

"So what do you think happened?"

"That's what I need you to tell me." He looked at me, holding my eyes. "What were you working on with Peter Morris? Why did he call you? Did whatever it was get him killed?" Well, here we were again. Horns locked, my neck on the chopping block. My neck . . . memories of last night.

Maybe, I thought, remembering the frightening little episode in the parking lot, it was time to tell Lansing at least some of what I knew. Maybe I didn't know when I was getting in over my head. Maybe I should take last night's warning seriously.

"Will you help us, McPhee?" he asked.

"I need a little time to think about it," I said, wanting to sort it out in my own mind first. "I'm not saying no. I just need to think it through." I waited for the thunder and lightning.

Instead of erupting in anger, however, he accepted my answer.

"Okay," he said. "How about this? While you're thinking about it, I'm going to take the boat out. Would you like to come? You might think better out there."

"I've never sailed before," I told him. "I wouldn't have the faintest idea what to do."

"You don't have to do anything, unless you want to. *Second Wind* is set up so I can sail her by myself, remember. You can just enjoy the trip."

"Okay," I accepted, delighted at the thought of going out on the boat with him. "I'll try to stay out of your way."

"You haven't been able to so far," he said, laughing. "Why should I expect you to start now?"

Twenty-two

I watched in fascination as Lansing got the boat ready to go out, uncovering the mainsail, taking out a second sail he said was a spinnaker, and attaching it to the thin cables—sheets, he called them—that ran from the bow up to the mast. When everything was the way he wanted it, he came back to the cockpit, started the engine, and expertly maneuvered the boat out of the slip and into the creek that emptied into the Potomac.

It wasn't until we had passed between the last of the red-and-green channel markers and a big green buoy with the number 77 on it and had reached the deeper part of the Potomac itself that Lansing put up the mainsail and turned off the engine. As the breeze caught and then filled the sail with a sharp snapping sound, suddenly pulling the boat along with it, my pulse quickened with excitement. Within minutes I was a convert, deciding that this sailing stuff had it all over the powerboats, with their noise, fuel fumes, and rougher rides. As I watched Lansing's attention move from the water to the sails that gathered and spilled the wind, as he deftly fine-tuned everything with a nudge of the wheel or a slight change of the tension or placement of a line, I began to understand what a heady mix of the physical and cerebral sailing must be for those who did it.

The sun, the water, the wind—it was a new experience for me to feel it all this way—and it drained me of any residual tension from the previous week. From time to time I would look over and see Lansing watching me quietly. Finally, he spoke.

"So what do you think?" he asked.

"This is wonderful," I told him with honest enthusiasm. "I'm just sorry no one introduced me to this before now."

He smiled, satisfied with my answer, and for another few minutes we sailed along in silence, except for the hiss of the water against the hull and the wind against the sails.

Finally, he changed the direction of the boat, explaining what he was doing and using words like *reach* and *run,* which meant nothing to me. Then he put up the spinnaker, a huge blimplike sail that bellied off the front of the boat in bright splashes of royal blue and yellow. The boat went even faster, spectacular in her new finery.

After a long stretch on that tack (see how fast I was picking this up?), Lansing lowered the spinnaker and set off in a new direction. He explained how the boat used the sails like the wings on an airplane, balancing wind direction and air pressure against the size and shape of the sail to go in the direction he wanted to go; how, in sailing, going in a straight line often wasn't the quickest way to get somewhere; how one had to travel at an angle to the wind to make it all work. I was completely lost, but it obviously had become almost instinct with him. He sailed as much through the feel of the boat in his hands and the wind on his skin as through what his eyes told him. It was a pleasure to watch this man and his boat work together like one creature.

For two hours we went back and forth, up and down,

playing the wind, riding it for all it was worth one minute, tricking it into taking us somewhere other than where it wanted to push us the next. We spoke little. I didn't need to voice the enjoyment that I was certain was as evident on my face as it was on his.

By noon, as the now-heating wind began to die down and the sun was shifting into broil, Lansing turned the boat back toward Fort Washington and the marina. On the return trip, I was the one who watched him. After the third or fourth time of looking over to find me studying him, he said, "What?"

"Sorry," I said, laughing. "You're very different out here than I've seen you at work. I'm just wondering which is the real you."

He looked thoughtful. He reached over to make an adjustment to the sail, then sat down beside me, his right hand firmly on the wheel. "They both are," he said finally. "I throw just as much of myself into the work when I'm there as I do into enjoying the sailing when I'm here."

"No, it's more than that," I told him. "Out here, you seem at peace with yourself."

A shadow passed across his eyes. "The waters of the Lethe," he said. "River of forgetfulness."

I didn't know what to say, not because he was much more literate than most policemen I knew, but because I understood the reference to his wife. I just looked at him in uncomfortable silence.

"I took up sailing after my wife died," he said finally, looking up at the sail. "I had sailed a little as a kid, but not for years after, even in Virginia Beach. But after she died, I found myself drawn to the idea as a way to leave it all behind. It worked, for a few hours at a time anyway. Back then, it helped get me through the really bad times. Now I do it because I love it."

Again I was quiet, afraid anything I said would open old wounds. He looked back at me in silence as well. I could drown in those eyes, I thought, and die a happy woman. His gaze was unwavering. I caught my breath as Noah Lansing reached up to brush aside a lock of hair that had blown down into my face. As he brushed it back over my ear his hand touched the spot where my attacker had hit me. I flinched at the pain.

Instantly, his look changed into a scowl, and his fingers started to probe.

"Ow!" I yelped, jerking my head away.

"What the hell is that?" he asked. "You've got a lump the size of an egg on your head."

"I'm okay," I answered, blinking as the pain his hand had set off began to recede. "It's nothing."

"I think somebody coldcocked you," he said decisively, standing up to lower the mainsail as we reached the green buoy that marked the entrance to the channel up to the marina. "Which should come as no surprise," he added in a grim postscript.

Once the sail was down, Lansing reached up on top of the cabin and secured the billowing fabric with a couple of elastic tie-downs. Then he turned the ignition key for the engine, to take us back to the slip under power.

Neither of us tried to talk over the engine as we headed into the creek. Soon we were at the marina, where Lansing turned the boat around, put it into reverse, and backed it into the first slip, using a long pole with a hook on the end to keep the boat from bumping the pier. A man and a woman, whose boat was two slips farther in, ran over matter-of-factly to help. They expertly fended *Second Wind* off the pier with hands and feet, caught the lines Lansing tossed them, and tied the boat to the metal cleats that were bolted along the pier.

Lansing shut off the engine and jumped nimbly to the pier, where he thanked the couple for their help. I waited on board the boat while he secured lines all around, and then I caught the hand he held out to make sure I ended up on the pier and not in the water. Once I was on solid footing, he let go my hand and caught me by the arm instead. He stood close, looking down at me hard, but not, I realized, angry. Instead, I thought in surprise, he looked concerned.

"I'm going up to the store for a Coke," he said quietly. "I want you to come with me and sit down and tell me how you got that lump on your head." I thought about Peter Morris and about my little parking-lot adventure and decided he probably was right. It was time to let him in on as much as I thought I could.

"Okay," I said, unable to look away. He just nodded, and turned to go, using his hold on my arm to bring me up beside him. He dropped his hand and we walked together up the pier to the gate and across the parking lot to the marina building, where we climbed the steps to the deck.

"Grab a table," Lansing said. "I'll be right back. What can I bring you?"

"A diet Coke is fine."

He walked away to get the drinks. There was no one else on the deck, so I took a chair at a corner table, facing the water. Two minutes later he was back, canned sodas in hand, a napkin around the bottom of each can. He put one in front of me, then pulled out the other chair and sat down.

"Let's have it," Lansing said, popping the top on his soda and drinking some of it down.

"It's about Ann Kane," I said, using the napkin to wipe off the top of my soda can before opening it.

"What about her?"

"Do you have any idea yet how she died?" The diet Coke was cold and biting as I took a swallow. It felt good in the now midday heat.

"We know how she died," Lansing said, somewhat impatiently. "Someone gave her a drug that didn't mix with one she was already taking."

"No, I mean do you have anything to tell you who was there when she died?"

"No," he answered, clearly irritated at the department's lack of results. "We don't have a goddamn thing!"

"Peter Morris thought he knew. He thought he knew who gave her the Demerol and who was there when she died. Or at least one of them. And I think he was right."

Lansing lowered his soda can slowly and held it in his hand, his arm on the table.

"How would he have known that—unless he was there?" he asked.

"No, he wasn't part of it. But a few weeks before, one of his patients brought a young woman to him in the middle of the night, a woman who also worked on the Hill, who had been given the same drug Ann Kane got later and who had gotten sick from it. Morris pumped out her stomach and made sure she would be all right. When he read about Ann Kane, all the pieces fell into place for him. He was convinced that it was his patient who drugged Ann Kane and who dumped her body when she died."

"Who was his patient?"

"Senator Ed Lloyd."

"What? You're joking!"

"No, I'm absolutely serious. Deadly serious, in fact, after what happened to Dr. Morris . . . and after this." I gestured to my head.

Lansing sat and looked at the water for a couple of minutes. I could see he was trying to fit Ed Lloyd into the picture he had carried in his mind of the men who had let Ann Kane die. Finally, he turned back to look at me.

"Tell me what Morris knew," he said, "what made him think it was Lloyd."

Step-by-step I took him through Morris's reasoning and my own. I told him about the woman Lloyd had brought to Morris and Morris's impressions of her. I told him about Morris remembering that he had prescribed Demerol for

Lloyd, and how, when he had read about Ann Kane, he also had remembered that Lloyd's rare blood type was the same as one of her assailants. I told him about Lloyd's reputation on the Hill and among the media. I was sure he had heard about it, but I wanted him to realize that the truth of it probably was even worse than he knew.

"The worst part," I said, "is that I really don't believe Dr. Morris killed himself, and I'm afraid I'm the one who got him killed."

"What makes you say that?"

"Morris was safe as long as Lloyd thought Morris had kept his secret. But when you stopped me at the cemetery on Friday, I had just asked Lloyd how well he knew Ann Kane. He didn't ask who she was, didn't look confused. He just looked really pissed off. That's when I started to believe that Morris was right, that Lloyd really had done it."

"And you think he killed Morris, too, for talking to you?"

"I don't know, but I think somebody killed Morris. I don't believe he killed himself."

"Why not?"

"I went over there because he called me. He was upset and scared. He said something had just happened and that he really needed to talk to me about it. He was afraid, not suicidal."

"And what was it that had happened?" Lansing's mind was still running my theory through his mental calculator.

"I don't know. He wouldn't talk about it over the phone. But I think Lloyd came to the logical conclusion that Morris had talked to me. Morris was the only one who knew about the other woman, who had enough information to make the connection between her and what happened to Ann Kane. I think Lloyd must have called Morris and threatened him, then decided the only safe way was to shut him up before he could say any more."

"Did Morris tell you who this other woman was?" Lansing clearly was following my logic.

"He didn't know." Although it was the truth, it was only part of it. But I left it at that. I might have to tell Lansing this much, to get him off my back and myself off the hook, but I wasn't ready yet to give away the whole store, to give him Maggie Padgett.

"He thought she probably worked somewhere on the Hill, like Ann Kane did, said she was pretty, with dark hair and violet eyes." Let Lansing and his guys make their own effort to find her, I thought.

"And your head?" he asked. "You want to tell me about that?"

"Someone grabbed me in the parking lot of my building last night when I got home from dinner, and hit me on the head."

"What makes you think it was connected, that it wasn't a mugger or a rapist who picked you out at random?"

"He had a message for me. He told me to lay off if I knew what was good for me."

"Lay off what?" Lansing asked.

"He didn't say. Apparently, I was supposed to know."

"Could it have been in connection with something else you're working on? Another story?"

"I don't think so. The only other thing I have going is Janet Taylor, but it's certainly no surprise to Hub Taylor that people are wondering if he killed her." Again the truth, but only part of it. He didn't have to know about my speculation that Hub Taylor might have been with Lloyd when Ann Kane died, or that his wife somehow had found it out.

Lansing pushed his chair back from the table to face the water and crossed a leg over a knee, thinking.

"So, do you think I'm nuts?" I asked when he looked back at me.

"Yes, but that's not the question," he said, his eyes smiling a little, in spite of the serious mouth. "The question is, do I think you're right? The answer is, I don't know. It's all pretty circumstantial to try to hang manslaughter or murder charges on a senator with. On the other hand, I can't take a chance on not following up in case you are right. But we'll have to move carefully. If Lloyd was involved, I don't want to tip my hand to him until I can nail him.''

"Not to mention the pressure he could bring to bear if he finds out you're looking at him,'' I added.

"True. No, I think we'll have to go after it quietly. I can try to get a warrant to search Morris's patient records. No judge will be happy to give me carte blanche to go through them, but I can make a case for his death looking suspicious. If I can get into them, I can confirm Lloyd's blood type, and maybe there'll be something else somewhere about the woman he treated, something that will help us find her. In the meantime we had better go back and do a lot more asking around up on the Hill. Talk to anyone we can find who knew Ann Kane at all, see if we can figure out who the other woman might have been.''

"So what will you be telling the rest of the press about Dr. Morris?'' I asked, knowing any hint that the police suspected something other than suicide would confirm for Lloyd that I—and probably Maggie Padgett—were loose ends he might want to tie up once and for all.

Lansing thought about it. "Until we say otherwise,'' he decided, "it's still an apparent suicide. His ex-wife is taking the body to Boston for a funeral and burial there, so I would think any other media interest in his death will die off pretty soon. But that does bring up one more thing.''

"What?'' I thought I had given him enough to placate him.

"Your safety. If you're right, and Lloyd or someone he sent grabbed you last night, you're running a real risk. I think you should let us put somebody with you for a few days. We could protect you if Lloyd does decide to go after you next, and if we could catch him at it, it would be one more case against him.''

"Thanks for the concern, but no thanks," I said firmly. A police escort would be the death of my efforts to go after Lloyd myself, as well as any future conversations with Maggie.

"Be sensible," he said, sounding irritated that I didn't like his idea. "You've got someone out there—whether it's Ed Lloyd or someone else entirely—who thinks you're a threat and who already has warned you once. What are you going to do if they decide to make good on their threat? I want you to drop this whole thing right here and let us handle it. And let me put someone with you. Bill Russell and I can make sure you get first dibs on information, if you're worried about that.''

Don't you ever learn? I thought as my macho meter climbed into the red zone.

"And in the meantime they can report my every move back to you?" I asked angrily. "Forget it. I'm not dropping this story, and I'm not having a baby-sitter. If I let myself get scared off by a knock on the head, I might as well quit my reporting job right now. So forget both those ideas.''

"I wasn't trying to plant a spy on you," Lansing replied testily, now just as angry as I was. "I was trying to make sure nothing happened to you. If you weren't so damned pigheaded, you'd see it's for your own protection.''

"I don't need you to protect me. I can do just fine without your help." The conversation was really heating up.

"Oh yeah?" he said nastily. "Well, your little episode in the parking lot sure doesn't sound like it.''

I could see this was counterproductive, especially since I was coming out on the short end.

"Look," I said, standing up from the table. "I've tried to be helpful. I've told you about Morris and about Ed Lloyd. What you do with it is up to you. But don't think that gives you the right to tell me how or when to do my job. It doesn't, so don't even try."

Lansing stood up, too, pushing his chair back violently. So much for our pleasant morning.

"I'm just trying to do mine," he said. "And if you weren't so determined to misinterpret everything I say, you'd see that!"

"Detective," I said, getting a grip and lowering my voice as a couple of people down on the docks turned to look at us, "I think we're at an impasse here. I think the best thing for both of us is just to get on with our jobs and try to stay out of each other's way." Which was really the last thing I wanted, but being around him always ended in an argument, so what was the point?

"Thanks for the sailing lesson," I finished lamely. "I actually did enjoy it." I turned and walked in the direction of my car. Behind me, I heard his muffled curse, followed by a clang as he threw the soda cans into a metal trash can on the edge of the deck.

I was down the steps and crunching my way across the graveled lot, when he came quickly up behind me, grabbed my arm, and spun me around.

"McPhee," he said fiercely, his face and body inches from mine.

"What?"

We stood there, looking at each other, the narrow space between us filled with tension. I wondered whether he was going to hit me or kiss me; his face looked like he wanted to do both. Then he appeared to realize what he was doing. His expression changed to one of embarrassment. He dropped my arm and took a step back.

"Sorry," he said, still looking at me. He turned and walked back toward the piers and his boat. I sighed heavily, from the release of the tension and in frustration with him, then turned, too, and went to my car for the trip back to Alexandria.

I spent the rest of the afternoon and evening reading the *News,* as well as the Sunday editions of the *Post* and the *New York Times,* and wondering what I should do now and whether Lansing would call to continue our argument. As much as I didn't want to fight with him anymore, I knew my voice was right when it sarcastically pointed out that I was disappointed when the phone didn't ring.

Monday

Twenty-three

I knew I had better start the week off with a stop to see Bill Russell. I couldn't let my problems with Noah Lansing get in the way of either my professional relationship or my friendship with Bill. Both were too important to me.

When I arrived at 8:30, Bill was already in his office, working his way through a mug of coffee. I stopped at the open door and knocked on the door frame. Bill looked up from a stack of papers he was marking up on his desk. He just shook his head from side to side in a what-are-we-going-to-do-with-you gesture.

"You might as well come in," he said, motioning me in from the hall. I crossed the threshold into his simple, uncluttered office: industrial-strength charcoal carpet on the floor, white miniblinds on the window, a wooden desk of unknown vintage, a couple of metal armchairs with black vinyl seats, and a four-drawer filing cabinet where I knew everything was neatly organized and filed away.

"Coffee?" he asked as I sat down in the second chair.

"No thanks," I declined. "I just wanted to check in to

see what's going on and make certain you're still speaking to me.''

"In answer to your second question, of course I'm still speaking to you," he said, looking a little amused. "In answer to the first . . . well, about the most interesting story I've heard this morning is one about a not-very-smart reporter who got hit on the head in a parking lot a couple of nights ago.''

"You've talked to Lansing?" So much for getting my version on the record first. I could just imagine what Lansing must have had to say about it all.

"Um-huh." Bill nodded. "I called him an hour ago to see if he had spoken with you again about Dr. Morris. He gave me quite an earful about what you've really been up to. I have to say that if it's all true, it'll make great headlines. But you're taking a big chance here, Sutton, maybe even with your life. Would it really be so awful to let Noah Lansing at least try to keep you from getting hurt?''

Bill, I could see, was genuinely concerned about me. It was hard to get angry at that.

"You know I can't let it go, Bill," I told him honestly.

"I know," he agreed, "and it really has very little to do with your favorite line about having a job to do. It's really about you. You're just like Lansing." That thought made him smile again.

"What does that mean?"

"The both of you are a pair. Even though you can't get within twenty feet of each other without fighting, one of you is just as stubborn as the other. I sure would hate to be the one who let Ann Kane die, because the two of you are relentless. Neither of you can rest until you have all the answers to all the questions. It's not just a job, with either of you, it's become a personal contest between you and the culprit. You can't stop, not until you've proven that you're smarter and faster than anyone around, including whoever is guilty.''

Lansing and me alike? I certainly hadn't seen any evidence of it so far.

"I thought you said we were like oil and water," I reminded Bill.

"You are," he replied, obviously beginning to enjoy enlightening me about my personality and Noah Lansing's. "Oil and water aren't all that different. Both are liquids; one's just a little heavier than the other. The reason they don't mix is because they'd each like to be on top, but neither of them will give a molecule to the other so they can both win."

Shit, I thought, he's right.

"Gee, Bill, you're a regular Mr. Wizard, aren't you?" I said, not wanting him to know his little analogy had hit a nerve. "Next thing I know, you'll be dragging out the Junior Scientist Chemistry Set you probably have in your file cabinet and giving me a little demonstration."

Bill laughed, but he wasn't dropping it.

"Just ask yourself whether the byline or getting to the answer before Lansing does or anything else is worth your life," he said, becoming serious once more. "You're my friend, Sutton. I'd like to see you live a long time. And if you're right about Ed Lloyd—and I think Lansing believes in his gut that you are—you're messing with a very powerful guy. He won't think twice about slapping you down if he thinks you're a threat."

I got up from my chair, walked over to the door to close it, then stepped behind his desk to give Bill a completely unprofessional kiss on the top of his head.

"I'll be careful," I told him. "I don't want to become another Peter Morris. But you're right about one thing. I can't let it go, either. I guess it is some kind of personal challenge match. I can't rest as long as some asshole thinks he's gotten away with it. And I don't think Ann Kane can rest until people know she was an innocent victim, not some nympho who liked her guys in pairs."

It was a pretty honest self-analysis. I had been stubborn all my life, but with my sister's murder, a new factor had entered the equation of my personality. When Cara was killed, I had been unable to rest or think about much of anything else until I had found the bastards responsible and had laid her death publicly at their door. Once they were arrested, however, and Rob had decided to move me to the police beat, I also found myself equally unable to let it go when some other innocent met an undeserved end.

Once again Bill shook his head, knowing nothing he could say was going to change my mind or my determination. I told him good-bye and went out to my car, where I called Lansing's office. He was out, no doubt trying to figure out who Peter Morris's mystery woman could have been. I wanted to go back to see Maggie Padgett, too, but I knew I had better put in an appearance at the paper first. Rob Perry needed to be let in on a few things.

"McPhee," Rob said, when I walked into the newsroom, "how nice of you to grace us with your presence." His voice carried clearly across the mostly empty room, where there was little going on as yet.

As a morning paper, the *News* has evening deadlines, a whole series of them that begins at 7:00 P.M. with the deadline for the most distant of the several zoned editions we publish. That means that the afternoons are the busy time as reporters come in from their various beats to file their stories for the next day's paper. It also means that the mornings usually are much quieter. There is only a handful of editors who work in the mornings and early afternoons. Because they regularly work until 11:00 P.M. or midnight, the majority of the editing staff doesn't come in until mid-afternoon. Rob, however, often puts in much longer days, as much as fifteen or sixteen hours much of the time. With his daughters grown and married, and his last ex-wife long since moved away, there isn't much else to distract him.

Besides, he had told me once over drinks, it finally became clear to him after his third divorce that what all his ex-wives had said was true: He's married to the newspaper. So why not spend all his time there?

"I had nothing better to do on Monday morning," I responded to his dig. "I figured I could be bored here as well as anywhere."

"Well, I can fix that," he answered. "Snyder wants your teen gunslinger piece for the magazine a week from Sunday, so you need to get it finished and into the system before the end of the day."

So much for going to see Maggie Padgett today. Elaine Snyder is the Sunday-magazine editor, a tall, willowy, green-eyed redhead, and a terror. The magazine is her personal fiefdom, and not just anyone is good enough to be allowed in. Once a reporter who isn't on the magazine's regular staff gets Elaine to agree to accept a story, they had better not come up subsequently with excuses about why the copy is late or not up to Elaine's standards. She doesn't believe in second chances. Fortunately, I was almost finished with my piece anyhow.

"I'll get it in," I reassured Rob.

"And while you're here," he went on before I could turn to go to my desk, "I think it's time you and Hale filled me in on what's going on with the two of you. If John Aldritch is going to start yanking everybody's chains, I probably need to know what you're doing so I can either defend you or throw you to the wolves. Hale said he would be back from the board meeting after lunch, so I want you both in my office as soon as he gets in."

I gave Rob a grim smile and a Nazi salute and went over to my desk to get busy on the magazine piece. I still had a couple of people to reach for quotes before I could finish a draft good enough to submit to Elaine.

At 1:30, as I was polishing the next-to-last page of my story, Ken arrived. I looked up as I heard Rob call his name, and Ken flashed me a triumphant smile and a thumbs up across the newsroom. I took that to mean his baiting of Hub Taylor had had promising results. Ken stopped at Rob's desk, they exchanged a few words, and Rob stood up and motioned for me to follow them into his office. In some ways, the grilling that ensued was much more draining than anything I had suffered at Noah Lansing's hands. When Rob heard who we were after, he knew the repercussions for the paper could be of major magnitude—in either direction. He wasn't taking any chances that we were in over our heads.

"Okay," Rob said, when we had given him the initial synopsis of what we thought had gone on, "take me through it again, step-by-step. Don't leave anything out, and I mean anything." He did. So we didn't.

When I got to the part about my parking-lot run-in, both he and Ken looked alarmed and asked simultaneously, "Why didn't you tell me?"

"Because it was late at night, it was the weekend, my head hurt, and it was only a threat."

"How can you be sure of that?" Ken asked, still looking worried.

"If the guy had wanted to kill me then and there, I couldn't have done a damned thing about it," I said, still not happy about how vulnerable I had been.

"Nevertheless," Rob said, "I want the two of you physically together on this as much as possible from now on. I don't want either of you taking unnecessary chances. Forget your regular beat stuff. I'll find someone to cover anything we can't ignore. I want you on this like buzzards on road-kill. If Ed Lloyd and Hub Taylor did this thing, we're going to nail their asses to the side of the Capitol for everybody to see."

Rob's disdain for politicians in general knew few bounds and went back to his days of covering Alabama and Southern politics for the Associated Press. He always said he was much more likely to be surprised that a politician wasn't a sleazeball than that one was. He loved nothing better than getting another one's tail in the wringer in as public a way as possible, and yet he didn't let his personal bias make him any less adamant about having the facts to support what he believed. His reporters knew better than to try to get supposition into his pages. That was why Maggie Padgett, who kept nudging the back of my mind, was so important to this story.

"Okay, so what else can you tell me?" Rob said, returning to his interrogation.

"Well, I had an interesting morning with Hub Taylor," Ken said, grinning.

"Yeah?"

"I started out the morning by stopping him just as he was walking into the meeting room and saying very quietly that I had heard the police apparently had reason to think he was somehow involved in Ann Kane's death. He just looked at me for a second, and I could see the sweat starting on his upper lip. He spent the whole rest of the morning on the dais, wiping his face repeatedly and giving me these nervous looks. He was clearly not himself. He was fidgety and distracted, and the other supervisors had to keep repeating their questions and comments to him. When the meeting adjourned, he was out of the room like a shot. He didn't stop to talk to anybody or shake a single hand, and just brushed off anybody who tried to talk to him. So I decided to see what he did."

"Which was?" I asked, crossing my fingers that Ken had managed to throw Taylor into a panic.

"First, he went over to a bank of pay phones down the hall and made a call. He kept looking over his shoulder like he was afraid someone would overhear, which I guess explains why he didn't call from his office. I hung back down by the meeting room where people were still gathered so he wouldn't think I was watching him, but as soon as he hung up the phone and started out of the building, I followed him. In fact, I followed him all the way into the District until he lucked into a parking space in the block before the Senate office buildings. So I just double-parked and watched him go up the block and inside. Three guesses who he was going to see in there in such a hurry.''

"Ed Lloyd," I answered, a statement, not a question.

"Makes sense to me," Ken replied.

"I don't suppose you might have seen them come out together?" Rob asked hopefully.

"No," Ken said. "For the first time in the history of the D.C. Police Department, a cop came up and made all the double-parked drivers move along. I went around the block a couple of times, but Taylor's car was still there. I decided I couldn't accomplish anything more by waiting for him to come out. Clearly, they were talking in Lloyd's office, so I gave up and came back here to report in. But there's no doubt in my mind that he went running straight to Lloyd over what I said to him about Ann Kane. I think he's barely hanging on, which has to have Lloyd worried."

Rob sat back in his swivel chair and thought for a while. He began taking us back through our stories again, following the connections, confirming in his own mind what we knew for certain and what we thought.

"Sounds to me like we still have a way to go before we can do anything with this," he said finally. "What do you two plan to do next?"

"I think we had better go back to see Maggie Padgett tomorrow," I told him. "Maybe Ken will have more luck convincing her to talk than I did."

"Good idea," Ken agreed, nodding thoughtfully and obviously considering what strategy to take with Maggie.

"Okay," Rob said, "get finished with anything else you're doing—Sutton, your magazine piece, and Ken, if you've got anything that has to be finished today—and then go see this woman. I think she's the only concrete thing you've got. If you can't get her to talk to you, you don't have the story.''

We all three stood, knowing the conversation was done and we were getting closer to deadline. Rob came around the desk as Ken and I moved toward the door, and put a hand on my arm.

"Sutton," he said, in a rare moment of letting his feelings show by using my first name, "be careful. I don't want anything to happen to you."

"Now, Rob," I said, reaching up and squeezing his hand, "you're starting to sound like the police, and you know that would be a fate worse than death for you."

He snorted a laugh and followed me out into the newsroom, to his patiently blinking computer full of stories that all needed his attention at once.

At three o'clock, my phone rang. For a minute I considered not answering it, knowing I had to get my magazine piece finished. But I thought better of it, never knowing what kind of news might be on the other end. I picked up the receiver.

"Sutton McPhee."

"McPhee, it's Noah Lansing."

"Detective Lansing," I said, surprised. "To what do I owe the honor?"

"I decided to let you in on something," he said neutrally.

Okay, I thought, I'll drop the sarcasm for the sake of curiosity.

"I'm listening."

"I got the search warrant for Morris's records," he said.

"Congratulations."

"Yeah, it took some convincing, but we finally got the judge to agree."

I waited for the other shoe.

"You still there?" Lansing asked.

"Still here."

There was another pause. I could tell he was leading up to something and was having some trouble spitting it out.

"Go ahead," I said finally, "I promise not to bite your head off."

"Is there anything else I should know about what Morris told you before I start going through the patient files?"

Lansing asking me for help instead of giving me orders? That was a novel experience. All sorts of answers popped into my head, but I bit my tongue and gave him a civil one.

"As a matter of fact, you might want to expand your search a little and check for a file on Hub Taylor," I told him. "I think you'll find one, and it might tell you what blood type he has."

"What?" Lansing asked, obviously surprised by my answer.

"Call it a hunch," I told him. "If his records are there, I'd be willing to put money on his blood type being O-positive."

"Jesus Christ!" he said, realizing just where my thoughts were going.

"It's really logical when you think about it," I went on. "Who else is closer to Lloyd? Who would be most likely to be invited to join him?"

"You got anything other than a hunch to base this idea on?" Lansing asked.

"Just some odds and ends that aren't adding up," I said, thinking about the things Taylor's secretary and his neighbor had said. "But I really think you ought to at least check it out while you've got access to the files. Now there's just one thing, Detective."

"What?"

"Not that you owe me any thanks for steering you in the right direction, but after you've checked, I want to know what you found out."

"I'll think about it. This is a police investigation, you know."

"Lansing, listen to me," I said, getting irritated. "I've been ahead of you guys all along on this thing, and you know it. So if you want to find out any more about what I know, I expect some consideration here. It's the way the world works, in case you hadn't noticed."

"Oh yeah, I've noticed all right," he responded, not sounding particularly happy either. "Okay, I'll let you know what I can—if you're right."

"Fair enough," I said. "Happy hunting."

We both hung up. I sat back for a moment, crossing my fingers that my guess about Taylor's blood type would pan out. I was hoping that if I could get Noah Lansing talking about anything to do with the case, there might still be a chance of establishing some sort of long-term communication with him. Otherwise, my future covering the Fairfax County police could become a chronic battle.

I finished my magazine piece just as the first deadline was arriving. I sent it to Rob's queue, yelled across to him that it was there, heard him yell back that he would read it when he was off deadline, and went over to make plans with Ken.

"Are you about done?" I asked.

"Yeah, just finishing up a couple of other things," he said, hanging up the phone in mid-dial.

"So how do you want to handle tomorrow? I'd like to get over to the Hill and corner Maggie Padgett again."

"I agree. Why don't I just pick you up here at . . ." He thought for a moment. "Say eleven, and we'll drive over there together. Rob did make me promise to hold your hand and watch your back, you know."

"Okay, eleven o'clock, out front," I agreed. "Oh, and Ken?"

"Yeah?"

"Blow it out your ear!"

I walked away to the sound of his laughter.

Twenty-four

At 8:00 P.M., I had just started my ski-machine routine when my phone rang. I long ago had decided not to interrupt my exercises for much of anything, so I let the answering machine get it while I listened.

"Heyya, McPhee," a male voice said. "It's Sy Berkowitz."

Oh great, I thought, what does that prick want?

"Now that I've had someone check tomorrow's lineup and I know you aren't in it, just thought I'd let you know I have it on good authority that if you don't have a blockbuster piece about Janet Taylor in tomorrow's paper, then by Wednesday, the story will be mine. So get your notes together, babe, and prepare to hand them over."

Like hell, I thought as he hung up. That bastard! He had some nerve. I would quit before I would let him have any story—or any notes—of mine.

I realized that in my anger, I had speeded up my pace on the ski machine. I kept it there, knowing that if I didn't work off my fury at Sy before going to bed, I would be up half the night, stewing. I hadn't gotten another ten minutes into my workout, however, when the doorbell rang.

Now who the hell could be at my door at this time of night, I thought, stopping the machine and grabbing the hand towel I had put on the bed. Wiping my face, I went into the living room and over to the door, where I looked out through the eyepiece and thought I must be seeing things. Noah Lansing stood in the hallway outside, looking back in my direction.

I opened the door, groaning inwardly at what I must look—and smell—like.

"May I come in?" he asked abruptly. "We need to talk."

Wordlessly, I stepped back and held the door open. Lansing walked in, stopped in the middle of the living room, and looked around.

"Nice view," he said lamely, his back to me as if he suddenly realized he wasn't completely comfortable.

"Have a seat," I said, watching him from the foyer. "Would you like something to drink? Beer? Wine? Iced tea?"

Lansing turned to face me.

"Frankly," he said, "I could use a beer."

"Guinness okay?"

He actually looked surprised.

"You keep Guinness?"

"I don't just keep it," I told him. "I drink it."

"Amazing," he said. "You're the only woman I've ever met who would drink the stuff. Actually, a Guinness would be great."

I nodded and ducked into the kitchen, giving myself some one-of-the-guys points, and took a bottle of the thick, smoky Irish stout out of the refrigerator and a cold mug out of the freezer. Back in the living room, I put both down on the coffee table next to where Lansing still stood, and I sat down in one the two burgundy tub chairs opposite the sofa. Finally, Lansing sat, too.

He took a minute to pour the Guinness, then looked up.

"Thanks," he said, holding the mug out in a toast and then drinking.

"So what's up, Detective?" I asked, stumped by what could have brought him to the enemy's camp.

"You were right about Ed Lloyd—and about Hub Taylor," he answered. "Both of them were Morris's patients, and I confirmed their blood types."

"So, don't keep me in suspense."

"Lloyd is AB-negative, just like Morris told you, and Taylor is O-positive."

"I can't say I'm real surprised," I responded. "Of course, there's still a problem."

"How do I do anything with it?" he asked, finishing my thought.

"Right. It doesn't prove anything."

"Not a goddamned thing," Lansing agreed angrily, but this time I knew it wasn't me he was mad at. "I still can't connect Lloyd or Taylor to Ann Kane. DNA testing could do it, but we're a hell of a long way from having any grounds for ordering either one of them to submit to that. I can't even nail Taylor for killing his wife. I think he did it. And he looks more strung out over it every day. But the fact that the guy has no alibi isn't anywhere close to a motive or proof."

He took another swallow of his beer and stewed.

"So now what?" I asked finally. I still hadn't figured out why he was here telling me all this.

He looked at me.

"I want to offer you a deal."

"I'm listening."

"We share information. For real. No secrets. No competition. I'll keep your information to myself. In return, none of the rest of the press will get anything out of me until you have it first."

"Why?" This was a major capitulation on his part. It must have been painful. I had to know what motive was big enough to drive him to it.

"Because the sons of bitches are going to get away with all this, unless I find a way to hang it on them. Unless we find a way."

"Does it matter that much to you?" I asked.

Lansing leaned forward, resting his forearms on his thighs, looking into his beer mug.

"Yes," he said quietly. "It does." He paused, giving me a measuring look. "My wife . . ."

"I know what happened," I said. "Bill told me."

He looked up questioningly, then seemed to answer his question for himself.

"No one was ever even charged," he explained. "The bastards tortured her and killed her and got away with it. Oh, they were tried and convicted for drug trafficking. I had enough on them to help put them away for that. But nobody ever paid for what they did to Sarah. It all got real personal for me after that. It was the last time I had to let a case go unsolved . . . until now. And I'll be damned if I'll let this one go. One way or another, I want these assholes!"

I pondered his proposal. I could see the advantages for me, of course: direct and immediate access to whatever the chief investigator knew about two major stories. But there were also disadvantages. I would have to be just as forthcoming with what I already knew—such as Maggie Padgett's identity—and anything else Ken or I turned up. And Ken might not appreciate my committing him to such a pact with the devil without asking first. Still, both stories were going nowhere fast. My gut told me this might be the only way I would have anything else substantive to say in print about either one. And it probably was the only way to keep Sy Berkowitz off my ass.

"So you've really decided to trust me?" I asked Lansing as he drained the last of the Guinness from the glass.

"Let's just say that the other thing Bill told me was about your sister. He says you were the one who found the scum who killed her when our guys were up against a blank wall."

"Oh really? And what else did Bill say?" I deliberately didn't mention Cara's murder to any of the cops I covered if they didn't know about it already. I neither wanted them feeling sorry for me because my sister was murdered nor interpreting my involvement in solving the case as some sort of slap at the police.

"That you have as many reasons as I do to want to see these guys exposed. And that I was wrong for calling you a voyeur that day in my office."

Clearly, I was going to either have to thank Bill or tell him to mind his own business—as soon as I figured out which.

"Never mind all that," I said, really wanting to get off this subject. "If you mean it, we've got a deal. But let me emphasize here that it had better go both ways. The first time I find out I'm the only one sharing, the deal is not only off, so is the cease-fire."

"Okay," Lansing agreed. "The bottom line is that we'll have to trust each other. So ask me what you want to know."

A possibility for a lead occurred to me.

"What about phone calls to Ann Kane?" I asked. "Did you check the phone records?"

"We did. There was nothing. Certainly nothing that would link Ed Lloyd to her. We tracked down every number she called and every number that she got calls from for six months before she died. Several from her own office. A couple from pay phones in the Russell Building. No way to know whether that could have been Lloyd."

I knew it was time to come clean about Maggie.

"You should know that I've located Dr. Morris's mystery woman," I said. "The one Lloyd brought to Morris's office."

"Who is she?" Lansing asked, his expression intensifying. "How did you find her?"

"Her name is Maggie Padgett. She works for Senator Black, the other senator from Florida. Morris found Black's business card in her coat pocket at his office that night, so I went to Black's office thinking Black might have been the second guy with Ann Kane. Maggie is Black's secretary. I ruled Black out after talking to his staff, but as soon as I saw Maggie, I knew she was the woman Morris had treated. His description of her was very specific, and she has these incredible violet-colored eyes that you can't miss."

Lansing reached inside his jacket and pulled out his small notebook and pen and began taking notes.

"So you talked to her?" he asked. "Did she confirm Morris's story?"

"No, she wouldn't tell me anything, but it was clear she was frightened. There's no question in my mind that she was the one."

"I'll go down there first thing tomorrow, see if I can convince her to talk."

"No, wait," I cautioned. "Let me have one more run at her. I think a cop will just scare her that much more. She knows how powerful Lloyd is. For all she knows, he has influence over the police. She can't be sure you aren't just making certain Lloyd will never be caught. But I think I may be able to get her to talk eventually."

I had another idea.

"What about her phone records?" I asked. "Maybe Lloyd got cautious only after Maggie got sick on him."

"There's nothing to base a subpoena for those on, unless she's willing to file some kind of charges against Lloyd."

"Okay," I said. "I'll work on it. I may be able to get

the information, even if it's not official. It could at least
tell us if there's really a connection between Maggie and
Lloyd.''

''It's worth looking at,'' Lansing was saying when his
pager began beeping. He unclipped it from his belt and
pressed a button to see who was trying to find him.

''Can I use your phone?'' he asked.

''Sure. There's one right there in the kitchen.''

Lansing went around to the phone and held a brief conversation, then came back to the living room but didn't sit
back down.

''That was the station,'' he said, standing next to my
chair. ''They say they've got some college kid there asking
for me who says he may have some information about the
day Janet Taylor was killed. But that's all he would tell
them without me there.''

''Did it sound like he's for real?'' I asked, unfolding my
legs from underneath me and standing up.

''Who knows?'' he answered. ''But I guess I'd better go
back out there.''

He turned and walked to the door. I followed to open it
for him. In the doorway, he stopped again.

''Will you be at the station in the morning?'' he asked.

''Early,'' I told him. ''You can fill me in on whether
there's anything to the college kid's story, and then Ken
and I are going to see Maggie Padgett.''

''All right, I'll see you in the morning,'' Lansing said.
''Ah—thanks for the Guinness, and for . . .'' He stopped,
looking uncertain about what to call our bargain.

''You, too,'' I said, feeling somewhat awkward myself.
''We'll talk in the morning.''

He nodded, took two steps down the hall toward the
elevators, and then stopped and faced me again.

''Interesting look, by the way,'' he said, referring to my
gym shorts and leotard. ''Think it'll catch on?''

I gave him the finger, went inside, and closed the door,

leaning against it for a moment in lust and frustration. Then I went to the phone.

It was time for a chat with another source I had, this one an employee at Bell Atlantic whose nephew had been arrested last year in a murder case. The family had convinced me that it couldn't have been Marcus, who was at a family party when the murder took place, an alibi the police had chosen to disbelieve because all the witnesses were relatives. Three months later Todd Fitzgerald, who covered the D.C. cops for the *News,* and I had pieced together enough in the way of eyewitnesses and other information to point the finger at a member of a D.C. street gang and to get Marcus released. At one point in our efforts, the uncle had gotten us copies of certain phone-company computer records that had been important in focusing the investigation on the guy who had done the killing. The result of it all was that I had friends for life in Marcus's family and a direct line into the phone company when I needed it.

Ralph White's twelve-year-old daughter answered the phone, and I told her who it was and that I needed to talk to her dad.

"Sutton," Ralph answered a minute later in his warm baritone. "It's good to hear from you!"

"You, too, Ralph," I responded. "Listen, I'm calling to impose on you for help with some information."

"Name it, Sutton," he answered unhesitatingly. "If I can get it, it's yours."

I gave him Maggie Padgett's name and told him she lived in Arlington.

"I need to know all the local calls she made and received in the last six months, and I need you to tell me whose numbers they are. Keep this to yourself, but I'm particularly interested in whether there were any calls to or from any office or home number for Senator Ed Lloyd, even if the home number is unlisted. I know this is a lot to ask, Ralph, but it's really important."

"I'll get it for you in the morning. You want me to call right away if I find anything especially interesting?"

"Yes, the sooner the better," I told him, hoping it would give me some ammunition to take to my next conversation with Maggie Padgett. "Call me as soon as you have anything. I need a printout, too, if you can swing it. But that's not as urgent."

We went on to talk about the rest of his family and how they were. Marcus, who had been nineteen when he was arrested, was now a sophomore at the University of Maryland, with plans to go to law school. The whole thing had had a pretty profound effect on him.

Eventually, our conversation wound down and we hung up. I went back to finish my exercise session and to ponder Lansing's change of heart.

Tuesday

Twenty-five

When I woke up Tuesday morning, the buzzing of my alarm clock gave me a dull, throbbing headache where Lloyd or someone he hired had whacked me over the head. I also realized I had been having a dream about Noah Lansing.

Don't kid yourself, my voice said as I struggled to the shower. *Just because he changed his mind about your working arrangement doesn't mean he's changed his mind about you.*

I turned the shower on full force to drown the little bastard and stuck myself under the hot needle spray. Twenty minutes later, feeling a little closer to human, I got out, toweled off, and tried to decide whether today was a dress day or a slacks day. Slacks finally won out.

At 7:30, I was at the Great Falls police station and was telling Jimmy Turner I needed to talk to Lansing when he walked in the front door behind me.

"Morning, McPhee," he said, walking over to open the inner door as Jimmy buzzed him in. "Come on back."

I followed him through, but not before glancing back to see Jimmy raising one eyebrow in a sardonic question. I grinned, shrugged my shoulders, and walked down the hall behind Lansing.

In his office, he hung his jacket on the coat tree and asked if I would like coffee.

"Love some," I answered. "Just black, thanks."

"I'll be right back," Lansing said, and left me alone in his office, which I took as progress. Two days ago he wouldn't have trusted me for ten seconds around his files or computer. I smiled to myself and warned my voice not to say a thing.

In a couple of minutes he was back, setting two steaming cups of coffee on the desk. He sat down and leaned back in his chair.

"Well, I spent an interesting night after I left your place," he volunteered. Give the man an A for effort, I thought, allowing myself to hope that this trust thing might actually begin to work.

"The college kid?"

"Yeah. The bottom line is he can place Taylor's car, or one exactly like it, at the house at one-thirty."

"Jesus! How?"

"He was putting out flyers in the neighborhood for a pool service. You know, going door-to-door and sticking them in the door handles. The Taylor house was the next-to-last one he did before he had to stop and go off to his classes at George Mason University. That's why he was watching the time. He says he's a chemistry major."

"Maybe he killed Janet Taylor," I suggested.

"We said the same thing to him. Nearly scared the crap out of him. I don't think it had occurred to him he could be a suspect. I asked why it had taken him so long to come in. He said he doesn't read the papers every day and it wasn't until yesterday he realized the Taylors lived in the neighborhood he had been working. Believe me, we grilled him pretty thoroughly, and he stuck to his guns. Even described Taylor's car without any prompting from us. We also ran him on the computer.''

"And?"

"And he came back clean. No record. Not even a parking ticket.''

"So you believe him?"

"Yeah, I do. He agreed to take a lie-detector test and is coming back this afternoon to do it. We told him it would rule him out completely as a suspect in case we arrest anyone and he has to testify. But I don't expect it to show anything. I think he's for real.''

"You think you can use this to get the truth out of Taylor?"

"I don't know, but it's worth a shot. We've tried a couple more times to question him again, and he refuses to talk to us. Says his attorney has advised him not to answer any more questions. We've also got a tail on him as of last night. He looks pretty ragged from what we've seen, so maybe this will help push him over the edge.''

"What do you have in mind?"

"I'm not sure yet, but we swore the college kid to secrecy, and I told the guys working the case that if his existence gets out, I'll have their nuts. When I do make a run at Taylor with this, I don't want him to be ready for it. So what about you, anything new?"

"Not yet, but I should have a handle on any phone calls to Maggie Padgett later this morning. If there's anything there, I'll know before Ken and I go talk to her.''

Lansing looked thoughtful.

"You know, don't you," he asked, "that if you're not able to shake her loose this time, I'm going to have to step in?''

"Just hold off for today, okay? Just until I know she's a lost cause for me. She's already scared. If you show up, I'm afraid she'll bolt.''

"Okay, you've got a day."

"Thanks. And, Detective?"

He looked at me.

"I mean that."

He nodded.

You suck-up, my voice said.

"I'll get out of your way now," I said, drowning the voice out and standing up. "I need to get in to the office."

"You'll let me know what happens with Maggie?"

"As soon as I can, although I really would rather talk about it in person than over the phone. Will you still be around at five or six?"

"Most likely."

"Okay, I'll call to let you know whether there's anything for me to come back and talk about."

We said our good-byes, the peace accord still maintaining its somewhat less tenuous hold. I did need to get to work. I needed to think about how to approach Maggie before Ken got there, and I realized I needed to neutralize Sy Berkowitz, who was counting down the minutes before taking over my story.

At 9:30, I was in the library at the *News.* At 9:45, I was at my desk and dialing Sy's extension. When he answered, I lapsed into my mostly-gone-but-not-forgotten south-Georgia accent.

"You don't know me," I said, "but I know you from reading your stories in the paper. I decided you're the only reporter there good enough for me to tell this to."

With his ego for bait, I threw out the hook. I proceeded to tell him a tale about the White House chief of staff having ties to an offshore company in the Cayman Islands that was a front for the Mafia in New Jersey. I named names, all of them garnered from my research in the library. I gave him dates of supposed meetings. I told him amounts of payoffs. I told him my name wasn't important but that

I worked in a position to see the evidence firsthand and that I couldn't live with my conscience any longer if I let these people continue to get away with their corruption and influence peddling. There wasn't a word of truth to any of it. But with his years in New Jersey and his time in Washington, I knew the fact that the people I mentioned and the company in the Caymans were real would keep him busy trying to nail it all down—and out of my hair—for the next few days anyway. And if I were real lucky, he would tell his editors about it too soon and end up looking like an idiot.

Sy was still trying to get me to tell him who I was when I cut him off and hung up. Rob Perry wasn't in the newsroom at the moment, and for a change, my voice mail light wasn't on. I was in the middle of making notes to myself about how to convince Maggie Padgett to talk to us when my phone rang. It was Ralph.

"I've got something for you, Sutton," he said, and I could hear he was pleased with himself. "First thing I did was get the home phone number for that certain VIP we talked about and match it to the records for the young lady. Seems he called her more than a dozen times between the middle and the end of March. One night he called three times. There are a few nighttime calls from his office, too."

Gotcha, I thought.

"Oh, yeah," Ralph continued, "the calls were all one-way. She never made any to him."

"This is good news, Ralph. Real good news. Can you make hard copy for me?"

"No problem."

"I'll pick it up from you sometime in the next few days. Just hang on to it until you hear from me. And Ralph? Thanks. I owe you."

"Not yet you don't," Ralph said. "We're not even close to being even yet. 'Bye, Sutton."

" 'Bye, Ralph. You're good people."

Rob still had not appeared when I hung up from Ralph's good news, so I took some time to put together a summary of the most recent events and sent it to his private computer directory, the one that only he could access. I didn't say how I knew what I knew, but I wanted him to know that even though Ken and I didn't have enough for another story yet, we might very well have a hell of a good one in another day or two. Then I went downstairs to wait for Ken.

Promptly at eleven (How can he plan it so closely in this traffic? I wondered), Ken pulled up in his tan Honda Accord and put up his hand in a wave. I came around the front of the car, let some traffic pass, opened the passenger's door, and climbed inside.

"Hi, Sutton," Ken greeted me as he pulled back into the traffic, looking impeccable as always.

"Hey, Ken."

"Do you think we should have called ahead to tell Maggie to make herself available?" he asked.

"No, I think it might send her into a panic. I think she's scared, really scared of Ed Lloyd. She's afraid no one will believe her story and that if she breathes a word, Lloyd will crucify her. She wouldn't tell me a thing on Saturday, and I could see her point. But today's different."

"Oh?"

"Today I have copies of her telephone records and all the calls Ed Lloyd made to her from his house. He would be hard-pressed to claim it was official business. Today, we might be able to sway her."

"Good work, lady," Ken said. "It's worth another try, especially since it's all we have."

"Well, actually, it's not."

"No?"

So I told him about Noah Lansing's visit the night before, about his confirmation of Lloyd and Taylor's blood types and about the college kid with the pool flyers.

Ken whistled softly.

"Jesus, Sutton, this thing is getting creepier by the minute. So," he said, looking at me shrewdly, "what was your quo for Lansing's quid?"

"I had to tell him about Maggie."

He raised a surprised eyebrow, then thought about it for a few seconds while he maneuvered past a string of double-parked limos in front of one of the downtown hotels.

"You really think Lansing is serious about telling you what he knows in return?" he asked finally.

"I think so. He agreed to give us another day with Maggie before he contacts her. He didn't have to tell me about the kid with the flyers. I already had told him about Maggie when the call came in. He could have passed it off as anything, but he didn't."

"That kid may just fry Taylor's ass."

"He may," I agreed. "No doubt Taylor will think it feels that way."

"So what's Lansing's motive for all this openness?"

"His dead wife, I think." I filled Ken in on Lansing's history and the murder in Virginia Beach. "Bill Russell made a comment once that he thinks Lansing has a hard time letting a case rest until he's closed it. I think maybe it's real personal with him these days, especially given the circumstances in this case."

"Yeah, he sounds pretty driven. But his wife getting raped and murdered probably would have that effect on a guy," Ken replied. "Okay, Sutton, if you think he's being straight with us on this, I trust your instincts."

"I think he is," I answered, also trying to reassure myself. "I think he wants to get these guys much worse than he wants to argue with us. I think the idea that they might get away with it upsets him more than the idea of dealing with me."

Twenty-six

We continued to wind our way through the beginnings of the lunchtime traffic crunch and over to Capitol Hill. After circling for the third time around the areas near the Senate office buildings, Ken finally happened on someone pulling out of a parking space next to the Folger Library and wasted no time in wheeling into it as they drove away. We walked the three blocks to the Russell Building and went up to the second floor to Senator Black's office.

It was 11:30 when we walked in, and Maggie Padgett was standing in the reception area talking with Susan Barrett. She turned when Susan's attention shifted to us and paled when she realized it was me again.

"Hello, Maggie. Hi, Susan," I said to the two of them. "This is my colleague Ken Hale." Ken nodded to each of them in turn, and they murmured soft hellos. "Maggie," I went on, wanting to take full advantage of having arrived unannounced, "do you think we could talk with you for a few minutes?"

"Well, I . . . we're very busy right now," she said, looking as if talking to us was just about at the bottom of her list of things to do.

"I know," I said soothingly. "Sorry we didn't call ahead, but something has come up that made it very important we talk with you as soon as possible."

She looked around the office, where a couple of people sat in chairs, apparently waiting to talk with someone there themselves.

"Do you mind if we talk in the hall?" she asked finally. We agreed and followed her out the door.

"Look," I said, once we were out in the busy corridor, "this is way too public, too, and you really are going to want to hear what we have to say. How about if you tell Susan you're going to go have lunch with us?"

"I don't know what you could say that I want to hear," Maggie answered. "Especially since I have no idea what you're talking about." She was still hoping that somehow this would all just go away.

"You may as well talk to us," Ken said, speaking for the first time. "We've learned a lot since Sutton saw you on Saturday. We understand you're scared. But if you help us, we think we can help you, too."

Maggie held Ken's eyes for a long moment, a searching look that tried to delve deeply into the truth of what he was saying and that made her fear and sense of helplessness more painfully obvious.

"I'll go for a walk with you," she said finally, and I sensed a note of defeat in her voice. "Wait just a moment."

She went back into the office, apparently to make her excuses to Susan, then rejoined us.

We went down the elevator and outside without speaking, then crossed Delaware Avenue to the park, where we found a bench.

"Why should I talk to you?" Maggie asked once we were seated. "No one will believe me. It's my word against his. I can't prove a thing."

"But we may be able to," Ken told her quickly. "You won't be in this alone."

"For starters," I chimed in, "we have proof that Lloyd called you repeatedly at home in the couple of weeks before he showed up with you at Dr. Morris's office. I've got the phone records, with the calls from his home and his office."

"And we have proof that his blood type is the same as one of the men who assaulted Ann Kane before she died," Ken added. "If we're able to come up with enough evidence against him, the police could force him to submit to a DNA analysis that could prove conclusively whether he was there."

Maggie looked as if every word we said to her pierced her like a sword, especially when Ken mentioned Ann Kane.

"There are a couple of other things you probably don't know," I told her, more softly now, partly out of sympathy and partly in an effort to make her see us as her friends. "Ann Kane isn't the only one who's dead because of Ed Lloyd."

Maggie groaned, a hurting sound that came up from the solar plexus and stood my hair on end. This was no fun at all, but I went on.

"You already know about Dr. Morris, the man who went out of his way to help you. Even the police are convinced now that his death wasn't suicide, and we all know who had a motive to keep him from telling what he knew."

Maggie looked from one of us to the other, her eyes wet. I went on.

"What you don't know yet is about Janet Taylor."

"Wasn't she the one who was married to that . . . ?" she asked, her question tailing off.

"Right," I said, nodding, "the supervisor's wife out in Fairfax County, the one who was murdered last week."

"But I thought Lloyd was a friend of theirs. Why would he kill her?"

"He didn't, but the police think her husband did, and we have reason to believe it was because of something she found out, something to do with Ann Kane." She didn't have to know just how flimsy the evidence for our "belief" was.

"With Ann?"

"Maggie," Ken said, putting his hand on her arm, "we think Hub Taylor was the other man with Ann that night she died. The blood type matches there, too. And there's a witness who can put Taylor at the house when his wife died. We think she found out about Ann somehow, and he killed her."

"Oh, God," Maggie said, looking at Ken's hand. She sounded ill. I could feel her mind picturing the line of bodies getting longer and longer. She started to cry for real.

Ken put his hand on her shoulder while I searched through my purse to get a tissue, which I handed to her.

"Maggie," I said, and she raised her tear-streaked face to look at me. "We have to stop him. Please, please help us."

Her eyes showed it when she made up her mind to talk to us. She used the tissue to wipe her eyes and blow her nose and then she told us what she knew.

"Ed Lloyd goes after anything in a skirt," she said angrily.

"We've heard," Ken told her dryly.

"The problem is he isn't one who takes no for an answer. There's been more than one secretary and aide around here who's been let go or who left in disgrace because she refused to go out with him. He carries a lot of weight on the Hill, and he doesn't hesitate to throw it around. There are even more who've given in to him just to keep from getting him angry with them. We all know the wisest thing is just to stay away from him because he's relentless once he decides you're the one he wants next.''

Already my stomach was turning sour at the sordid profile she drew. Ed Lloyd was a predator, a jackal, who preyed on those unable to protect themselves.

''He started calling,'' Maggie went on, ''after Senator Black introduced him to me at a reception. In fact, I was talking to Ann at the time. Paul introduced us both to Lloyd. Lloyd called me later that evening at my apartment and asked me to come have drinks with him.''

''What did you say?'' Ken asked.

''I had heard too many stories about him. I wanted nothing to do with him, but I didn't want to make him angry. I told him I wasn't feeling well. I hoped by the next day he would find someone else more interesting.''

''But he called again,'' I said, not needing to phrase it as a question.

''Yes, practically every night for the next couple of weeks. And he called me at the office a couple of times, too. I told him I didn't like to go out with people I worked with, that I wouldn't be comfortable with the idea. I hoped that way he wouldn't take it personally.''

''Did you tell anyone else that he was bothering you?'' Ken asked.

''No, I was too mortified by the whole thing. I didn't want anyone to know. I kept hoping he would get tired of me and go away. But he wouldn't give up. He said he just wasn't going to accept defeat, even if it meant he had to do something serious like have a word with Paul.''

''From what I've heard about Senator Black, it doesn't sound like he would have expected you to go out with Lloyd,'' I told her.

''I know that, now,'' Maggie said, ''but Lloyd was just driving me crazy. I couldn't think straight about him anymore. All I could think of were the stories I had heard and how to get him to leave me alone. Finally, I thought that if I went out with him once, maybe he would find me so boring that he would want nothing more to do with me.''

"So you went out with him?" Ken asked, sounding as if the answer he was expecting was making him feel ill, too.

"It was stupid, I know, but I finally agreed to have dinner with him. I figured what could happen over dinner in a restaurant? But he drove over himself to pick me up, and it wasn't until we turned into his neighborhood that I realized he wasn't going to a restaurant. We went to his house instead.''

"Were there other people around? A maid? A cook?" I asked, thinking about potential witnesses.

"No one," Maggie answered. "He told me first thing that we were alone, that he had given the maid the night off once she made dinner. It made me uncomfortable, but it just didn't occur to me that he would try to hurt me. So we went ahead and had dinner. He had quite a bit of wine, but I barely touched mine. I wanted to keep my wits about me. It wasn't until after the liqueur he served with dessert that I knew I was in trouble.''

"He put something in the liqueur." Again it wasn't a guess on my part.

"I think so," Maggie went on. "We had the liqueur and dessert in his living room. I was on the sofa and he was across from me in a chair. I . . . I remember thinking that he hadn't done anything out of line all evening, that maybe it would be okay, and then I started to get very warm in the room and I just was not feeling well. Lloyd was talking, and I realized he had put his hand on my . . . my leg and was stroking it.'' She looked down at her leg as if she could still feel Lloyd's hand there.

"He won't hurt you again," Ken told her, sensing that the memories of that night still were painfully real for her.

"I told him I had to go to the bathroom, that I was going to be sick, and I stood up quickly. But I lost my balance

and fell back on the sofa. I think . . . I think I may even
have blacked out for a few seconds. When I came to, Lloyd
was on top of me, kissing me and trying to put his hands
under my clothes. I pushed him off and tried to get away,
but I couldn't get my legs to work right. I kept falling
down. It was all very confused. Part of my brain knew he
had done something to me, but I couldn't get the rest of it
to work very well. And he kept coming after me, putting
his hands on me and trying to kiss me.''

"So when did he take you to Dr. Morris?"

"I think I started having these muscle spasms, like my
arms and legs began to jerk and tremble. It must not have
been what was supposed to happen. I guess it scared him.
He finally left me on the floor for a minute and came back
with my coat. He put it on me and half carried me out to
his car. I think I passed out again in the car. I don't remember anything else until I woke up in the doctor's office.
I saw Lloyd there and he frightened me. He made it clear
I wasn't to say anything in front of the doctor. Later, when
he took me home, he told me he would see to it I was fired
and that I would never get another decent job, that everyone
would know what a slut I was if I told anyone what had
happened.''

"And you believed him?" Ken, too, sounded angry.

"Absolutely," Maggie said vehemently. "I knew he
could do it and he would. And then, when Sutton told me
about Dr. Morris, it frightened me even more. I realized
Lloyd was capable of murder, that he wouldn't hesitate to
destroy me one way or the other if he thought I was a
threat.''

"So did he bother you anymore?" I asked.

"No," she said, sighing, "but a week or so later I got
a call from Ann. She wanted to have lunch. So we went
out, and she told me Lloyd had started calling her, asking
her out.''

My stomach kicked up some more bile. Maggie kept talking.

"I know now I should have told her what he did to me," she said sadly. "I lie awake at night thinking she might not be dead if I had just spoken up. But I didn't. I was too embarrassed. I just told her he was really bad news, to stay away from him, not to go anywhere with him. She said she had no intention of seeing him. She thought he was a worm."

"So he probably showed up unannounced at her apartment instead," I speculated. "Hub Taylor in tow."

"Probably said they just wanted to have a drink," Ken added disgustedly. "Even though she couldn't have alcohol, Lloyd somehow managed to put the Demerol into whatever she did drink. It knocked her out, and while they were having sex with her it killed her."

Maggie began to cry again, softly but brokenheartedly. I realized that she had been holding herself responsible for what happened to Ann Kane.

"It wasn't your fault, Maggie," I said, trying to comfort her. "But there's something else you have to do."

She looked up again.

"You have to tell the police what you know. It's the only way Ann is going to have any justice or peace."

"But I can't tell the police," she protested. "If I do, Lloyd will know!"

"Not until it's too late for him," I tried to reassure her. "The detective who's in charge of the case . . . I think you can trust him, Maggie. He wants to see Lloyd pay as badly as you do. And he's not going to do anything to jeopardize his best witness."

"You're the link," Ken added. "The one who can make the connection to Ann, the one who can break this thing loose. Detective Lansing will do whatever it takes to see that nothing happens to you."

Maggie remained tearfully silent, looking down at her

hands. Eventually, when we didn't go away, she made up her mind.

"All right," she said tiredly, raising her eyes to look at us again. "I'll talk to him. I'll do it for Ann."

I looked at Ken, knowing my face probably held the same look as his as one more of Ed Lloyd's escape routes closed.

"I think you should come with us right now, to talk to him," I said, turning back to Maggie. "We'll call him from the car, and you can call your office and give them some excuse for not coming back this afternoon."

She nodded silently, apparently no longer having the energy to argue with whatever we suggested.

We made the walk to Ken's car in virtual silence as well, each of us lost in our own thoughts about just what Maggie's decision to talk to the police might—or might not— mean, just how much leverage it would provide against Lloyd and Taylor.

As Ken started the car and maneuvered back into the lunchtime traffic, I called the Great Falls police station. Lansing wasn't there.

"I need you to page him," I told the dispatcher. "It's important. Tell him it's Sutton and that I'm on my way there with a woman from Capitol Hill he's been wanting to meet."

Maggie called her office then and told them she had a small emergency at home and would be out for the rest of the day. Then she settled into the backseat and stared quietly out the window throughout the drive to Great Falls. From time to time I saw her lift a hand to wipe her eyes, but whether her tears were for Ann Kane or herself, I couldn't tell.

By the time we arrived at the police station, Lansing was waiting for us. Jimmy, who was manning the desk as usual, didn't comment when I asked him to call back for us, but his expression said he could hardly wait to hear what this was all about.

Lansing came out immediately and ushered us back to his office. Only then did I make my introductions.

"Detective Noah Lansing," I said, "this is Ken Hale from the paper. We've been working this story together. You may remember Ken from the press conference at the Taylors' house." The men shook hands.

"And this," I continued when they finished showing what good manners they had, "is Maggie Padgett. She has decided to tell you her story about Senator Lloyd."

Lansing shook Maggie's hand also, studying her closely.

"Thank you for coming down," he said. "I know this isn't easy for you."

"No," she agreed, studying him with equal intent. She was about to put herself and her future in his hands, and it was clear she didn't want to make a mistake in doing so.

"If you'll have a seat here for just a minute," Lansing went on, motioning to his guest chair, "I'll see these two folks out and find us a more comfortable room to talk in."

Maggie nodded and sank into the chair gratefully. She was looking more drained by the minute, and I knew she still had a grueling afternoon in front of her. Lansing's "more comfortable room" no doubt would be an interrogation room where his conversation with her would be videotaped, and he would make sure he got everything from her that she had to tell. My heart went out to her at the thought of her having to tell her sordid story again, but I knew she had to if Ed Lloyd was going to be stopped.

Ken and I stepped back out into the hallway ahead of Lansing, who closed his office door as he followed us out.

"How'd you manage this?" he asked, as soon as the door closed.

"You know people just can't resist telling me things." I grinned.

Lansing rolled his eyes. Then I gave him a serious answer.

"Actually, I think it was the phone records," I told him. "I've got proof of a whole shitload of calls from Lloyd's home and office to her apartment over a couple of weeks before the night he showed up with her at Morris's office."

"So she decided there may be some evidence to support what she says?"

"That and the guilt trip Sutton put on her over Ann Kane," Ken chimed in.

"I can picture it," Lansing said drolly.

"I didn't say a thing that wasn't true," I told them huffily. "And besides, she was already on a major guilt trip of her own before I ever showed up!"

"Well, we'll take it from here with her," Lansing said. "With any luck, she'll prove to be one more nail in the coffin."

"Speaking of which," I asked, "anything else on the guy with the flyers?"

"He passed the lie detector test with flying colors. We've told him to keep himself available and his mouth shut. But he looks like bad news for Hub Taylor."

"Good," Ken spoke up. He was as bad as Lansing and myself about not wanting the guilty to go unpunished—or a prizewinning story to go unwritten.

"Anyway, we'll be as gentle as we can with Ms. Padgett," Lansing said. "She looks like she could fall apart any second."

"Just remember, she's a victim here, too," I added.

"I will. And McPhee?"

"Yeah?"

"Thanks."

"You're welcome, but you owe me one."

"Come back about six o'clock. I may be able to even things up a bit."

I looked at him shrewdly. "What do you have?"

"All in good time," he replied. "Just be here."

"Count on it."

Lansing turned and opened the door to his office to go back inside. Ken and I showed ourselves out of the police station. As soon as we were in the car, Ken turned to me.

"Is there something going on between you and Lansing that I should know about?" he asked.

"No," I answered honestly while my inner voice made a few references to things like lust and hypocrisy. "In fact, I'm probably one of his least favorite people."

"That's not the way he looked at you," Ken said, a knowing smile coming across his face. He turned and reached down to start the car.

"You have an overactive imagination," I answered, wishing I could believe otherwise.

"So where to now?" he asked, feigning innocence, as we drove away from the police station.

"Why don't you drop me back off at the Russell Building? I think it might be time to pay a visit to Ed Lloyd."

"Be careful with him," Ken counseled. My hand went to the gradually shrinking lump on the side of my head, and I knew he was thinking the same thing I was, that I had already had my warning.

Twenty-seven

In the Russell Building, I took the elevator up to the third floor. As a powerful Senate figure, Lloyd had what was probably one of the largest and most ostentatious offices I had seen in the building. It was luxuriously furnished in what looked to be either expensive period reproductions or the real things. In this office, unlike Senator Black's, all the inner-office doors were closed, and quiet prevailed.

There was no one in sight except a middle-aged man in a navy-blue suit who sat on a floral-print sofa, a pad of paper on his lap, making notes with a Mont Blanc pen, and the receptionist, a silver-haired woman in her fifties, who, I could see when she stood up, had a steel beam for a spine and probably made mincemeat of lesser mortals on a regular basis. When I entered, she quickly sized me up as inconsequential. While her mouth smiled at me ever so politely, the smile didn't touch her eyes. Lloyd couldn't have guarded access to himself any better with a pit bull.

"Yes?" she said.

"I'm Sutton McPhee from the *Washington News*," I told

her, and saw her opinion of me drop another couple of notches. "I'd like to see Senator Lloyd if he has a few minutes. It's urgent."

"What is it about, please?" the ice queen asked.

"I really think the senator would rather I discussed this in private with him."

"I'm very sorry," she replied, without pause, "but the senator is quite busy, and unless you can tell me what this concerns, I just don't see how we could work you into his schedule for at least a couple of weeks."

"This is very important"—I looked down at the name-plate on her desk—"Mrs. Rose. I really think Senator Lloyd would want to hear what I have to say."

"No, it's just not possible," said Mrs. Rose, who by any other name probably would have been just as unyielding. "Perhaps you should call ahead next time. And talk with Mr. Robbins, the senator's press secretary. I'm sure he could assist you."

Just as she finished what was supposed to be her final brush-off, Lloyd came around the corner with another man, left arm around the man's shoulder, right hand shaking his hand.

"So call me, George," Lloyd was saying. "Let's get in a round of golf." George was nodding happily, his audience apparently having gone well.

When he saw me, Lloyd stopped where he was, hatred and something else—menace, I thought—lancing across the space between us.

"Mrs. Rose?" he said, asking in that short phrase tinged with rebuke what I was doing there.

"Mr. Stevens is here for your next appointment, Senator," Mrs. Rose said smoothly, as if I didn't exist. Mr. Stevens, the man on the sofa, got up immediately and walked over to Lloyd, who took him in hand and went back down the hall, but not before casting Mrs. Rose a last, meaningful look. I knew what it meant: Get rid of her. But I decided I wasn't going.

"Thank you for coming by," Mrs. Rose said smoothly, turning her attention back to me. "Do call ahead next time."

"I'm sorry," I told her, even though I wasn't, "but I'm afraid I'm going to have to stay right here until the senator agrees to see me." I sat myself down in Mr. Stevens's spot and tried to look unruffled.

"Look," Mrs. Rose said, the steel creeping from her backbone into her voice, "I've told you the senator has no time."

"You tell the senator I think he should make time," I responded, still keeping my own voice polite but serious. "You tell him I want to talk to him about the woman with the violet eyes. I think he'll change his mind."

The outer door opened and an elderly couple walked in. Mrs. Rose studied me for a second and then turned to ask if she could help the new visitors. They told her they were constituents and were hoping to get passes to the Senate's visitors' gallery.

When Mrs. Rose had finished taking care of them and had seen them out, Mr. Stevens and the senator returned to the reception area, their brief meeting apparently concluded.

"Charlotte?" Lloyd asked the secretary when he saw me still in his reception area, halting abruptly and looking at me with more than mere annoyance. Mr. Stevens stopped, too, confused.

Charlotte Rose quickly stepped between Lloyd and Stevens and spoke quietly to the senator.

"I see," he said. "All right, take her back."

Mrs. Rose came over and said, "Follow me, please." I did. While Lloyd exchanged good-bye pleasantries with Mr. Stevens she led me down the hall. As we passed, the door to another inner office opened and a blond-haired woman of about my age stepped through, nodded at us, and left. One of the senator's staffers, I guessed.

Charlotte deposited me on a sofa in Lloyd's office and left me there without saying a word. I was calculating just what the antique desk and tables and the Italian leather sofa and chairs might have cost the taxpayers when Lloyd returned, closing the door angrily and wheeling to face me.

"What the hell is this?" he barked, his demeanor full of menace and meant to intimidate. All trace of the smooth, genial host who had dealt with George and Mr. Stevens was gone.

"I have some questions to ask you, Senator," I said calmly. I knew things he didn't know I knew. His bluster was wasted on me. "I didn't think you would want to answer them in front of Mrs. Rose or your other visitors once you knew what they were."

"This had better not be any more of the nonsense I heard at the cemetery," Lloyd warned, walking over to stand near the sofa. "I told you I don't know what you're talking about!"

"Oh, I think you know exactly what I was talking about," I told him, smiling. "But first let me ask you about another woman. Maggie Padgett. How well do you know her?"

"In the first place, I don't know her. In the second place, even if I did, it's none of your affair!"

"I don't believe you, Senator. I think you know—or at least wanted to know—her very well. So well, in fact, that you took her to your house for dinner and then drugged her drink."

Lloyd threw back his head and laughed. I had to give him a gold star for his acting ability.

"Don't be absurd," he said. "Do you really think someone in my position has to go around drugging women to get a date?"

"Of course you don't. That's exactly what makes what

you did to her so sick. You could have plenty of women. But when Maggie and Ann Kane turned you down, you couldn't take no for an answer.''

"This is slander, of the vilest kind! You don't have an ounce of proof for any of this. If this Padgett woman told you this, she's lying.''

"Wrong again, Senator. I've got copies of your and Maggie's phone records. There were repeated calls from you to her apartment and her office.''

"She works for another senator, for God's sake! Anyone in my office could have made those calls.''

"Most of them were calls from your house. And how do you know where she works if you don't know who she is?''

Lloyd's eyes sparked, but he didn't miss a beat.

"Because I just remembered after all that I was introduced to her somewhere. Some reception, I think.''

"It's too bad you didn't leave it at that,'' I went on. "If you had been able to keep your pants zipped, Dr. Peter Morris might still be alive.''

"What does he have to do with the woman? Besides, Peter Morris killed himself! The police said it was suicide.'' He looked almost smug.

"But you and I know it wasn't, don't we? Was it because you figured out he had told me all about Maggie? About the night you had to take her to him for help? Is that why you did it?''

"Are you saying I killed him?''

"Did you?''

"Are you insane? You're talking to a United States senator!''

"Yes, I am, and it makes me sick to my stomach to think a scumbag like you sits in this office.''

Lloyd's face reddened, and his hostility ratcheted up several notches.

"You'd better watch your mouth, little sister,'' he said,

his voice lowering as he dropped the bluster, taking on a tone of truly serious intent. "It's going to get you in a whole heap of trouble!"

"Oh, you mean like the little love tap you gave me in the parking lot a few nights ago?"

"I mean like trouble there's no getting out of, no coming back from."

"Make all the threats you want, Senator. But your sick little peccadilloes are about to bring it all crashing down around your ears. I know you were there when Ann Kane died. I know Maggie Padgett came close to ending up the same way. I know Peter Morris didn't kill himself. Pretty soon I won't be the only one who knows."

Lloyd's eyes were glittering with hatred. He reached down and grabbed my arm, pulling me half up off the sofa.

"Your mouth just signed a check I'm going to cash for you. Now get out of my office."

I fell back as he dropped my arm, then stood up and went to the door.

As I opened it he spoke.

"You take care now," he said with smooth menace.

"You, too," I replied, hoping my smile was coming somewhere close to matching his in malevolence.

Charlotte Rose ignored me when I got back out to the reception area. I thought for a moment about stopping to bait her, but decided my wit would be wasted on her, and besides, Lloyd had been frightening enough that I really wasn't in the mood. I let myself out.

I caught a taxi back to the paper's parking garage, and as I drove out of the District I called Ken to let him know how my chat with Ed Lloyd had gone.

"Do you really think that was such a good idea, Sutton?" he asked in a worried voice. "What if he comes after you again?"

"I'm on my way back out to Lansing's office," I told

him. "Lloyd would have to climb over a lot of cops to get to me there."

"But you don't live there, Sutton. What about the rest of the time?"

"Don't worry. I'll be fine," I said, hoping I sounded reassuring. "I'm forewarned. I'll be very careful. I promise. I won't let him get that close to me again."

"That son of a bitch!"

"I'll be okay, Ken. Really. But I've got to go see Lansing now. We'll talk later."

Twenty-eight

Traffic into Virginia was already pretty backed up by the time I got across Memorial Bridge, and the day had turned hot. It made me ask myself for the umpteenth time why I was driving an un-air-conditioned car in the South, but I knew I was far too attached to the Bug and to its low gas and repair bills to trade it in for something newer, cooler, and more upscale. So I rolled down the windows and crept along.

Finally, at 6:10, I pulled into the station parking lot. At the front door, I could see Lansing in the lobby, talking to the evening duty officer. He saw me, too, and crossed the lobby to come outside.

"We'll take my car," he said, without any preliminaries. "It's over here."

Wordlessly, I followed him over to a gray unmarked sedan, which he unlocked, and we got in. The rolled-up windows made the inside like an oven, but I expected the souped-up police engine would enable the air conditioner to solve that problem in no time.

We were out on Crimmons Avenue, already-cooling air blowing in our faces, when I decided I couldn't stand it any longer.

"So, are you going to tell me where we're going?" I asked. "Or am I going to have to guess?"

"Oh, sorry," Lansing said sheepishly, his conscious mind surfacing from wherever it had been. "I guess I didn't tell you, did I? We're going to see Hub Taylor."

"Really? Has he decided to talk to you?"

"Yeah," Lansing said, smiling grimly, "he just doesn't know it yet."

"So where are we meeting him?"

"His house. I called him an hour ago at the county building and told him we needed to have a private conversation—completely off the record and no attorneys—and that we could either do it at his office, where people would know who I was, or do it at his house. He agreed to meet me at the house."

"To meet you. I take it that means he doesn't know I'm coming along."

"No."

"He's not gonna like you springing me on him."

"Listen, by the time we're done, you'll be the least of his worries. This whole thing, including you being there, is off the record and very unkosher. But if I play this thing right, in the long run, none of that will matter."

Well, Lansing certainly knows how to pique a girl's interest, I thought.

And that's putting it mildly, my voice added.

Leave me alone, I groaned.

"What?" Lansing asked.

"Nothing," I said, embarrassed, "just talking to myself."

In another five minutes we were turning up the drive to the Taylor house. Lansing was finishing his instructions on

how to comport myself—in short, just stay quiet and listen—when he pulled up at the front door.

The maid, Maria, was there and let us in without argument when Lansing gave her his name. She did look a little
surprised to see me there again, but she kept whatever
thoughts she had about it to herself and took us back to the
family-room area with all the windows. Hub Taylor was
sitting in an overstuffed armchair when we walked in. He,
however, didn't take Maria's silent approach about my
presence.

"What is she doing here?" he asked angrily, standing
up from the chair. "I didn't say you could bring any
press!"

"Forget about it," Lansing told him. "She's just here to
listen and in case one of us needs a witness to this conversation later. Nothing she hears will leave this room unless I say so. She'll do what I tell her."

I turned to look at Lansing in astonishment, only to see
him give me a surreptitious wink that told me to swallow
hard and stay quiet.

Lansing sat down on the end of the sofa nearest Taylor's
chair, and I helped myself to another chair across from him.

"So what do you want this time?" Taylor asked impatiently, returning to his chair. "I've got a lot of work to
do."

But Lansing wasn't to be rushed. He sat back on the sofa
and looked around the room.

"Did Mrs. Taylor do much of the decorating herself?"
he asked. "This room looks a lot like what I expect she'd
have liked, given everything I've heard about her." He
didn't even know Janet Taylor, but I had to give him credit
when I realized what he was doing—invoking her presence,
bringing her to life again in the house and in Hub Taylor's
mind.

"Yes," Taylor said uncomfortably. "She did."

"A very special lady, everyone says," Lansing went on,

his expression the very picture of innocence.

Taylor said nothing, and I had the feeling the memory of his dead wife was gnawing at him again.

"Okay, Mr. Taylor." Lansing spoke again. "Let's get down to why I'm here."

Taylor just looked at him. Lansing went on.

"I want to offer you one last chance to change the story you told us about the afternoon your wife died, about where you were."

"There's nothing to change," Taylor spoke up gruffly. "I told you where I was. I was out driving around."

"Okay, Mr. Taylor," Lansing said, looking sad now, "let me tell you a different story. I think you may start to remember some things you've apparently forgotten."

I knew then what Lansing was about to do. He was going to lay the whole thing out for Taylor.

"What we have, Mr. Taylor," he said, "is a United States senator, a very powerful man, who can't leave good-looking women alone. But somewhere along the line, he goes a little over the edge. Somewhere he gets the idea that no woman he's interested in should be able to tell him no. So one night, when a woman he has the hots for continues to turn him down, he drugs her so he can fuck her."

Lansing's blunt language drew a flinch from Taylor. He had used the word very deliberately, I knew, to emphasize the ugliness of what Lloyd had done. Lansing went on.

"The plan is that once she's unconscious, he can do whatever he wants with her. And even if she knows later what happened, what can she do about it? Considering who he is, no one will stick their neck out for her, and he can make life miserable for her.

"The only problem is, he uses too much of the stuff and it makes her sick. So instead of screwing her, he has to call a doctor friend to meet him at the doctor's office. The doctor pulls the senator's chestnuts out of the fire, and the woman is too afraid to talk.

As Lansing spun his tale I watched Taylor's face. I suspected that even Taylor hadn't known this part of the story, that he hadn't known Lloyd had already put at least one woman's life in danger before Ann Kane. Nor had he known there was a witness: Peter Morris. Taylor already was watching Lansing's face as if hypnotized by a cobra.

"So a few weeks go by," Lansing was saying, "and the senator's got his eye on another sweet young thing who wants nothing to do with him. Why not try the mickey on this one? he thinks. Only this time he somehow convinces his friend, a county supervisor, to come along for the fun."

Taylor started, then dug his fingers into the chair arms, his knuckles whitening as if he were holding on for dear life.

"No doubt," the detective went on, "the senator tells his friend it's all perfectly safe. Or maybe he doesn't tell his friend anything until the woman starts passing out. Whichever, they go to the woman's apartment, talk their way in on some pretext, and have some drinks. The senator puts the mickey in whatever the woman's drinking. He doesn't know she isn't drinking alcohol because of another drug she's taking. And so she passes out, and the boys have their fun."

Taylor's face, by this time, was suffused with color. Hard to tell if it was fear, embarrassment, or both.

Lansing sat forward with his forearms on his thighs, his hands clasped between them. He looked at Taylor intently, and Taylor couldn't seem to pull his eyes away.

"But then the poor woman starts to have convulsions, and then she dies," Lansing said, "So the senator and his friend the supervisor take the woman's body, wrap it in a sheet, and dump it out at Mason Neck, where it's found the next day. The senator tells his friend not to sweat it. No one saw them with her. There's no way to connect them. Forget it."

"This is all bullshit." It was Taylor speaking, finally.

His voice was hoarse and breathy. "I don't know anything about any of this."

"Let's not get into denials, yet," Lansing said. "There's more to the story." He paused for a second and then continued.

"In the meantime there's a tragedy. Someone kills the supervisor's wife. The supervisor says it wasn't him. He was out driving around. Neighbors and coworkers say he and his wife were having problems, that he went home that day because his wife was upset about something. But he still says he didn't do it.

"At about the same time the doctor who helped Lloyd out begins to get suspicious about the senator. He calls a reporter at one of the newspapers and has a long talk with her about what he knows. He points the finger at the senator in the death of the second woman, and even has some evidence to back it up—like the senator's blood type and a prescription for a certain drug that he had written for the senator.

"So the reporter goes to the senator and asks what he knows about it. The senator denies it all, but very shortly, the doctor—a Dr. Peter Morris, who I think you know, by the way—turns up dead, supposedly a suicide, but the police don't think so. And that same night, the reporter is attacked and she's told it's a warning to drop the story. Still, there's no real proof in either of these cases. It looks, Mr. Taylor, like your wife's killer and the men who let Ann Kane die are all going to get away."

At that, I saw a glimmer of hope come into Taylor's eyes. But Lansing quickly doused it.

"Then the police get lucky," he said. "What the senator doesn't know yet, Mr. Taylor, is that the woman he drugged first has come forward with her story. And we have telephone-company records to back it all up. So listen carefully, Mr. Taylor, and I'll tell you what I'm going to do." Lansing moved forward in the chair, even closer to Taylor.

"I'm going to hang the senator out to dry. I'm going to get a warrant for blood and hair samples, and I'm going to run every test there is, and I'm going to match his hair and his blood and his DNA to the evidence we found on Ann Kane's body. And do you know what I'm going to do then?"

For a moment there was no response to Lansing's question. Finally, as if the words had taken a while to penetrate, Taylor shook his head no.

"Then I'm going to offer the senator a deal in return for the identity of the second man with him that night. And I can tell you what the senator is going to do. He's going to take my offer, and he's going to point the finger at you, and he's going to say it was all your idea."

"No!" Taylor spoke up, as if jerking himself awake. "He's my friend. He wouldn't do that!"

"Oh, I think he would," Lansing said, smiling as if the thought pleased him. "The other thing you don't know, sir, is that I now have an eyewitness who can put you at this house at the time your wife died. If you're already in jail on murder charges, the senator has nothing to lose and everything to gain by laying it all at your feet. He's going to sell you out!"

Taylor leaped up from the chair, his eyes wild and panicked.

"No!" he shouted. "No!" He looked wildly around the room, as if searching for a way out.

Lansing jumped up as well and shouted back at him.

"Sit down!" he ordered. "And listen to me!"

Taylor focused on Lansing's face and then did as he was told. I was riveted to my chair, fascinated by the whole performance, by a side to Lansing I hadn't seen, and I was eagerly waiting for him to drop the other shoe.

Taylor was sitting in the chair once more, gasping for breath as if he had been doing wind sprints.

"Here's what I think, Mr. Taylor," Lansing said, calmly

again, as he sat back down, too. "I think your wife's death was accidental. I think you tried to make it look like murder to hide your own involvement. I think that we're going to offer you a deal in exchange for the truth. I think what you're going to do is tell me exactly what happened the day your wife died. And then you're going to help me nail your friend the senator!"

Taylor's chin dropped to his chest, and as tears ran down his face and onto his shirt, great broken sobs issued up out of him, shaking him and grating on my nerve endings like sandpaper.

Lansing waited calmly, his eyes leaving Taylor's face only once, to look at me with an expression that told me there was satisfaction in what he had done, but little joy.

When Taylor finally managed to stop crying, he spoke to Lansing.

"I didn't mean to hurt Janet," he said. "It was an accident, like you said."

"I know," Lansing told him. "But don't say any more right now. I want you to come down to the station and tell your story there. We can tape your statement for the record. And you should call an attorney to meet us there. I don't want any questions later about violating your rights. But let me give you a piece of advice, Mr. Taylor."

"What?"

"Get a new attorney. John Aldritch can't represent you and Lloyd both, and you and I both know where he's going to throw in his chips."

Mutely, Taylor shook his head. I was busy admiring the workings of Lansing's mind. With his warning to Taylor about Aldritch, he had neatly managed to neutralize the one person who might have tipped his hand to Lloyd before Lansing was ready to go after him. Now Aldritch would have no more warning than Lloyd would.

Good-looking and smart, too, my voice said. For once, I couldn't disagree with it.

Twenty-nine

After some thought, Taylor called a lawyer he knew socially and asked him to come to the Great Falls station. Lansing and I took Taylor in to the station, none of us talking throughout the twenty-minute trip.

At the station, Lansing took us in through the back, in an effort to keep Taylor's presence out of public view—and, he hoped, out of public knowledge. He took Taylor to an interrogation room to wait for the lawyer. Then he took me next door to what I realized was a darkened observation room that looked in to the first room through a one-way mirror.

"You can watch and listen in here," he told me. "Just don't discuss anything that goes on with anyone else who comes in. We'll talk again when I'm done in there. Okay?"

"Yeah," I agreed. "I'll behave."

Lansing smiled at me then, a real smile, not the calculated ones I had seen at Taylor's house. He turned and left the room, and I sank down in a chair in the back corner,

wondering how I could think about my love life in the
middle of what was going on.

I cleared the hormones from my brain and settled in to
watch Hub Taylor wait. He was like a man dissolving, bit
by bit. Every so often a new wave of tears would start in
his eyes and run down his face, which now looked pale
and doughy. A couple of times he sat forward and put his
head in his hands. Cynic that I am, I had to wonder how
many of his tears were for his wife and how many for
himself.

Probably ten minutes had gone by when the door to the
observation room opened, and several people, some in uniform and some not, came in and sat down. The last one
was Bill Russell. He did a double take when he saw me
there. Then he walked over and sat down next to me.

"Lansing know you're here?" he asked in a whisper.

"He invited me."

At that, Bill's eyebrows rose in even greater surprise.

"It's a long story," I told him, feeling smug myself for
once. "Let's just say he and I are getting along a little
better today."

"All right," Bill agreed as we saw Lansing lead a group
into the interrogation room, where Lansing sat down at the
head of the table. "But I expect to hear the real story eventually."

I gave him an affirmative shake of the head, and as we
turned our attention to the other room, a man I didn't know
walked over to Taylor and put a hand on his shoulder, then
sat down next to him. One of the two other plainclothes
detectives in the group stood by the door as the second one
sat down opposite Taylor.

"Hub," the lawyer—Sam Ross, according to the whis-
pers of the two cops in front of me—said to his client, "I
think you and I should talk privately before you talk to the
police."

"No!" Taylor said. "I want to get this over with."

"But, Hub, I can't—"

"I said no! I want to talk about this, and I want to do it now!"

"All right, Mr. Taylor." Lansing stepped in smoothly. "If you're ready to talk to us, the recording system is working and we're listening."

So Taylor told his story . . . all of it. He told them about how Ed Lloyd gradually had sucked him into his latest little game. Lloyd had started by sympathizing with Taylor that his wife was only "half a woman." He loved his wife, Taylor said, but as Lloyd had talked about it more and more, he had begun to feel his wife's paraplegia was cheating him of real sex. So he had started going out with Lloyd to parties, and then to little private parties at Lloyd's house, where there were just four of them—Lloyd, Taylor, and a couple of attractive young women, although never the same young women.

"I knew it was wrong," Taylor said, "and Janet knew something was going on, but once I started, I couldn't seem to stop. And Ed was always there, telling me I deserved to feel like a real man again."

Then came the night, he said, when Lloyd took him to Ann Kane's apartment. It was clear when she answered the door that she wasn't expecting them and was less than happy to see Lloyd there. But Lloyd talked his way in— "Just for a nightcap and then we'll go," he had said—and Ann Kane finally relented, probably hoping it would get rid of them sooner than continuing to argue. She fixed the two men drinks at Lloyd's request, but declined to have one herself, which irritated Lloyd. He badgered her about it until she agreed to have a soda. Once the drinks were on the living-room coffee table, Lloyd asked if she had any sort of snack, some crackers maybe. Obligingly, Ann went into the kitchen, and while she was gone Lloyd put some type of powder in her soda.

"I asked him what the hell he was doing," said Taylor,

"but he told me to shut up, and then she came back with the crackers."

It couldn't have been, he continued, more than fifteen or twenty minutes after she drank the soda that she passed out.

"It scared the shit out of me," he said, "but Ed told me to relax, that he had done this before and she would be fine."

Lloyd had carried Ann Kane into her bedroom, where he put her on the bed and undressed her, then raped her.

"And you watched?" Lansing asked him. "You saw him have sex with Ms. Kane?"

"Yes," Taylor answered, almost in a whisper.

"Holy Christ!" Bill muttered beside me.

"I wonder how much of this was really Lloyd getting his jollies and how much was a test for Taylor," I mused.

"And then what happened?" Lansing was asking.

"Then I had sex with her, too," Taylor admitted.

"Why?"

"It was Ed. He was telling me how great it was, being able to do anything I wanted to her. He kept at me, and finally I did it. He was my friend, the one who got me started in politics. He told me if I did whatever he said, he'd see to it that I ended up in Congress, maybe even the Senate. He said he had to know if I really had the balls for the job."

"So you had intercourse with her," Lansing said. "And then what?"

"And then she . . . she started having convulsions."

Taylor described Ann Kane's death, by which time Sam Ross was looking rather green around the gills. When the convulsions started, Taylor said, neither he nor Lloyd had any idea what to do. Within a minute or two Ann stopped convulsing, but she also stopped breathing. Taylor tried pounding on her chest, but nothing happened, and they gave up.

They sat there for a few minutes, Taylor said, he in

shock, and Lloyd calling the woman every name he could think of for dying on them. Then Lloyd wrapped her up in a sheet, and the two men went into the living room and wiped down every surface either of them could remember touching.

It was a Sunday night and quiet in the small apartment complex where Ann Kane lived on the ground floor. At Lloyd's direction, Taylor went out and moved the car up to the door and opened the trunk. With Taylor making certain no one was around, Lloyd put her body in it.

"He went back in and came out with her purse," Taylor told Lansing. "He said the police would think it was a burglar."

They drove down to Mason Neck and dumped Ann's body in the trees off a small dirt road. Afterward, Lloyd drove Taylor home, handed him the purse, and told him to destroy it.

"But I didn't," Taylor said, starting to cry again. "It was late, and I put it in a closet, thinking I'd get rid of it later. But Janet found it."

"Did she go through it, realize whose it was?" It was Lansing again, keeping Taylor moving in the direction he wanted him to go.

"Yes," Taylor went on, "that's when she called the office. She was hysterical and not making any sense, so I went home. I went up to the bedroom, and she was holding the purse. She threw it at me when I came in, and then she started screaming at me, calling me names, telling me I was shit like Ed. She came over to me in the wheelchair and was pulling herself half out of the chair, trying to beat at me with her fists. I . . . was scared. I was afraid she would want a divorce, maybe tell what she knew. I just wanted her to be quiet so I could think, but she wouldn't stop screaming at me. So I hit her. But I guess I hit her too hard. She went over sideways in the chair and hit her head— hard—on the slate hearth in front of the fireplace."

"Why didn't you call an ambulance?" Lansing asked.

"I thought she was dead," Taylor told him. "I couldn't find a pulse, nothing. And then I panicked. I went downstairs for a while and went to pieces. I was afraid. Afraid it would all come out. When I finally looked at the time, it was one-thirty, and I knew I had to have an alibi. So I went back to the county building and the board meeting."

"What happened to the purse?" Lansing asked.

"I put it in the trunk of my car. I told Ed afterward that I finally had gotten rid of it, but I hadn't. It's still there."

Lansing looked down at his hands for a second. His body language told me he had just said a silent thank you.

"So you went back to your meeting," he said to Taylor, looking back up.

"I knew I had to be seen there," Taylor explained, "and then I had to go back home and pretend to find her."

It was when he returned home, Taylor said, that he put the scarf around Janet's neck.

"There was no blood from where she hit her head," he explained, "so I thought I could make it look like she was strangled from behind by someone who came in and surprised her."

Finally, he said, he went to the phone and called Mannie Sims and 911.

Taylor stopped talking. He slumped in his chair, a picture of misery and shame and fear. Lansing and Sam Ross each sat back in their chairs as if digesting all that they had just heard. The people around me in the observation room punctuated the air with soft curses and exclamations, and then Lansing began speaking again, and they stopped talking to hear what he would say next.

"All right, Mr. Taylor," he said, "here's what I want from you. We're going to prepare a statement based on everything you've told us, and I want you to sign it. I also want your permission to search your car right now so I don't have to wait for a warrant. In return, I will talk with the commonwealth attorney and try to have you charged with involuntary manslaughter in your wife's death instead of murder. You help us put Ed Lloyd in prison, and I'll also do what I can to get reduced charges in Ann Kane's death as well. If you don't, you're going to take the fall for all of it.''

Sam Ross had recovered from his shock enough to calculate the pros and cons of what Lansing was offering. He whispered briefly in Taylor's ear.

''I agree,'' Taylor said. ''You can search my car. I'll testify against him. Whatever you want.''

At that, Lansing and his associates left the room, telling Taylor and Ross to hang tight for a while. I knew the first thing Lansing would do would be to send an evidence team after the purse. I wondered how long he would wait to make his move against Lloyd. Not, as it turned out, very long.

Bill and I followed the rest of the observers out into the hall. Lansing was there in the middle of a crowd of officers, giving several of them directions. Finally, he saw us and came over.

''What's next?'' I asked.

''We bring in Ed Lloyd and lay it all out for him,'' he said grimly. ''I'm sending a detective out there right now to tell him to be in here at eight tomorrow morning, with his attorney, no arguments. And I'm sending two marked units along to sit at his gate and make certain he doesn't go anyplace that we don't know about.''

At least he won't be able to come after me, I thought.

''That was quite a performance you staged in there and at Taylor's house before,'' I told Lansing. ''I would have confessed to anything you said.''

''Thanks, but I didn't take any pleasure in it.''

''I didn't think so.''

''You took her to Taylor's house with you?'' Bill asked. He was approaching astonishment.

"Yeah, as an observer . . . and as a payback."

"For what?"

"It's a long story, Bill," Lansing told him. "Some other time."

Bill gave me another one of his looks. I knew I would have to spill my guts to him eventually.

"Look, McPhee," Lansing said, "the rest of it around here tonight is bureaucratic, redtape bullshit. We'll be getting Taylor's statement transcribed and booking him. I'm going to have him taken to the detention center and held in an isolation cell. I don't want anyone there giving the game away. So why don't you go home and get some sleep? Come back bright and early for the next set of fireworks."

"I will, but is it okay if Ken comes, too?"

"Yeah, just keep it between the two of you."

"Oh, you needn't worry about that," I assured him. No way was the competition finding out about this from me. "Thanks, Detective."

"You, too, McPhee," he said tiredly, but the smile was back.

"And I've got to call Chief Fielding and let him know what's happening," Bill said as I waved to the two of them. "He's going to have a coronary."

Ken, when I called him later from home, was overjoyed to hear about Hub Taylor.

"Oh, I'll be there, all right," he said, when I told him Lansing had invited us back to watch him take on Ed Lloyd. "This is amazing, amazing!"

"At least that," I agreed, my own adrenaline stores finally running out as I could hear Ken's shifting into high gear in excitement over my news.

"But are you sure, Sutton, that no one else is onto Taylor being picked up by the police?"

"No one knew when I left the station, and Lansing has

done everything he can to keep it under wraps until at least tomorrow morning. Not for me, of course. He was adamant that no one had better tip Lloyd's hand to what was going on.''

"Let's hope he's got it under control, then," Ken said. "Rob would have our heads on platters if he woke up to this tomorrow in the *Post* and we didn't have it!''

"Some things are too frightening to even think about, Ken."

"You're right. So I'll see you in the morning?''

"Yeah, meet me there by seven-thirty. Lloyd is supposed to show up by eight.''

We hung up, and I went to bed, to several hours of nightmares of Ed Lloyd trying to kill me and of every news outlet in the region having the Hub Taylor story tomorrow morning except the *News*. I couldn't decide which was scarier.

Wednesday

Thirty

At 7:25, I pulled into the Great Falls police-station parking lot, already having scanned the local news shows and the *Post* with relief. No one knew about Taylor yet.

Ken was already there, waiting for me in the parking lot, and we walked in together. Jimmy called back to find Lansing for us, and then went back to the telephone call he had put on hold, grinning at me all the while.

Lansing came to meet us and took us directly back to the observation room.

"I would just as soon Lloyd not see either of you wandering around when he shows up," he explained.

After Lloyd's threats to me the day before, I had to say I agreed with Lansing for a change.

"Thanks for letting us be here," Ken told him. "We owe you one."

"No," Lansing said, looking at me. "This is Sutton's payback for giving us Maggie Padgett. Without Maggie's statement, we'd have a much harder time tying all this to Lloyd."

Lansing left us there and was closing the door when Bill Russell reopened it and came in. He didn't look as if he had done any better in the sleep department than I had.

"Well," he said tiredly, sitting down in front of the two of us, "I guess this is why they pay me the big bucks."

"Rough night, huh?" I asked.

"Let's just say the chief is glad to hear we think we're about to solve all this, but he's less than thrilled to hear that we've got a supervisor in custody and a senator coming in for questioning. Lansing and I have to call him the instant they've finished browbeating Lloyd so Fielding can prepare himself for the next round of angry calls from John Aldritch and assorted other bigwigs. Aldritch started calling last night after the cruisers showed up outside Lloyd's gate."

I introduced Ken to Bill, and we were discussing what probably would happen to Taylor in court when the door to the interrogation room opened and Ed Lloyd walked angrily in, followed by Aldritch, Lansing, and the two other detectives from the night before. Lloyd stood stiffly by the table until Aldritch took him gingerly by the arm and told him to have a seat. The police officers placed themselves in the same spots they had taken before. Except for the fact that the detective by the door was in shirtsleeves this time, his holstered gun in full view, it looked like a rerun of Taylor's questioning. The other difference was the addition of a television and VCR at the far end of the room. I had an idea what it was for.

Lansing spoke first.

"I apologize for asking you to come down at such an early hour," he began, his voice cordial and friendly. I didn't expect that would last long. "But we need to ask you some questions that just wouldn't wait any longer."

"I must object to this entire episode!" John Aldritch told him heatedly. "My client has absolutely nothing to discuss with you, and I've already placed calls to Chief Fielding and to the chairman of the board of supervisors to complain about your completely unprofessional conduct! Putting policemen at the gates went totally beyond professional behavior.''

''Well, Mr. Aldritch,'' Lansing said, still smiling politely, ''since this isn't a courtroom, your objections don't carry much weight here. And since your client is in deep shit here, of the first order, we thought it was just good judgment on our part to make certain the senator was still available this morning.''

''Whatever you're accusing Senator Lloyd of, it's outrageous and completely unfounded!'' Aldritch said, his voice rising. ''My client is innocent of any ridiculous charges you've trumped up, and he has nothing to say to any of your questions! This is all just a waste of everyone's time, and when you let us out of here, we're going straight to police headquarters to file a formal complaint, and I'll have my staff researching a lawsuit before the day is out!''

''I tell you what, Senator,'' Lansing said, turning to look at Lloyd, ''before you and Mr. Aldritch here go back home in a huff, how about watching a little TV with us?''

''What?'' Aldritch shouted.

''Mr. Aldritch,'' Lansing said, his voice suddenly menacing and not polite at all, his eyes never leaving Lloyd's face, ''I would appreciate it greatly if you would shut up for a few minutes. This is between the senator and me.''

Aldritch's jaw dropped in outrage, and then he snapped his mouth shut.

''John,'' Lloyd said, speaking for the first time, a smug smile on his face, ''do what the detective says.'' Aldritch looked as if he had been slapped.

''You see, Senator Lloyd,'' Lansing continued smoothly, ''we had a visit last night from your friend Hub Taylor. Mr. Taylor apparently has been overcome by his conscience, and he felt the need to get some things off his chest. He talked to us for a long time, and I would appre-

ciate it, Senator, if you'd take a look at what he had to
say.''

Lloyd was shocked, I could see. But he wasn't about to
give it all away so easily. His smile disappeared, but he
kept any reactive expression off his face. Aldritch, too, remained silent, but unlike his client, he clearly had no clue
what he was about to see and hear.

Lansing picked up a slim remote control from the table
in front of him and started the VCR. In a few seconds the
VCR's tracking locked on and the screen showed Hub Taylor and Sam Ross sitting where Aldritch and Lloyd sat now.
At the sight of his friend in the interrogation room, Lloyd
slowly dropped his eyelids and then raised them, the only
indication that he was steeling himself for the bad news
that was coming.

On the TV screen, the police entered the room the night
before, Taylor and Ross had their little argument, and Taylor launched into his story. Ken, who had missed the original telling, was riveted by what Taylor was saying on the
screen. I, on the other hand, was free to watch Lloyd.

Lansing obviously had worked with the tape for some
time after I had gone home the night before. He wasn't
giving everything away. Instead, he had what apparently
were time cues jotted down on a notepad to which he would
fast-forward and show Lloyd and Aldritch just enough seconds of Taylor's most damning statements for them to realize that Taylor had sold Lloyd out completely.

Lloyd was an amazing actor. His face was carved of
marble. Not a muscle moved or twitched as he watched and
listened to his protégé spill his guts. Only the eyes changed.
As Taylor went through his story Lloyd's eyes grew colder
and colder. By the end, the expression in his eyes was murderous. I wondered if that was the look Peter Morris saw
just before he died.

John Aldritch was another story, however. He couldn't,
after years of representing Lloyd, have had any illusions

that his client was any sort of Boy Scout. He probably saw more of the real Lloyd than most. But by the end of Taylor's confession, the lawyer looked almost as ill as Sam Ross had looked the previous evening.

When the tape ended, Ken was sitting next to me exclaiming to himself in low tones. In the other room, Aldritch leaned over to whisper something to Lloyd, who looked at him impassively, saying nothing. Lansing pointed the remote at the VCR and stopped the tape.

"This is no proof of anything," Aldritch began, as soon as the loud hiss of the tape was silenced. "This is just the word of a man who's trying to draw attention away from his having killed his wife by slandering a U.S. senator!"

I had to give Aldritch credit. He might be in shock, but he was still a lawyer, and he still had a powerful client to protect.

"We're not done," Lansing said, once again ignoring Aldritch and speaking directly to Lloyd. "Before you rule out talking to us, Senator, you should know a few other things."

"Like what?" Aldritch asked.

"Like the fact that a woman named Maggie Padgett has given us a complete statement of how you drugged her just the way you did Ann Kane," Lansing answered, his look still directed at Lloyd and almost as hard as Lloyd's was. "Like the fact that we have phone records to show how relentlessly you harassed her until she agreed to go to dinner with you. Like the fact that she told us the doctor you took her to when she got sick was Peter Morris, who turned up dead in a phonied-up suicide soon after he talked to a newspaper reporter about what he knew."

"That's just this Padgett woman's word against the senator's," Aldritch interjected, still trying to do a job that was becoming increasingly difficult by the second.

"Oh there's more," Lansing said, a grim smile now touching the corners of his mouth. "Before you decide to go through your righteous-innocence act, Senator, there are two or three other things you should know. You should know that I've got a lot more than just someone's word against yours. For starters, I've got Ann Kane's purse. It was right where Taylor said, in the trunk of his car. And it's covered with fingerprints, Senator, some of which I think will turn out to be yours.''

The picture in my mind of Ed Lloyd in prison began to get much clearer.

"You should also know," Lansing continued, "that sometime in the next few minutes I'll have a warrant from a judge giving me permission to take blood and other samples from your person to match against sperm and hair samples taken from Ann Kane's body. We've already taken the samples from Hub Taylor. I'd say that the results of those tests ought to just about prove Taylor's story and make my case. I'm afraid, Senator, that your political career is in the crapper, as of now.''

The prison door was slamming shut on my vision of Ed Lloyd. But Lansing wasn't done.

"Senator Lloyd," he said, his voice now taking on an official tone, "I'm placing you under arrest in the death of Ann Kane. You have the right to remain silent. Anything you say can and will be used against you in a court of law. You have the right to an attorney. If you cannot afford one, one will be appointed for you—"

"He has an attorney!" Aldritch yelled.

Lloyd stood abruptly, as if realizing for the first time that this was really happening, that his empire was crumbling and nothing in all his power could stop it.

The detective at the door straightened, and Lansing and the third detective both stood as well. All three watched Lloyd intently to make certain he didn't do anything stupid. Lansing continued to read Lloyd his rights. When he finished, he reached behind his back and took out a pair of handcuffs with which he quickly cuffed Lloyd, hands in front.

"We're going to take your client to be booked, Mr. Aldritch," Lansing said, finally addressing the attorney again. "You're welcome to come with us."

As if they had rehearsed it numerous times, the detectives smoothly escorted Lloyd from the room, Lansing and the detective at the table each taking an arm, the detective in shirtsleeves dropping in behind them. Lansing opened the door with his free hand to go into the hall. That was when I made my mistake.

I suppose, in hindsight, I should have stayed in the room. But I had to see Lloyd. I wanted to see, without any mirrors or videotapes between us, the look on his face as the evil he had set in motion finally caught up with him. I bolted from the room and into the hallway where Lansing and the detectives were entering with Lloyd.

"Sutton," Ken called, coming out the door behind me.

At my name, Lloyd and the cops all looked up. Lansing's face told me I had done the wrong thing. But it was Lloyd whose face said the most. The marble that had held his face immobile all during the videotape melted, and his cold expression transformed itself into one of pure hatred and murderous fury.

"You cunt!" Lloyd screamed, and then with an inarticulate bellow of rage, he tore himself free of the detectives and bodychecked me, slamming me into the wall. The back of my head hit with a loud thud, and both of us fell to the floor. Lloyd was on top of me and used his handcuffed fists to backhand me across the left eye. When the cops and Ken pulled him off me, he had his hands around my throat, fully intending to choke the life out of me right there in the police station.

It was total chaos.

Lloyd was screaming at me, every foul, putrid name that lived in his vile brain. Lansing and the other detectives were trying to wrestle him to the floor to subdue him, but his rage made him incredibly strong. Cops were running in from everywhere. Ken and Bill Russell were bent over me, partly to shield me from Lloyd and partly to make sure he hadn't killed me.

Somehow, during their struggles with him, Lloyd managed to take the gun from the holster of the shirtsleeved detective who had stood by the interrogation-room door.

"Gun!" the detective shouted as he felt his pistol sliding out of the holster and realized what had happened. All three detectives immediately loosened their holds and backpedaled away from Lloyd, who fell to his knees, the police pistol looking huge in his hands.

The room was suddenly as quiet as death.

"Get back!" Lloyd screamed, waving the gun in wild arcs in front of him, forcing the detectives to step farther away from him.

When the gun in Lloyd's hands came to a stop, it was pointed at me. His eyes were enough to stop my heart.

You're dead, my voice said.

That makes two of us, I told it.

All I could do was stare back at Lloyd.

Lansing moved to stand between Lloyd and me. He had his own gun out, pointed at Lloyd.

"Don't do it, Senator," he ordered. "It's a standoff. You shoot her. I shoot you." Their eyes locked.

And then, with one more roar, Lloyd turned the gun around, and in one swift movement, put it in his mouth.

I screamed.

Lansing shouted, "No!" and dove to grab the gun. But his brain understood what was happening faster than his body could move to stop it.

Before Lansing could reach him, Lloyd had pulled the trigger.

It was a nightmare, a scene from some hellish abattoir.

"Goddamn it!," Lansing yelled, more than once, and pounded his fist impotently on the wall.

Lloyd's blood and brains were sprayed all over the cops and Aldritch and the floor and walls behind them. His body had folded to the floor, where the rest of his blood was now pumping out and puddling beneath his mutilated head. His eyes still looked at me, now vacantly, as if the incredible anger they had mirrored was draining away with the blood on the floor.

As I tried to sit up straighter and assess the damage Lloyd had done to me, I knew it was a scene I would wake up to in a cold sweat for weeks or months to come.

Obviously, the rest of the day proved to be a little hectic.

First, I had to sit still while Ken, Bill, and Lansing, and then an ambulance crew from the fire and rescue station next door made certain that my rapidly swelling and purpling eye was the only real injury Lloyd had inflicted. Thankfully, I got to go sit in the lunchroom while they inspected me. Getting my checkup a few feet from Lloyd's body would have been rough, even for me.

Once we knew I would live, Lansing said someone would be in shortly to get statements from Ken and me. He left to go back to the hallway, where crime-scene investigators already were beginning to process the evidence. Bill said the rest of the press pack had gathered outside already, but they were being given nothing substantive.

Ken and I used the time to call Rob from the pay phone in the lunchroom. Ken gave him the synopsis and my prognosis and then handed the phone, over which I could hear Rob yelling, to me. Rob ran out of expletives long before I finished filling him in on the details of what had happened.

"As soon as they'll let you out of there, you and Ken haul ass back here," Rob said, when I reached the end.

"Thanks for your concern over my well-being," I told him sarcastically.

"Stop breaking my ass, McPhee," Rob said. "Hale says you're fine, and you and I both know you're too goddamned hardheaded for anything to make a dent up there!"

It was, of course, the right thing to say. By pissing me off and throwing down a challenge, Rob ensured that I wasn't going to sit around brooding or feeling sorry for myself.

"Besides," he went on, "the cops won't be able to keep this out of the rest of the press. But by God, our stories will blow everybody else out of the water!"

He was right. They did.

Friday

Thirty-one

It was Friday afternoon before I got to talk to Noah Lansing again. We both had our hands full, he with putting together all the details of the case against Hub Taylor, and me with staying a jump or two ahead of the rest of the press on the follow-up stories to Lloyd's suicide and Taylor's arrest.

Bill Russell called me on Thursday morning, ordered me to have lunch with him, and then said I wasn't leaving the restaurant until I told him everything that had gone on during mine and Lansing's little tête-à-tête with Hub Taylor and my earlier visit to Lloyd. When I was finished with the story and we were having our last cups of coffee, he nodded his head up and down.

"Yep, that's pretty much what I heard from Lansing," he said, grinning.

"Well, if you already got all this from him, why the hell did you need to hear it again from me?" I asked, irritated. "And what are you grinning about?"

"Just looking out for you, Sutton. God knows someone

should! Although maybe it's time to let Lansing share in the responsibility."

"Kiss my ass, and you can pick up the check," I told him huffily, completely violating the ethical proscription that says reporters never take freebies from sources. Of course, some sources need disciplining more than others.

I didn't get any more phone calls from Sy Berkowitz about taking over my story, but Rob eventually did pass along the news that Berkowitz had gotten both his and Mark Lester's asses in a sling over some dipshit story Berkowitz had come up with about one of the big cheeses at the White House. Word apparently got back to the chief of staff that Berkowitz was calling up and down the East Coast, making noises about the guy having ties to the mob. Unfortunately for Sy, none of his "evidence" panned out. He and Lester got paid a memorable visit by some guys from 1600 Pennsylvania Avenue and from FBI headquarters that made them forget all about anything the rest of us were working on.

My biggest problem was that I was having bad dreams nightly in which I faced Ed Lloyd over the detective's gun again, and I soon was exhausted from lack of sleep. When Cara was murdered, I was grief-stricken and in mourning for a long time, but the fear I had felt when her killers attempted to kill me, too, eventually had been lessened by my testimony against them, testimony that put them in prison where they couldn't come after me again. With their threat to me neutralized, I had been able to lock the fear away in some mental closet where it couldn't reach me.

But Lloyd had forced open that closet door, and this time I couldn't seem to push my fears away through willpower alone. Even Lloyd's suicide and Taylor's arrest didn't seem to help me escape the effects of my brush with death, effects that continued to ambush me at unexpected moments and in dreams. Eventually, I decided to make an appointment with a therapist named Elizabeth Parks, a former high-school guidance counselor I had met when I covered the Fairfax County schools, who had gone back for a Ph.D. in psychology and now was in private practice. Her confident reassurance when I called her and described my problem made me feel less reluctant about going the therapy route. Admitting my vulnerabilities was not something I enjoyed.

It also helped that Maggie Padgett and Ann Kane's fathers both called to thank me for helping prove what Lloyd had done to their daughters, and I knew their thanks would stay with me much longer than the bad dreams or even the glow of satisfaction I got from our stories.

Ken and I wrote all the stories under a shared byline. For one thing, it was too hard to figure out where the Ann Kane story left off and the Hub Taylor story began. For another, there was plenty of glory to go around. Ken deserved it as much as I did.

In the newsroom after my meeting with Bill Russell, Ken and I finished up our latest stories for Saturday's paper and sent them to Rob's computer queue. I told Rob and Ken I wanted to go back to the Great Falls police station one last time before the weekend just to make certain nothing new had gone on with the story. Ken said he would hang around until Rob edited the Saturday pieces, and that he would call me on my cell phone if Rob had any questions Ken couldn't answer. The two of them waved me out the door.

It was after four when I got back out to the Great Falls station, so Jimmy had long since gone off shift. The evening duty officer called Lansing, who apparently told him to send me back, and the officer buzzed me through.

Lansing was signing papers when I parked myself in his doorway. He looked up.

"That's quite a shiner you've got there," he said, straight-faced. It was an understatement. My left eye was still puffy and partially closed, and the skin around it and across my check sported every color of black, blue, and purple in the spectrum. It was also sore as hell.

"I just have this effect on people sometimes," I replied, stepping inside the office and sitting down in one of the extra chairs.

"Yeah, I've noticed that," Lansing answered, now starting to smile. "I've even thought about doing the same thing a couple of times myself."

"I'm sorry about Lloyd," I told him, serious this time. "If I'd had any idea it was going to set him off that way, I wouldn't have come out of the observation room."

"Don't sweat it," he said. "I'll admit I was pissed off at you at first. I'd like to have seen him go to trial for what he did. On the other hand, there's no way now for him to deny any of it, no way for him to get off because of who he is. Are you sure you're okay? He really wanted to kill you."

"I think he would have killed me if you hadn't stepped between us. Kind of a stupid thing to do, wasn't it?"

"No, I'd have shot the son of a bitch myself if he hadn't saved me the trouble!"

He would have, too, I knew. For him, it would have been like shooting the guys who killed his wife.

"Does it surprise you that he killed himself?" I was still trying to put the pieces of what drove Lloyd together in my mind.

"Not really. He was a powerful guy, but he was a coward, too, a bully. He knew his career was down the tubes, that someone finally had stood up to him and was willing to call him what he was—in public. So instead of staying around to watch it all go in the toilet, he took the coward's way out."

"Yeah, and I suspect Hub Taylor is saying a few choice things about that right now, too."

"Hub Taylor," Lansing said, looking like he wanted to spit. "What a pathetic piece of shit he is! He sold his soul to Lloyd. I wonder if he thinks it was such a bargain now."

"Anyway, thanks for keeping Lloyd from shooting me.

I was surprised you didn't take longer to think about it."

"Listen, Sutton," he went on. It was the first time he had used my first name. I liked the sound of it. "About all that. I'd like to apologize for being so hard on you. I have to admit I was wrong about you. I'll be done here in another ten minutes. Just to show you I'm not a total asshole, could I buy you a Guinness someplace?"

"No," I said, "I don't think so." I wasn't supposed to drink with the pain medicine my doctor had given me, and besides, I just wanted to go home tonight and try to get some sleep. Lansing didn't know all that, of course. He looked taken aback at my refusal.

"No, if you really want to make it up to me," I told him, "you're going to have to take me sailing again."

He looked at me for long seconds, as if he were really seeing me for the first time.

"Tomorrow morning, nine o'clock, Fort Washington Marina?" he asked.

You sure you want to start this? What about your job?

My mind, I realized, was long since made up. I would deal with the job somehow.

"I'll be there, Detective."

"Noah."

"Okay, Noah."

When I went out the door, he was smiling. So was I.

That night, I dreamed I was in a meadow, walking, when Janet Taylor rode up on a magnificent bay horse. She was whole in the dream, her legs strong and healthy, and she was beautiful. She stopped the horse a couple of hundred yards away, and I stopped, too, uncertain what to do. She never spoke. She just looked at me for a long moment, then smiled and turned to ride away. The soft breeze brought me the scent of wild mint, crushed by the horse's hooves. I inhaled it deeply and drifted farther away, into dreamless sleep where, for once, memory couldn't follow.

Brenda English is a former newspaper reporter and healthcare writer-editor. She lives near Alexandria, Va., with her husband and daughter.